James River

Destiny

Laurie A. Boche

Beaver's Pond Press, Inc.
Edina, Minnesota

ISBN 1-59298-031-7

Library of Congress Catalog Number: 2003111925

Book design and typesetting: Mori Studio
Cover design: Mori Studio

Printed in the United States of America

First Printing: September 2003

06 05 04 03   6 5 4 3 2 1

Beaver's Pond Press, Inc.

7104 Ohms Lane, Suite 216
Edina, MN 55439
(952) 829-8818
www.BeaversPondPress.com

to order, visit www.BookHouseFulfillment.com or call 1-800-901-3480. Reseller discounts available.

Author's Note

The Plantation Trust and Winterview Plantation, subjects of this story, are completely fictitious, as are the characters involved with them. The plantation, in its appearance, is a combination of several of the James River plantations. Its location, if real, would be in the middle of two existing plantations.

The information about the James River plantations, however, is accurate, according to the literature published by each site. The information about Colonial Williamsburg and the Colonial Williamsburg Foundation is accurate.

I am a supporter of the Colonial Williamsburg Foundation and a member of the Raleigh Tavern Society, and I encourage anyone who is interested in learning more about the history of the United States to visit this special place. If you would like more information about Colonial Williamsburg, how to visit, or how to contribute to the Foundation's ongoing work, call 800-HISTORY, or go to *www.cwf.org*.

This book would not have been completed without the help and support of many people. My sister Susan allowed me to live with her and her family during these past years, and my mother, Beverly, gamely read, reread and edited my manuscript. My friends and sisters (Janet, Robyn, Maralee, Tania, Sally, Jean) read my drafts and gave support and suggestions. My friend Stephanie made the characters come alive by discussing them with me as if they lived down the street. Also, John's prodding and suggestions kept me working on the book. Thank you one and all! This has been a journey that was fun, exciting, frustrating and a great lesson for me.

One

At last, my new friend, here it is—my first e-mail. I have boldly mastered the technique after only six attempts. I am now a proper e-mail correspondent. Thank you for the encouragement. I will write again soon. Your friend, Marjorie Fulton

The coffee cup hit the oak floor with a thud, rolled and came to a stop in front of the startled Labrador retriever. Darcy didn't even notice as she stared at the letter in her hand, feeling the color drain from her face. "It can't be true," she whispered.

"What's all the noise?" Jane asked as she entered the kitchen. "I could hear you all the way down the hall." She stopped immediately. "Darcy, you're as white as that dish towel. What's the matter?"

"You remember Marjorie Fulton, the woman I became friends with when I went to Virginia two years ago and who has been my e-mail buddy ever since then, don't you?"

"Of course I remember her. You read me those funny e-mail excerpts practically every day."

"That's right." Darcy lifted the letter, its weight feeling heavier than the single sheet. "This notice from her attorney, Graham Hastings, states that Marjorie passed away in her sleep two nights ago. The funeral is Friday!" Reeling from disbelief, Darcy put her hands on the back of the kitchen chair to steady herself. "I can't believe she's gone. In some ways she was a replacement mother for me. We had so much in common, especially our passion for history and preservation. I can't believe this has happened."

"Oh, Darcy, I'm so sorry." Her friend's voice carried her sorrow and her concern. "It's always so hard to lose a friend or loved one. You've already had your share of that." Jane moved to Darcy's side and put her hand on her shoulder. "But tomorrow is Friday—Darcy Marie Jeffers, you're not going to try to get to Virginia by then, are you?"

She smiled at Jane's use of her full name. "I have to. Not only do I want to pay my last respects to my friend, but also the lawyer's letter says I have to be at the reading of the will. Apparently Marjorie left me some little thing. I need to call the airline and get my plans in order. Will you take care of Cairo while I'm gone?"

"As always, I am here to walk that mutt," Jane replied, fondly looking down at a pair of chocolate eyes in a black Labrador retriever body. "That dog isn't even mine and I get suckered in. Don't worry, I'll take care of everything around here while you're gone. Joel Gunderson is coming over this weekend to look at the hay field and make sure it's coming up as it should and the horses can take care of themselves. We'll be fine."

"You're a lifesaver, Jane. What would I do without you?" Darcy hugged her best friend. "I love this old farm, and you've helped me keep it going. I hope you know how much it means to me to have had your support and friendship these last years when I needed it most."

"Same here, Darcy. We're quite an odd pair in our own way, but it seems to work. Now, go get packed and make your reservations." Jane quickly turned away, uncomfortable, as usual, with Darcy's praise. She grabbed the leash and headed out the door, Cairo dancing at her heels.

Darcy watched the pair jogging down the quarter-mile long driveway. Jane Marshall had been her best friend since elementary school. They had done everything together from playing tennis and riding horses to playing pranks. They had drifted apart after college when Jane had been briefly married and Darcy had set out to conquer the world as a teacher, but they had been brought back together by the untimely death of Darcy's parents ten years earlier.

She thought of her parents, how full of life they had been and how dependent upon them she had been. She had been twenty-two years old when they were killed, living at home on the farm in Minnesota. She had just finished college and was set to begin her teaching career that autumn. Her parents had encouraged her to live at home until she got settled in her career, and she was happy to comply. Darcy made sure to earn her keep by working with the horses and in the garden while she was going to school. Things were going according to plan until that summer.

The sudden death of Darcy's parents in a car accident had left her devastated, not knowing which way to turn. Her only sister, Fran, had been engulfed in her own grief and had dealt with her problems by moving away from the family farm to an apartment in Minneapolis. She was no help to her little sister. If Jane hadn't come back into her life at the funeral, Darcy shuddered to think what would have happened to her sanity.

Pulling herself out of her memories, Darcy got up to confront the present. Funerals were still hard to take. She felt sorrow for the person for whom the service was held as well as her own losses. This one would be especially tough, as Marjorie meant more to her than she liked to admit. After spending so much time in the area, Darcy had even entertained the thought of moving to Virginia and working at Colonial Williamsburg. Marjorie had had great plans for restoration work at her home, Winterview, and she was thrilled that Darcy was so interested and wanted to help. Now there would be no need for her to move. Her friend, her second mother, was gone.

Jane sighed as she turned the corner onto the main road and headed away from the house. Her long, black hair swirled around her face as the wind caught it. She caught the errant strands and tucked them back behind her ear. Ahead of her, Cairo raced through the mud, his tail held high, a grin on his face. He was obviously enjoying the beautiful spring day. But Jane wasn't. She hated the thought of Darcy going off to this funeral. Darcy had gotten too attached to Marjorie, even after her friend tried to point out how she might get hurt. She tried to keep Darcy from suffering, her constant job for these last years. Jane couldn't bear to see her friend distressed and grieving over Marjorie Fulton.

She had known her own deep grief when her marriage had broken up. Her husband had cheated on her with one of her friends less than a year after they were married. He showed no remorse for his infidelity. He even blamed Jane for it by telling her that she was a failure as a wife. The cruelty of her husband's actions left her devastated and unsure of herself. She vowed that neither she nor Darcy would ever suffer such hurt again.

Glancing at the cows grazing on the short, spring grass, Jane sighed again. She loved being out in the country, walking down dirt roads, watching the cows, listening to the birds. To imagine any other place as home was unthinkable. She knew that Darcy had thought about moving from time to time, but she, like Jane, could not bring herself to leave their slice of heaven. Not that it's mine, Jane grumbled to herself. *Maybe someday I will actually own a piece of land like this, but for now I am content to share Darcy's bounty.* Cairo roared up to her side, looked up, then shook, covering Jane with a coat of mud and water.

"Thanks, Mutt, just what I needed—a mud shower!" she cried, as she turned and ran for home. "Come on, let's go get cleaned up." The woman and dog sprinted down the road.

By late that afternoon Jane was driving Darcy to the Minneapolis/St. Paul Airport, an hour's drive from the farm. The rush hour traffic slowed their progress. "I can't believe you got a flight so soon," Jane commented. "It doesn't seem like Richmond would be a big city for airplane traffic."

"They have one non-stop a day from here to Richmond, and it happens to be in the early evening, so I was lucky," Darcy answered. "Otherwise I'm sure you're right—there's not a huge call for flights to Richmond. Good thing we live fairly close to a big airport and that it's not winter."

"Darcy, you're the one who loves the snow and the cold, remember?" Jane pointed out laughing. "That's why we still live in Minnesota, right?"

"Home will always be Minnesota, you know that," Darcy replied. "Although after this past winter I might reconsider." Seeing Jane's look of disbelief she added, "It was just too long even for me. I'm ready for spring now. You know, one day I'll actually leave home and strike out on my own, but for now Minnesota is best, whether it's cold or hot."

Jane winced at her comment. Surely Darcy didn't want to leave her behind, did she? They had been friends far too long for that, she decided. If Darcy ever moved, Jane would go with her.

Darcy rattled on, oblivious to Jane's distress. "I called the school and left a message that I wouldn't be available to hold my preservation seminar until further notice. I hate doing that considering how well the group was going, but I can pick it up as soon as I return. I wish I could have found another full time college position, though," she sighed. "Hopefully next year I'll be back teaching regularly."

As they reached the airport and unloaded Darcy's luggage, Jane responded, "Don't worry about next year. Worry about making it through this trip. Everything seems to work out for you if you're patient enough." She gave Darcy's hand a quick squeeze. Take care of yourself, and come home soon." Jane got back into the car quickly and watched her friend enter the airport terminal.

Darcy was soon through airport security and on her plane. Settling back in her seat, she closed her eyes and thought about Marjorie Fulton. She was a lovely woman who had made a name for herself in Virginia as a staunch believer in preserving all aspects of the state's history. Her husband had passed away twenty years earlier, and after his death Marjorie had thrown herself into her volunteer work.

Marjorie was involved not only in the area preservation efforts, but she worked tirelessly on a literacy campaign. She worked daily on that effort, from volunteering as a mentor in the local schools to becoming a national advocate on the subject. She made regular trips to Washington, D.C. to lobby Congress on both issues. She had friends in high places, and Marjorie was a woman to be taken seriously. She was a strong role model to those around her. Darcy had admired Marjorie and knew there would be many others who would also miss this dynamic woman.

Two

I am finally home again. I look forward to spending time in the garden weeding out the vegetable beds. My home is my oasis, and when I get too involved in my work, I come to Winterview to find peace.

Darcy remembered her first meeting with Marjorie. She had been on vacation to escape the stress of her teaching job and the grief she felt every spring on the anniversary of her parents' deaths, so she had gone to Virginia. Darcy had always loved Virginia, but especially Williamsburg and the surrounding area, as it was so full of history and the birthplace of the nation. She especially enjoyed Colonial Williamsburg with its authentic eighteenth-century buildings and the re-creation of life in that century. She had visited several times as a child with her parents and sister and had become a supporter of the Colonial Williamsburg Foundation as an adult.

That spring, Darcy stayed in a bed and breakfast in a nineteenth-century plantation on the road east of the James River. It was close to many of the large plantations, including Berkeley, Shirley, Westover and Winterview. Her room was actually behind the main house in what had been the slave quarters. It was a separate building that had not only housed the slaves but the garden tools as well.

The room was small but wonderful, filled with antiques and stuffed animals. The double bed was high off the ground with a small step to get into and out of the bed. There was a bathroom right off the main room, so she had everything she needed in her snug quarters. And the breakfasts! The most scrumptious breakfasts she'd ever tasted included French toast topped with strawberries and whipped cream. It was just what she needed for the perfect get-away.

As she toured the plantations, Darcy had found herself more and more drawn to them. She loved the architecture and the way they still sat proudly on the banks of the James River, but she also admired the work and the stamina it had taken to make working plantations and magnificent buildings out of the Virginia wilderness. It was history coming alive, and Darcy basked in it.

One day she decided to take a tour through the gardens of Winterview Plantation. Like Westover, the house was not open to the public, but its grounds and gardens were open for everyone's enjoyment. She had not been to Winterview before, as it was tucked away on a long, gravel road and not easily found, but once she got there she'd realized it was all worth it. The Georgian plantation house sat majestically facing the James River, its mellow brick giving the big house a warm, welcoming feel. Trees two and three centuries old stood around framing it like a painting. Darcy walked to the side of the house, past the original detached kitchen that was now used as a gardening shed and nursery, to a huge walled garden. Since it was spring, the whole garden was in bloom, and what a breath-taking sight! A rustling in the bushes let her know she was not alone in the garden. Squirrels ran back and forth, flicking their tails, chirping at one another. Birds called from every tree, bees flew from one blossom to another, and the gentle breeze put the entire garden into the movement of life.

From the garden, the house was barely visible. Darcy felt cut off from everything around her, alone, at peace. Shortly, that peace was shattered by the sharp bark of a dog, followed quickly by the arrival of the perpetrator, a huge Golden Retriever. The dog bounded up to Darcy, licked her legs, accepted a few pats, then bounded back out of the garden toward the house where her master was calling. Darcy felt charmed by everything. Oh, she could stay in this place forever! A beautiful, secluded garden, a view of the river to die for, as well as an intense feeling of belonging. She had never been here before, but it felt like coming home.

Darcy visited other plantations, but she was drawn back to Winterview and returned the following day. As she was walking around the grounds, she noticed her dog friend sitting with its mistress, an older woman. The woman and dog sat in the shade enjoying the cool of the morning. Darcy stopped to pet the dog and say hello.

The slim, gray haired woman greeted her with a light Virginia accent and mentioned that the garden was in full bloom. "Garden Week is not for another two weeks," the woman noted. "You've gotten to see a sight today that all of those people will miss. By the time the others get here my garden will be past its prime."

Darcy thanked her and started to move on. The woman stopped her by continuing the conversation, "I see you are a photographer." She noted the camera swinging from Darcy's shoulder.

"I try," Darcy replied. "I'm better with landscapes than with people and animals." She smiled down at the dog lying under the table on the cool grass. She was rewarded with a thump of the golden-haired tail.

"Well, enjoy yourself. It's a glorious day." Darcy moved off leaving the woman and dog to their privacy. Perhaps the woman was the owner of this magnificent home and garden. She couldn't imagine anything more wonderful than being in that position.

Darcy spent more than an hour on the grounds, finding the far end to the tunnel that had been built even before the current house as an escape from Indian attacks. It was cleverly hidden in the slope of the yard and came out just short of the river dock. She found the opening just to the east of the main house in what had been the old well house. The other outbuildings of the plantation were on the landside of the house so as not to block the beautiful view of the river. Each building was of the same mellow brick, making the whole compound look uniform and tidy. She wondered where the animals had been kept and where the slaves had lived, but she saw no sign of those buildings.

Darcy finally moved back toward the house and the parking lot beyond. She again ran into the gray haired woman who was immaculately dressed in casual gray slacks and well-cut white blouse. She smiled at Darcy.

"What is your name?" she asked.

"Darcy Jeffers. I'm in the area visiting. I'm staying down the road at the bed and breakfast. And you?"

"My name is Marjorie Fulton, born and raised in Virginia. You're obviously not from around here. Where do you call home?"

"I'm from Minnesota, born and mainly raised within 45 miles of the Twin Cities," Darcy replied. "I lived in Maryland for a couple of years when I was a child and I loved our visits to Virginia, so this is where I came for my vacation."

"How wonderful. The Midwest is a wonderful place to grow up. My late husband was from Wisconsin, so I had many opportunities to visit the area. It's so peaceful and beautiful—except those winters, of course. They are too cold for my Virginia bones. You seem quite taken with my home here in hot Virginia," she added.

"It's fantastic. I feel like I've come home just walking around the grounds." Darcy stopped, feeling she had shared too much.

"That's lovely to hear. This plantation requires quite a bit of work to keep it running, and it's nice to know it is appreciated by more than my family." The dog trotted up to Marjorie. "Oh, and you've already met Molly. She's a good dog, aren't you, girl?" she said fondly as she ruffled the dog's furry coat.

"Ah, another plantation lover," a deep voice said from behind Darcy. "This place is not for sale or for commercializing."

Darcy flushed at the insinuation and turned around to confront the voice. She was astonished to find that hard voice coming from one of the most intriguing, handsome men she had ever seen. Before she could reply, her companion spoke.

"There's no need for that, Robert," Marjorie admonished. "Ms. Jeffers is just in the area visiting and enjoying the early blossoms in the garden. She doesn't deserve your snide remarks."

"Sorry, Mother. You just never know who you're talking to, do you?" He glanced down at the Darcy from a height well over six feet.

"Darcy, this is my son, Robert Fulton. Robert, this is Darcy Jeffers from Minnesota."

For the first time, Robert stared directly at Darcy, looking her up and down with his amber eyes. She became even more flushed and heated from the scrutiny. Obviously, he found her unsuitable as either a human being or a woman, for he merely nodded in acknowledgement of the introduction and moved away. The dog rose from her spot and followed him into the house.

"Take no notice of him, Darcy," Marjorie soothed. "He is very protective of his home. He loves it here and would do anything to keep it the way it is."

"That's understandable. With a piece of history that is so beautiful, I would do the same thing, I think," Darcy admitted. "That reminds me—would you like some of my photos if they turn out? I can send them to you." She tried to steer the conversation away from the handsome man who had just caused her heart to race.

"Please do. The address is on the brochure. It was a pleasure to meet you, Darcy Jeffers. Do you have a card? I can let you know about special events in the area if you like."

"That would be great." Darcy pulled a business card out of her purse. "My e-mail address is also on the card, so you can reach me that way, as well."

"I have not conquered the e-mail yet, but I have been meaning to try. You could be my guinea pig," Marjorie laughed. "I'll have to get Robert to set it up on the computer he bought me for Christmas. He'll be thrilled that I am finally interested in turning it on."

"Thank you for keeping this place so beautiful and letting us all enjoy it, " Darcy added. With a wave, she made her way toward the parking lot.

Darcy spent the next two days visiting all of the plantations on both sides of the James River and venturing down into Williamsburg. She stopped at the winery there, tasting the wines made from grapes grown on site and enjoying the new experience. She made a quick stop at Colonial Williamsburg, just to say hello to her friends at the Raleigh Tavern Society, one of the Colonial Williamsburg Foundation's donor societies. After her parents' deaths, Darcy had become an even bigger supporter of Williamsburg by joining this society. There she had made several friends with whom she had traveled to London, Paris, Prague and Dresden. The tours took them deeper into the cities than just the tourist sights and included examples of historical preservation and the chance to meet the people involved in these efforts. Darcy also believed in the Foundation's mission, "that the future may learn from the past", and she supported these efforts faithfully.

And then it was time to go home. Her Virginia idyll hadn't lasted nearly long enough. She had many new stories to share with her history classes when she got back to Minnesota. She could certainly make history come alive with the photos of these beautiful plantations.

As she was heading to the airport in Richmond, Darcy stopped by Winterview one last time to enjoy the gardens and the peace of the grounds.

"Here again so soon?" a voice mocked.

Darcy looked up into the amber eyes she had seen the last time she was at Winterview. The thin but handsome face was framed with military-short brown hair lightly sprinkled with gray. His well-tanned body had the lean look of an athlete. Realizing she was staring, Darcy replied, "I'm leaving today and I just wanted to see the Winterview gardens once more. Anything wrong with that?"

"The gardens at Westover are just as beautiful. Are you sure you're not here to see my mother again? You certainly tried to insinuate yourself into her good graces last time you were here. What else are you up to?"

Darcy bristled at the accusation. "I am not here for any other reason than to see the gardens. And for your information, I just came from Westover. How dare you say such a thing? I've done nothing but see the gardens and have a conversation with your mother. You know nothing about me and your accusations are ridiculous."

Robert gave a smug smile. "Quite a little speech. I don't need to know about you to know you are a parasite. My mother doesn't need anything you have to offer," he said, "She already has three children and does not want to sell the plantation. So, please leave as soon as you finish your tour of the gardens. You've been around here enough."

"Robert, where are your manners? Who gave you the right to speak to a guest at Winterview that way?" Marjorie asked from the entrance to the garden. "You owe Darcy an immediate apology."

"No, Mother, I do not. But if it will appease you, I will do so." Turning back to Darcy, Robert bowed formally and said, "I apologize for offending you." With that he stalked back toward the river. Darcy watched as the tall man strode away. She shivered at the venom that had been in his voice.

"My dear, I am so sorry for Robert's behavior. He thinks it is his responsibility to keep me safe from everyone who comes to see the grounds. I have had several run-ins over the past year with visitors who turned out to be interested in turning this land into a huge development of condominiums and large homes. So, Robert now assumes the worst of people. It's lovely for a son to be so concerned, but he goes too far. Did I overhear you say you were leaving today?" Marjorie asked.

"Yes, I'm on my way to the airport now." Relieved that Robert was no longer in sight, Darcy added, "Thanks again for allowing me to share your beautiful gardens. It was a memorable treat."

"You are most welcome. It is a joy to me to be able to keep the history of plantation life alive and open for others to experience. I very much enjoyed our chat yesterday, Darcy, and I do hope you will keep in touch. I see a lot of myself in you, and I love to talk to people with quick minds and a thirst for knowledge. It will be my challenge to actually sit down and use e-mail to stay in touch." The older woman laughed at the thought of herself at the computer. "You may be responsible for finally dragging me into the computer age."

"It will be my pleasure to keep in touch. I never seem to be short of stories about my farm and my students, so there's plenty to chat about. It was certainly a pleasure to meet you. Please take care, Marjorie, and I will wait for your e-mail." Darcy waved goodbye, then headed back to the car.

The words of the flight attendant brought Darcy back to the present. "We will be landing in Richmond in approximately twenty minutes. Please put away all personal electronics until you get into the terminal. Thank you for flying with us today."

Darcy wondered what awaited her at the Richmond airport. She had contacted Marjorie's friend and lawyer, Graham Hastings, to let him know when she would arrive. Mr. Hastings assured her someone would be at the airport to meet her and take her to the hotel. The funeral would be held tomorrow morning in Richmond before a private burial on the plantation grounds in the afternoon.

This could be difficult, Darcy thought to herself. *Not only does Robert not like me, but the other children will be none too happy to see me, either. After my last visit there is no doubt how they feel about me. I hope I can get through this ordeal without any problems with them. I just want to honor Marjorie and get back home.*

As the plane began its descent, Darcy recalled the previous December when Marjorie had invited her to spend Christmas with her family at Winterview. She had jumped at the chance to see her friend again and to actually see the inside of that wonderful Georgian home. She and Marjorie had faithfully exchanged e-mails, once Robert had set it up, and Marjorie had gotten the hang of it. The first e-mail was a funny story about Marjorie's first attempt at turning on the computer then conquering the Internet. After that there were also regular letters interspersed with the e-mails where Marjorie wrote about her three children. She was a typical mother, proud of the children, yet worried about each for different reasons. Darcy felt as if she'd gotten to know the children, all of whom were older than she, long before she ever met them.

Marjorie's writings were also filled with her hopes for the future of Winterview. She shared her dreams of further restoration and for making the plantation a real piece of history from which everyone could learn. Darcy was eager to discuss this more with her and to see personally the piece of history about which Marjorie was so enthusiastic.

When Darcy arrived at Winterview that Christmas, it was to find the temperatures balmy, by her standards, with highs in the 50s and 60s. George, the Fulton's major domo, opened the Winterview door. Moving into the house was like walking hundreds of years into the past. The Georgian style was obvious with symmetrical rooms on either side of the long hall that ran from the front of the house to the back. The parlor, resplendent in antique furniture, showcased a Chippendale divan and loveseat. The dining room, too, contained a Chippendale table and sideboard, with a three-tiered crystal chandelier providing light through the hundreds of prisms of hand-cut glass.

The other side of the house appeared more like a normal house. The rooms on this side mirrored those on the other in terms of size and shape, but here was the actual living room with overstuffed chairs, a sofa, a television and lots of photos and other family items. The deep green of the living room walls accentuated the greens and browns that made up the fabrics in the room. The room felt warm and snug. The other room on that side had been turned into the kitchen. It was large and modern with an island in the center for food preparation and room for a comfortable kitchen table and chairs for informal dining.

Marjorie had laughed as she watched Darcy's face when entering each new room. "I think that means you approve, doesn't it? You look a bit overwhelmed."

"I'm sorry. I'm acting as if I have never seen a beautiful home before," Darcy apologized. "It's just that I had no idea what to expect and you have done such an amazing job with this house, keeping its original style while still incorporating all of the modern comforts. It's absolutely lovely."

The back door opened and they heard several voices as people came in. "We're in the kitchen," Marjorie called out to the new arrivals. "Come meet my house guest."

Darcy turned and smiled at the four people who came through the door. They did not smile back, and she was confused until she saw Robert. She decided to go on the offensive this time. "Robert, how nice to see you again." Robert seemed to be caught off guard by her smile and the show of friendship. He even seemed a bit stunned by it, but he recovered quickly.

Ignoring the outstretched hand, Robert turned to the man beside him. "Jonathan, this is Mother's friend Darcy Jeffers. She's the one you've been hearing so much about this past year and a half, the person who is so interested in Winterview and in Mother."

Darcy studied the older man. As Marjorie had mentioned in her e-mails, he was many years older than Robert. Seeing him in person she realized he had none of his mother's grace and beauty. Jonathan's complexion was dark, as was his hair, and he resembled a bear with his wide, thick body. He was the complete opposite of Robert.

"Miss Jeffers," he began in a rich baritone voice. "I am glad we finally get to meet you. Mother has talked so much about you and Robert has added his opinion so we have been anxious to find out who you really are."

"Please call me Darcy. I hope we will get to know one another during my visit."

"What's that supposed to mean, Dad?" a lanky teenage boy asked as he came into the room. He wore a bright red t-shirt under a button-down oxford shirt on top of baggy pants that swept the floor when he walked. "How's she going to get to know you better?" he asked with a smirk.

"Knock it off, Lucas," Jonathan ordered, "and come meet Darcy. She is your grandmother's guest, so be nice." He added a stern look that had no effect on his son. "Darcy, this is my son, Lucas," he tried to continue the conversation.

"Yeah, whatever," Lucas replied. "Isn't she the one you and Aunt Beth and Uncle Robert think is trying to get Gram's property?" He looked around smugly at the shocked faces of the adults around him. Smiling, he took a CD player from his pocket and put on the headphones. "I'll be outside if anyone wants me. Oh, by the way, welcome Darcy!" With a laugh and a wave Lucas left the room.

A silence followed Lucas' statement. Finally, the petite blonde woman next to Marjorie spoke. "Darcy, I am so sorry about that. Lucas' statement wasn't exactly accurate. He just loves to stir up trouble whenever he can. He's a typical teenager. By the way, I'm Beth Page, and this is my husband Andrew." She nodded at the well-dressed man beside her. "We hope you enjoy your holiday here." Marjorie's daughter looked very much like her mother except that she was shorter. Her husband appeared to be uncomfortable in this setting and kept putting his hands in the pockets of his pressed khaki trousers. He shifted his weight from foot to foot as he continued to watch what was unfolding in the kitchen.

"I don't know what to say to you, my dear," Marjorie said as she took Darcy's hand. "From the first time you came to Winterview one of my children has been rude to you, and it looks like that trend will continue. Please know they are good people, but they worry about me and they worry about their heritage and their inheritance. Sometimes way too much," she added glaring at each of the children in turn. "After all, it is only your inheritance if I give it to you."

Turning back to Darcy she continued, "Let's take you upstairs and get you settled into your room. In the mean time, children, try to calm down so we can all start over when we return," she ordered.

Darcy remembered that the rest of the stay was as awkward as the beginning. It was quite clear that none of the children wanted her anywhere near their mother. She was an interloper who was taking their mother's time away from them. However, Marjorie was happy to have the younger woman with her. She certainly enjoyed having a mother figure to talk to for a few days. They spoke of many things from Darcy's problem with her sister to the pros and cons of living in the cold. What Marjorie couldn't stop talking about throughout her stay was what she wanted to see done with the plantation. She felt strongly that preserving its history was most important, and restoring the rest of the plantation should be top priority, but her children didn't seem to be interested in pursuing that agenda. She had found a soul mate in

Darcy and the two spent several nights talking about the plantation's history.

"Do you know why it's called Winterview?" Marjorie asked. After Darcy shook her head, she continued. "Well, when the first settlers came to this section of Virginia, they looked for a place to build their compound along the river. Nothing caught their eye on the first trip, but when they returned in January, they found their site. Standing on this hill looking across the James River they were greeted by the sight of thousands of birds wintering in the marshes on the far bank of the river. All of those birds were not only beautiful but would provide food for the settlers indefinitely. The birds weren't there in the summer, so it was the winter view that made this plantation."

"How interesting!" Darcy exclaimed. "It makes sense now, but I did wonder about it. Just another fun fact to know about Virginia." The two women continued their talks well into the night for the length of her stay.

Christmas at Winterview mirrored the ones she had known growing up in Minnesota. On Christmas Eve the whole family had a large dinner, attended candlelight services at the Westover Episcopal Church just down the road, then they all returned to Winterview to open presents. On Christmas Day, each family had their own celebration in the morning, so Marjorie and Darcy celebrated together. The rest of the family returned that afternoon to have a late meal of leftovers. Although she was clearly an outsider, she had enjoyed the feeling of family that surrounded that holiday. She had enjoyed her time with Marjorie, despite the children's animosity.

As the airplane taxied in, Darcy thought about how poorly the children acted toward her when their mother was present. She didn't even want to think of how they would act toward her now. With a small shudder, she picked up her purse and headed out of the plane and into the world of the Fulton family.

Three

My children are the light in my world. However, they are grown and have their own lives. My reason now for living is quite simple. It is for the preservation of Winterview.

Darcy made the trek to the Richmond baggage claim area, stopping short when she saw who was waiting for her at the carousel. He hadn't spotted her yet, so she took the opportunity to closely study Robert Fulton. Although he was lounging against a post, he looked as though he were tightly wound, ready to spring at a moment's notice. He was as tan as she had ever seen him, which only emphasized his glowing amber eyes and his narrow face. With perfectly proportioned features, Darcy imagined he could be a model for an outdoor magazine if he wanted to do so. What did he do for a living that left him so tan and fit, she wondered.

As she finished her appraisal, her eyes met his in silent salute. He held her gaze a moment longer before breaking the silence. "Ah, Ms. Jeffers, how good to see you again." His voice was mocking.

"Robert, I am so sorry for your loss," Darcy countered, not wanting to spar with him on this occasion. "I can't believe Marjorie is gone. I know how it feels to lose a parent, and I sincerely wish you did not have to feel that pain."

Robert was silenced by the sincerity in her words. She could see from the shift in his glance that he was deciding whether to believe her sympathy was real, or whether she was just acting for his benefit.

"Thank you," he finally acknowledged her words. "Now where's your luggage? We need to get back to the house right away."

"I'm not staying at Winterview, Robert," Darcy exclaimed. "I have a reservation in Richmond. The funeral is here in the morning anyway, so it's better this way. That's why I'm surprised to see you. I thought Graham Hastings would have just sent a car for me."

"Plans have changed," Robert said coldly. "It has been determined that my mother wanted you to be treated as one of the family, so you will be with us tonight as well as during the funeral and the reading of the will tomorrow. Let's get going."

"I can't intrude on your family's grief! You may think many things about me, but I would never, ever do such a thing. Please, just take me to the hotel and I will be at the service in the morning. Marjorie couldn't have wanted me to be at Winterview with all of you since she knew how much you dislike me," she added petulantly.

"No matter. It is part of her will. She choreographed her funeral and everything surrounding it, so none of us has a say in anything that happens between now and the reading of the will. Is this your bag?" Robert picked up the suitcase Darcy had taken off the carousel and headed toward the exit. Frustrated, Darcy had no choice but to follow.

The drive to Winterview was silent except for the sounds of the highway and the night creatures of summer. Darcy didn't dare even look at Robert, as she could feel his tension next to her. In what seemed like forever, they finally turned into the drive. "Go on in," he said. "I need to go over to the farm and check on the horses."

Check on the horses? Robert? Darcy didn't have time to mull that one over except to wonder at him having anything to do with a farm. His appearance always struck her more as a jetsetter than a farmer.

George came down the steps to take her bags. "Welcome back to Winterview, Miss Darcy," he said solemnly. "I wish your return could have been for a happier occasion."

"Thank you, George. I wish I were here for any other reason than this. I really loved Marjorie and respected her. I will miss our conversations and correspondence so much. She was like a second mother to me," Darcy replied with a catch in her voice. "I'm sorry, I guess the reality of the situation is really hitting home with me being here."

George started up the steps to the house. "Follow me, Miss Darcy, and we'll get you settled in right away. Then you can have some time to collect yourself. The family members are scattered about the house so I don't believe you will run into them until morning." Darcy followed the short, plump, gray-haired man into the house. He was still spry for his age; she had trouble keeping up with his quick strides.

His news about the Fulton family was the best of the evening. Darcy could wait forever for her encounter with the other Fulton children and families. She hated being here when they needed their privacy, but Marjorie was still dictating to the family from beyond the grave, and there was nothing she could do but go gracefully with the instructions.

Darcy was given the same room she had had at Christmas, and it was like coming home. At once comfortable in her surroundings, she decided to wash up and go right to sleep. Morning would come all too soon.

Robert closed the stall door and brushed the sweat from his face. The last horse had been fed and he could now go home to bed, but he was too restless to think about sleep. He missed his mother already and didn't know how he was going to get through the funeral in the morning. Robert not only lived the closest in proximity to his mother, since he lived on the plantation farm, but he was also the closest to her emotionally. He would never admit it to his sister or brother, but their mother's death would leave a large hole in his life. She had supported his decision to join the Marines, she had been there to help him recover from his losses and she had always made him feel that he made her proud.

Turning from thoughts of his mother, Robert thought about Darcy Jeffers. She was a good-looking woman with short, sassy blonde hair and a face that was open and fresh. At another point in his life he might have been interested in her as a woman, but now he was only interested in why she was in Virginia. His mother had orchestrated Darcy's presence here, but he instinctively knew she would have made the trip anyway. Whatever else he thought about her, the young woman had cared for his mother. Clicking off the light switch in the barn, Robert headed toward his home.

"Well, well, here's sleeping beauty," Jonathan remarked as Darcy came into the kitchen the following morning. "We didn't know you had even arrived until Robert informed us just now. Sorry to have missed the chance for a tête-à-tête last night," he added sarcastically.

"Stop it, Jon," Beth ordered her older brother. "That's not going to help anything. We all have to get through today, so let's just be civil. Mother obviously wanted Darcy with us, and we need to respect that." She turned to the other woman. "I'm sorry about all of this. We're all on edge."

Darcy noticed the lines around Beth's eyes in an otherwise flawless face. She looks so much like her mother, Darcy thought, as she noted Beth's slim figure in an immaculate black suit.

"You don't owe me any apologies or explanations," Darcy responded. "If I had my way, I would be in Richmond so that you could all have your privacy. Marjorie was a good friend to me, but she was your mother, and you deserve to grieve in peace. I'm sorry she has put all of you through this." She moved to the coffee pot. "I'll just grab a cup of coffee and be out of the way. If you can let me know when we are leaving for the funeral, I won't trouble you further." Darcy grabbed her cup and headed out the back door, but she heard Robert speaking.

"I have no idea why Mother wants Ms. Jeffers with us, but I have a feeling it has something to do with her will. I think we had better be civil to her until we find out what's going on. I'll just tell her when we're leaving." He walked out the back door, Molly at his heels, and Darcy continued toward the garden.

Darcy wandered around the walled garden and tried to pull herself together. The attacks from Marjorie's children every time she met them left her wondering what in the world she was doing here. She had her own grief, but nothing compared to theirs. She wanted to pay her respects, but the price was a bit high.

Strolling up the path through the gates, on a tree-lined path, made her feel as if she could forget the present. The breeze was cool, and the sun was hot. She imagined the garden looked just as it had over two hundred years ago. The only things out of place were the noises: an occasional car door slam, the drone of the lawn mower. All around, yellow tiger butterflies flitted through the air like falling leaves. There was peace.

The grass in the center of the garden was dark green and filled with clover. The old trees, lining what must have once been a road to the kitchen when it had been a separate building, were split open, their insides filled with brick and mortar to keep them from toppling over. The air smelled sweet with the scent of flowers, like perfume, and Darcy could hear the sounds of the mighty James River in the distance. The river's course had obviously altered over the centuries, as the house now overlooked smaller back channels and marshland on one side, with the main river running directly in front of the house.

Robert stopped at the garden entrance and stared at the woman standing like a statue in the midst of the flowers. The sunlight glinted off her blonde hair, and the breeze picked up the ends and blew them about her face. Her deep hazel eyes were wary, but she looked completely comfortable and somehow right standing in the middle of the garden. Not liking where his thoughts were taking him, Robert announced, "It's time to go. The cars will be leaving in about 15 minutes. If you'd like, you can ride up with me so you don't have to deal with Jonathan," he added.

Darcy, surprised by his voice, simply nodded her head in acknowledgement. She watched Robert shuffle back to the house, Molly at his heels. The retriever looked around as if to find Marjorie, but she wasn't going to let Robert out of her sight. Her tail drooped, she looked miserable. Taking a deep breath, Darcy squared her shoulders and prepared for the day's ordeal.

The ride to Richmond was quiet and somber with both occupants of the car lost in their thoughts of Marjorie. The funeral service was held at a large United Methodist church in downtown Richmond. It was obvious from the number of people in attendance that Marjorie was a very special, beloved person. The sanctuary, crowded with flowers, made a stunning backdrop for the service. Several people rose to pay tribute to this unique woman and all of the work she had done in the community, and when Robert spoke of his mother, Darcy finally broke into tears. It was so obvious that he had loved his mother and missed her terribly.

After the service Darcy found Marjorie's lawyer, Graham Hastings, and accompanied him, along with his son, Grant, back to Winterview. She did not want to intrude further on the Fulton family. Robert hadn't seemed upset about the change of plans and he had been engulfed in mourners when she slipped quietly away. The interment in the Fulton family mausoleum was a quiet affair with little fanfare. After saying their final goodbyes to Marjorie, the group headed back to the house.

Winterview had been opened up to those who had been at the service as well as other friends and neighbors who wanted to pay their respects to the family. Darcy watched the people come and go from a corner of the parlor, trying to stay out of the main body of mourners. When curious people did finally locate her, she slipped through the side door and into the quiet ballroom, located in a building adjoining the main house. The room was dark and cool, and the paintings of Marjorie and her ancestors on the walls calmed her soul. This room had once been a separate building on the south end of the house, and it had been connected to the main house in the nineteenth century when the plantation office had been attached at the north end. The ballroom was obviously not used often, but it was a beautiful room.

Finally, the crowd wound down, the doors were closed and Darcy made her way back into the main house.

"I know you have all had a long day," Graham Hastings announced, "but we do have one more piece of business. Why don't you all get comfortable and meet me in the family room in ten minutes." As Darcy started to walk upstairs, he added, "You too, Ms. Jeffers. You need to be present at the reading of the will."

Astonished, she replied, "If you insist. I just want to go upstairs and freshen up."

Once in her room she reached for the telephone and dialed Jane's number. Her friend answered on the second ring.

"Oh, Jane," Darcy sighed. "I'm so glad you're home. This has been the longest day of my life and it's not over yet." She went on to explain what had happened both the night before and today. "And now for some reason they want me at the reading of the will. I know that's gone over big with the family."

"Darcy, it doesn't matter what the family thinks," Jane replied. "Marjorie was your friend and you're grieving, too. Just hang in there a little longer. You can come home tomorrow and things will be back to normal."

"I hope so, but I have a bad feeling about all of this. I'll call you tomorrow and let you know just when I will actually be coming home. Thanks for being there and listening. You're the best."

"Take care of yourself, girlfriend," Jane said as she disconnected. Darcy didn't notice the other click on the phone as someone in the house put down the extension.

Darcy found the family gathered in the family room, the forlorn dog at Robert's feet. It was obvious the dog missed her master, and no one else was paying attention to her. Darcy reached down to scratch Molly's head as she walked to the only available chair in the room. The dog got up and followed her, turning all of the heads of the family members toward them.

Graham Hastings got up from behind the desk. "I see we are all here now. Unless there are objections, I will read Marjorie's Last Will and Testament."

No one uttered a word, and the lawyer took this as assent. "As most of you know, Marjorie left a very large estate. There are millions of dollars involved, and she was quite adamant about how they were to be divided." He paused to glance around the room. Clearing his throat, Graham continued, "There are the usual preliminaries with which I will not bore you. You already know that Marjorie insisted on Ms. Jeffers' presence in this house, so I will start at the bequests. Marjorie writes:

> There will be many questions about what I have done in this will, but I hope that in time all of you, my family and friends, will come to see that what I have done is best for everyone. Before I make my wishes known, I want you to know that I value you as people and as my family members and friends. I fervently hope you will respect my wishes.

> To my loyal workers, George and Anita Marshall, I leave a lump sum of $250,000 and a position in this household for as long as you both desire it. Even after you retire, you may choose to continue to live on the house grounds until your deaths.

> To my oldest son, Jonathan. You were burdened early with the expectations of carrying on the family business and the family name. Thank you for trying your best to carry on that tradition and for bringing Lucas into our lives. You are both very special men. I leave you, Jonathan, a trust that will help keep you in the style to which you are accustomed and the job of Chairman of the Board of Fulton Foundation for as long as you want it. However, should you give up sitting on the Fulton Foundation board, you will give up your trust. Hastings & Hastings will administer the trust.

> To Elizabeth, my beautiful daughter. You are lovely and talented, and I am sorry I have not lived to see your children. I am sure they would have been exceptional with you for a mother. To you, I leave all of the paintings in the house except those in my bedroom. I also leave you a trust dedicated to letting you pursue your dream of becoming an artist. However, this trust will be revoked if any of the money is used to pay your husband's debts, or if you choose not to pursue your dream. You have the talent to do it, now you have the means.

To my Robert, my son who has kept so much going on the plantation. I know it was hard for you to give up your military career and come home to farm; however, you have more than proven you are the man for the job. To you I leave the home farm, all equipment, animals, buildings, etc. It is yours to continue the farming tradition. A trust has been set up to keep the farm running, and if you choose not to do it yourself, there will always be money to hire people to keep the farm in operation. It is my dearest wish that you continue to work the farm in the tradition of our ancestors, but if you choose another occupation, the farm will always be your home.

To my grandson Lucas. You are young and full of fire. I hope you use that fire to good end. Do not think your grandmother's money will keep you from hard work! I leave you a trust, in the care of your father and Graham Hastings, the principal of which cannot be touched until your 28th birthday. That will give you enough money to play with but not enough to get you into trouble. The condition of your trust is that you work, even part time, at a job until your 28th birthday, and hopefully beyond. I also leave you the car collection that has been your fondest wish since you were 6 years old. The cars are yours to do with as you please.

With regard to the house and surrounding acreage, other than the home farm, I leave that in the care of a new foundation, The Plantation Trust. This means that the house and gardens can never be sold or taken over and that as long as there is a trust, Winterview will continue to be a well cared-for piece of history on the James River. The new head of the Plantation Trust and the person whom I choose to live in my house is my newest, dear friend Darcy Jeffers. She will also receive a lump sum of $100,000 and a yearly income for her stewardship of the plantation.

A collective gasp escaped the lips of the family members and they all turned toward Darcy. "How can this be," Jonathan shouted, as his face turned a deep red. "This is our house! She is not part of the family!"

"Calm down, Jonathan," the lawyer said quickly as Jonathan ran out of breath. "Let me finish the will and then we can talk about it." Jonathan subsided back into his chair, but the color of his face deepened. Grant Hastings discreetly moved behind the chair to help with any further outbursts.

> I know this will come as a shock to my children. However, I feel the house needs to be cared for and paid for by my new trust to ensure that it goes on as a part of history. All of my children are entitled to anything that is in their rooms and anything that is in the boxes labeled with their names on them in the storage room. However, the furniture and the rest of the household items will stay with the house. You will also have access to the house as long as it is cleared with Ms. Jeffers.

> Darcy, I would guess you are as shocked as everyone else about this gift. I know it means a great change for you, but I need your help to help secure our heritage. I hope you will move to Virginia as soon as possible and begin work with the Plantation Trust, as I further instruct that the interest from the Trust be used to repair other plantations in Virginia and throughout the South. You will find a list of board proposed members and an idea of my vision in the papers Graham Hastings will give you. Your background as a teacher of history and preservation, as well as being an active preservationist, will serve you well in this new endeavor. You are my hope for Winterview's future, and I wish you well.

> If for some reason Ms. Jeffers refuses to live at Winterview and take up her position as head of the Trust, the plantation will still continue on under the care and operation of the Trust and Ms. Jeffers will

choose a new Chair for her replacement. If that happens, she will retain a seat on the board for her lifetime and a lifetime stipend from the trust to match that salary.

My Children, before you all decide to contest this will and go to court, you should know it is legally binding and you will have a hard time breaking it. If you attempt to do so, the trusts set up for each of you will become null and void and the money will be added to the assets of the Plantation Trust.

I love all of you and I love our heritage. Please remember that it is mine to do with as I see fit, and I think I have done what is best for everyone through this will. Be good to one another.

"So ends the Last Will and Testament of Marjorie King Fulton." Graham put down the will and set his glasses down on top of it. "Now, are there any questions?"

Four

I believe that each of us has to find our place in the world. There are key moments when we have to make a decision that will change our lives. Don't be afraid to make the decision for your happiness and your future.

Darcy finally found her voice. She was shaking at the monumental nature of what had happened in the last few minutes. "Mr. Hastings," she began as all eyes turned in her direction, "what do you think about me turning the Plantation Trust over to someone else? The will says I can do that, right?"

"Yes, Darcy, it does," the lawyer answered gently, "but I hope you will consider Marjorie's request. It was her fondest wish, as she thinks you are the perfect person to keep her dreams alive for Winterview. You two discussed those dreams, didn't you?"

"Well, yes, we did. Marjorie had very specific ideas for the plantation going forward. It's a shame she won't be here to see them come to fruition."

"If you don't take this job, they may never come to fruition," Graham responded. "You are the only one with whom she shared those dreams."

"Now wait a minute," Robert interrupted. "We all know Mother wanted lots of changes for Winterview. Why do you think she only talked to Darcy about these ideas?"

"Because she told me that's what she did," Graham replied. "She talked to you children about some of the ideas and you weren't too thrilled. Marjorie wanted things done in a certain way and I think she felt someone outside of the family would be needed to make it happen."

Andrew Page, who had been silent through the whole pro-ceeding, finally stood up. He was wobbly from too many drinks, but he could speak. "The old gal's got no right to take this house away from you kids," he thundered. "And she didn't leave me a damn thing!" He collapsed back onto the couch and onto his wife. "Where's the justice in that?"

Andrew had broken the dam of silence and everyone began talking at once. Only Darcy sat in silence and tried to process what had just happened. In one moment she had found her purpose and had added to the wealth left to her by her parents. But how could she accept knowing that Marjorie's children were so against the idea? Darcy thought of her friend and all of the letters she had received full of her hopes for the plantation's future. How could she not accept?

Realizing all was quiet Darcy turned around and found herself the center of attention once again. This time it was Robert who spoke. "Darcy, do you have any idea what you are going to do?" he asked softly. "What you do affects us all."

She looked up into his solemn, handsome face. "I know it does, Robert," she replied. "But this is a big shock to me. I had no idea I would have to decide the rest of my life on this trip. You all need to give me a little time."

"Witch!" Lucas cried. "You're making a mess of everything! They had it all worked out and you weren't a part of anything!" He glared at her as he stood. "This should've been my inheritance, not yours!" He stormed out of the room leaving a heavy silence behind him. Darcy saw Jonathan watch his son leave, a worried look on his face.

Elizabeth turned to Jonathan. "What right did you have to let Lucas think this house would ever be his? None of us was ever promised the house by Mother. How dare you give Lucas such hopes?"

Turning to Darcy, the furious woman continued. "And as for you, I have nothing to say. You will, I believe, accept the terms of the will because you were Mother's friend and believe you are doing the right thing. But this will only cause you pain and sorrow. You can bank on that." Her green eyes burned with jealousy. "How dare you flaunt your relationship with our mother? Do you think you were one of her children? Well, let me tell you that she was using you to get to us. She never could deal with her own children, so she went out and found one she liked better. We'll fight you on this in any way we can."

Darcy felt as if someone had punched her in the stomach. There was so much malevolence in these people. How could she possibly stay here? Standing slowly, she said, "I know you are all unhappy about your mother's bequest to me. I know nothing of your relationship with Marjorie except that she spoke lovingly to me about all of you. As for the will, you all received enough money to let you live a good life, as well as either having a job for life or the opportunity to follow your dreams. How can that be bad? This will is Marjorie's dream for protecting your heritage. I could back out, but someone else would be put in my place, isn't that right Mr. Hastings?" At the lawyer's nod in the affirmative she continued, "Why can't you let your mother have her dream? You are the coldest group of people I have ever met."

"We're all quite passionate, actually," Robert replied from behind her. Feeling the heat radiating from him, Darcy turned to him as he spoke. He held himself rigidly, fire in his eyes. "And as for Mother's dream, any one of us could have made it work. Beth is right that she put you into the mix to stir things up. But don't you underestimate any of us. We'll make sure you don't get anything more than what we think you should get. Beth is right. We will fight this situation any way we can." His voice trailed off.

"Is that a threat?" Darcy asked. She looked around at all of the people in the room. Even Graham and Grant Hastings looked as if they wanted her gone. "Well, you know what? I don't respond well to threats. Threats make me want to get right into someone's face." She turned back to Robert. "So, let's be clear about this. I don't need Marjorie's money or the job at the foundation, but I am going to accept them because it's what she wanted. If that's a problem for you or your siblings, you're just going to have to learn to deal with me or get out of my way." As regal as a queen, the new trust director crossed the room and exited, leaving six astonished faces behind her. Darcy had gotten the last word in this round.

"Well, I guess that says it all," Graham found his voice. "Looks like you will need to learn to deal with Ms. Jeffers living in this house and controlling it." He looked at each person in turn. "She will need to pick a successor for the trust position and that person should be someone in the family. So, if any of you can manage to be civil for a while, you may eventually end up with all of this. You all need to calm down and deal with this situation. Grant will be in charge of the Plantation Trust while I will continue as attorney for the rest of you."

Shaking from her shock and anger, Darcy made it into her bedroom before collapsing into the nearest chair. She had known only a loving family and she couldn't imagine anyone she grew up with being so self-centered and greedy as the family downstairs. Even now when she was virtually estranged from her own sister she had never felt so alone. She needed time to think this through, but she had done it again—leaped before she looked—and had committed herself to staying on at Winterview.

Darcy sighed and reached for the telephone. The line was already in use. An unfamiliar, rough voice was speaking rapidly. "I can take care of everything. Don't worry about it. By the end of the week it will be over."

Another indistinguishable voice, that Darcy was having trouble hearing, replied, "Good. Report back if there are any problems." The line went dead. Darcy wondered what that was all about. It seemed rather sinister, but then everything today was being blown out of proportion. She forgot about the conversation as she got a dial tone on the next try and punched in Jane's telephone number.

Jane answered immediately, and Darcy took her time explaining the events of the day. After an hour's monologue, Jane finally spoke. "Wow. I can't believe all that happened today. Sounds like a story right out of a book. But it's just like you to end up with a mansion and a lifetime job and income! You always land on your feet, don't you Darcy? I told you yesterday that your job situation would all work out. Now you can use your new position not only to preserve the past at Winterview, but to continue educating people as you were born to do." Her voice held a sharp, jealous edge.

"What's wrong with that? I know there have been wonderful people and events in my life, but I've had my share of knocks," she said, her voice rising. "Marjorie was my friend and I intend to stay and make her dream a reality. You know I've been looking for my place in the world, and I think I've found it." She paused, then added more calmly, "The family may not like it, but I'm confident we will eventually come to some agreement. I don't want to cheat them out of anything, but I am going to do what Marjorie wanted done with this plantation."

"Watch out, Darcy. From what you've said those people could be dangerous. They might even try to get you out of the house somehow. Just watch your back."

"Now who's the one sounding like a bad movie plot? No one is going to come after me. They might try to scare me away or just be so rude I won't want to stay, but no one's out to get me personally." She hoped that last statement remained true, but Elizabeth Page's earlier threat still rang in her ears.

"OK, OK. You may be right," Jane conceded. "But how about Robert? He's the one who's around the plantation the most, right? How's he taking it?"

Darcy thought about the glitter in Robert's eyes when he had spoken downstairs and the tingling she felt as he gazed at her. "Oh, I think he's pretty put out by all of this, but I don't think he's the physical revenge type. I think he'll wage a psychological war with me."

"Sounds interesting. Is this guy good looking? I hear something extra in your voice when you talk about Robert." Jane laughed.

"Very funny, Jane. Yes, Robert is a good looking man and very single, but do you remember how he treated me when I first met Marjorie? And again when I visited last year? I don't think you have to worry about my virtue with Robert Fulton."

"But do be careful, Girl," Jane said seriously. "You are now a very wealthy and powerful person, and there are people who are going to resent that and try to take advantage of it. Promise me you'll look out for yourself."

"I promise. And, I'll be home soon to get my belongings together for my move. In the mean time, will you take care of things for me?"

"As always, I will keep things running for you, Darcy," Jane replied quietly. "Your home and your animals will be fine, but come home soon."

Darcy skipped dinner that night and fell into a deep but fitful sleep. She was awakened the next morning by a brisk knock on her door.

"Ms. Jeffers," the maid called out, "Mr. Robert is downstairs waiting for you. He wants to show you around the plantation."

Cracking open her eyes she looked at the clock. It was 7 A.M. Well, she thought, the fun begins now. "Thank you," Darcy called out to the woman. "Can you please tell him I'll meet him in the kitchen? And is there some coffee? I think I'm going to need it."

The maid, a young woman who came in twice a week to help Anita, giggled then responded, "Yes, the coffee is ready and there are rolls as well. I will have Mr. Robert meet you in the kitchen."

Darcy got out of bed and stumbled to the bathroom. After a quick shower and a comb through her wet hair, she put on jeans and a t-shirt and was working on socks and shoes when another knock came. Thinking the maid was coming to get her, she opened the door without thinking. It wasn't the maid, but Robert with a mug of coffee in one hand and a plate in the other. He looked marvelous in skintight jeans and a t-shirt that had seen better days. Darcy stared at the stubble of a beard on his face and wondered what it would feel like under her hand.

"Like what you see?" Robert asked, his tone sarcastic. "Is it me or the coffee that has you in a trance?"

Darcy jerked back to reality. "The coffee, of course," she grumbled. "What are you doing up here? I was going to meet you in the kitchen."

"Just saving time. It's going to be a hot day, so the sooner we get started the better. I assume you want to survey all that is now yours," he challenged.

"It's not mine, and you know it. It will never be mine. It's the property of the Trust." She looked up to see him smiling. "It's not fair to antagonize me before my first cup of coffee," she said, grabbing the mug from his hand. "That's an unfair advantage."

Amused, he watched as she drank from the mug. He liked the way she looked in the morning, even before that first cup of coffee, and how she had no pretense about the way she looked. Maybe she would once she was more coherent, but for now he found her charming, a feeling that didn't quite sit well with him. She was the enemy, wasn't she? He would have to keep control of himself and watch his step.

Darcy noticed the shift from friendly to distant even as it was happening. She was sorry to see it, as she enjoyed sparring with this man. It had been a long time since there had been a man in her life, and she wondered if they might ever be friends. Glancing up into his face now, she doubted that would ever be possible.

"Let's go, Darcy," Robert ordered. "Or do you prefer I call you Ms. Jeffers now?"

"Darcy is fine. I'm ready to roll. Let's go see this magnificent plantation you are all so fond of. How many acres did Mr. Hastings say is part of the Trust property?"

"Only the quarter section, one hundred sixty acres. The rest of the original plantation is part of the farm and is still being used to raise crops and animals."

"So that translates into how many acres for you?" Darcy asked, smiling sweetly.

Robert glowered at her, then slowly answered, "The farm is now four hundred forty acres. Some of the original land was sold off in the late nineteenth century."

"So, that means you have over twice the amount of acreage that the Trust was left, isn't that right, Robert?"

"You can play with the best of us, can't you, Darcy? I won't make the mistake of underestimating you now, or in the future."

"See that you don't. That way we can all try to live together in some kind of peace. Isn't that best for everyone?"

"Certainly for you. But you know from yesterday that my family isn't just going to let this rest. You'd better be ready for anything."

"Another threat?"

"No, just a friendly warning," he replied as he stopped the pick-up truck. "Here's the first stop on the tour. Everybody out!"

Darcy finally took notice of her surroundings. They were deep into the woods to the far side of the main house. The road they had traveled was dirt and gravel, and they stood in a clearing with several dilapidated structures around the periphery. Most of the structures were in complete ruin, but a couple could still be entered.

"Where are we, Robert?" Darcy asked. "What are these buildings?"

"This is the slave village, or at least that's what it was called by the plantation owners here," he replied. "They had their own village by the late eighteenth century, as it was the easiest way to keep them all together. It's not far from the house and it's even closer to the farm house, so the slaves could get to their work easily," he explained.

"Wouldn't they have tried to escape from this village? Seems so remote."

"The trees weren't so overgrown when the slaves were on the plantation and there were always foremen and others who patrolled the property on the lookout for slaves trying to escape, as well as trespassers. The slaves were often born and raised right here so this was their home. They didn't want to escape, had nowhere else to go."

"So this is what Marjorie was talking about," she remarked excitedly. "What she wanted rebuilt and made available to the public. I had no idea it was such a large place and that it would need so much restoration. I'll have to get help from the Colonial Williamsburg Foundation. They would know how to go about all of this."

"Aren't you getting a little ahead of yourself, Darcy? You don't even have a board of directors for the Plantation Trust yet, and you're already off and running."

"You're right, first things first. But it's great to know this is here and what it looks like. I'd like to come back with a camera so I can record the condition of the buildings and the area."

"Maybe later, he said brusquely. "Right now, let's get on with the tour. I need to get back to work."

For the next hour the two toured the property, most of which was wood or water. There were remains of other buildings that had long ago been abandoned, and there were also extensive tracts of land where the trees had been cut for lumber and now had regrown. Darcy was most impressed.

As Robert started back for the house, Darcy stopped him. "May I see where you live? Can I see the farm? I can walk back to the house from there, can't I? Then you can get right to work."

Robert grudgingly complied. As they pulled into the farmyard Darcy was overwhelmed with memories from her childhood. This house was older than the one she had lived in, as it was from the early 1800s and very much a brick farmhouse, but it was big and welcoming with a porch that wrapped around most of the structure. Not too far from the house was a huge old wooden barn that had been lovingly restored and returned to its usefulness. Several more outbuildings made up the rest of the farm, all of them nearly 200 years old. A few new buildings had been erected as well, but they had been placed behind the other buildings and back into the trees so as to be almost invisible. Darcy sighed with pleasure.

"Oh, Robert, this is wonderful," she said as she got out of the truck. "I love farms. I've lived on one almost all of my life although it was nowhere near the size of this one. Do you have animals here?"

Robert was silent and stunned by the look of pure joy on Darcy's face. "You love farms? You must be pulling my leg." She made no response except to head toward the barn. "Yes," he answered gruffly, "there are animals. Come on, I'll show you." He led the way into the dark building.

In her enthusiasm and ignorance of the man's obvious suspicion, Darcy shouted with joy when she got into the barn and saw two rows of stalls full of horses. "Oh, my, horses! I love horses. I miss my horse. Oh, Robert, do you think I will be able to find a place to keep my horse when I move down here?"

"You own a horse?" he asked. "I find that hard to believe. You don't strike me as an outdoor girl. I would have guessed more of a mall rat."

"Well, believe it. He's a big old thoroughbred, grandson of Secretariat. He qualified for the Kentucky Derby but injured himself doing it, so he was on the dressage show circuit for years. Like his famous grandfather, he's a big chestnut, but now a gelding. These days Cassidy is just a big old teddy bear that I can ride."

"You can keep him here, of course," he replied. "The rent will be minimal."

Darcy's head came up at that. Coolly she replied, "Why of course I'd pay you rent, Robert. I know the farm is yours and I would never impose upon you otherwise." Seeing his face begin to turn red, she decided a retreat was called for.

"Thanks for the tour. I think I'll get on back to the house. I need to pack for my flight tomorrow. Can you point me in the right direction to walk?"

Robert watched as Darcy's curvaceous form retreated down the dusty road. She walked with authority and ownership, but seemed so at ease at the same time. He had to give her credit; she was never dull. He didn't think she'd be able to outlast his family, but she was a worthy adversary.

As Darcy walked back to the plantation she thought about the move she was about to make. It was a huge decision and, as usual, she had made it without much thought as to the consequences. Moving here would mean leaving Minnesota and her home, leaving behind the lakes and woodlands that were so dear to her. She would also have to face the hot and humid weather and leave behind the winters full of cold and snow. Well, that won't be too much of a hardship, she laughed to herself, but leaving home would be hard. Still, she knew it was the right thing to do. Darcy had been feeling the need to break out on her own for some time, and as Jane so rightly pointed out, she had landed on her feet once again with all of the pieces falling neatly into place.

Five

I love Virginia with its history and its natural beauty. However, danger and peril are also a part of Virginia. You have to respect the heritage.

Andrew Page stood looking out the window at the golf course in front of him. He thought about getting in a round this morning before heading into the office, but he just wasn't feeling too well. His head pounded and his hands shook. All because of Marjorie Fulton, he thought. The reading of the will had been devastating to him. That his mother-in-law left him nothing was bad enough, but to restrict his own wife from helping with his debts had been humiliating. Good thing the old bird is gone already, he thought, or I might have done her in myself!

Beth looked at her husband's back as he stood silhouetted in the window. They shared a tasteful, new, two story brick home on the golf course in Williamsburg. She had used her artistic talent to decorate each room. The result was a showplace of which she was proud.

She shook with a wave of frustration. There was nothing she could say to make her husband feel less embarrassed about what had happened yesterday. She had been thrilled to receive money to pursue her dream of becoming an artist, but it was overshadowed by her husband's distress. Not to mention the thought of Darcy Jeffers getting the house. She growled at that thought, and Andrew swung around.

"Are you all right, Beth?" he asked, concern in his voice. "You look a little flushed."

"I was just thinking about the newest thorn in our side, Darcy Jeffers," his wife replied. "We need to talk to Graham at once about whether we can break the will or do anything about this situation. We also need to have a family meeting. Can you talk to Jonathan about that when you go into work?" She smiled up at him. "Your help will be invaluable to us, you know. You really are one of the family, Andrew."

He looked down at Beth and wondered, not for the first time, whether she really believed in him or if it was all an act. Deciding not to worry about it, he leaned over and kissed her. "I'll talk to Jon as soon as I get in. Don't worry, Dear."

"George, can you help me with my suitcases?" Darcy called down the stairs. "I just don't seem to have enough hands!"

George was quickly at her side and relieved her of several bags. "The car is waiting for you. The driver will drop you off at the Richmond airport in plenty of time, Miss Darcy," he replied in his thick Virginia accent. "With a sunny day like this the trip should be quick and easy."

Darcy looked back at the house as she entered the car. Could it really be true that she was now the mistress of such a piece of history? She allowed herself a small smile until she heard the throb of a pickup truck coming up the drive.

Robert parked quickly and walked over to Darcy. "I could have given you a lift to Richmond," he said. "You didn't need to get a driver for that, or have you already become the lady of the manor?" he added sarcastically.

Darcy counted to ten before answering. "I had nothing to do with arranging this car. I thought you were probably sick of me and had it arranged," she answered as calmly as she could. "But obviously it was someone else who wants to get me out of town as fast as possible. There are so many of you, it's hard to keep track." She leaned back in the seat and smiled sweetly. "See you soon, Robert. I know how much you will look forward to that!" Turning to the driver she said, "Let's get going. I don't want to miss my plane." With that the driver started the car and left Robert standing on the steps of the house beside George.

Darcy closed her eyes. She was tired of fighting already and these had only been skirmishes. The war had yet to begin in earnest. She had heard from Graham Hastings' son, Grant, that the Fulton siblings had had several meetings with attorneys over how to proceed with the matter of the will. Darcy had even heard about a meeting of the four that had taken place fairly late one night at Jonathan's house in Williamsburg. They were obviously plotting strategy while she was leaving the battlefield. Not the greatest tactic, but Darcy needed the break to regroup and get things ready for her move. She sighed audibly and looked up to find the driver staring at her in the mirror.

"Oh, I'm sorry to be so rude," Darcy remarked. "My name is Darcy and I appreciate you driving me to Richmond. And who are you?"

"Name's Nick," said the driver. "Shouldn't take long 'tall to get you to the airport. Just sit back and enjoy the ride." His smile was more a sneer.

Now that he had her attention, Darcy took a long look at Nick. His hair and eyes were a deep black, and he was built solidly, like a wrestler. His hands were meaty and held tightly to the steering wheel, and he had an air about him of someone waiting for something to happen. Darcy idly wondered if Nick had a jumpy personality, and if so, how he had ever become a driver. Oh, well, Richmond wasn't far away. He should be able to make it that far without trouble. She closed her eyes again and settled in for a nap.

A fierce jolt and the scream of metal upon metal woke Darcy with a start. Luckily she had put on her seat belt or she would have been thrown into the front seat and probably through the windshield. Shaking her head to clear it, she looked around to see where she was and what had happened. A stabbing pain in her left foot caused her to see that it was pinned beneath the driver's seat that had been pushed back by the impact into her lap. Darcy tried to move her foot but was unable to dislodge it from under the seat.

Nick was nowhere to be seen. It seemed that the car had been hit on the driver's side by another vehicle or something metallic, but neither that vehicle, nor Nick, were anywhere that she could see. Darcy scanned the area frantically for someone to help her, then stopped cold. She sniffed the air. The car was leaking gasoline. Suddenly a small explosion occurred in the engine compartment. If she didn't get out of the car fast she was going to be toast, literally!

Frantic now, Darcy grabbed at her leg trying to shake her foot loose. No luck—it was only making things worse. As the fire in the engine got brighter, she willed herself to be calm, to think this through. She looked down at the seat once more and realized the handle to move the seat forward was still intact. Pulling the lever and pushing the seat with her other hand, she managed to move the seat less than an inch, but it was enough to wriggle free her foot. Her shoe remained where it was lodged as she threw open the door and hobbled as fast as she could away from the smoldering car.

Her heart banging a million beats a minute, Darcy fell to the ground and turned back toward the car just as the gas tank exploded. It filled the clear sky with smoke, heat and flames, and all she could do was stare. She could have been killed. What was going on here?

The sound of a vehicle approaching made her turn back toward the road. For some reason she was not surprised to see Elizabeth Page's Mercedes pull up to the scene.

"Darcy, are you all right?" Beth asked as she viewed the fire. "Oh, my gosh, were you in that car? You could have been killed!" The immaculately groomed woman seemed genuinely distressed as she gazed at the fire and the wreckage.

"I'm fine, but we need to call this in, then I need to get to the airport," Darcy replied. "Can you help me take care of this? Beth? Do you hear me?" She grabbed the other woman's pant leg and pulled her around to get her attention.

"Sorry," Beth mumbled. "I've just never seen a car on fire like that. I've always been afraid of fire, and I lost my focus. I've already called 911 so the police and fire should be along shortly. And of course I can take you to the airport, but shouldn't you go to the hospital first?"

Darcy gazed at her swollen foot. She should have it x-rayed, but she wasn't willing to miss her flight home. Now more than ever she wanted to get back to Minnesota. "No, I don't need a hospital," she replied quite definitely. "After the police arrive and I give them my story, I want to get to the airport."

"Well, here comes the sheriff now, so it shouldn't take long." After a moment Beth turned and said, "Whose car is that anyway? Is it a rental?"

Darcy tried to stand next to the other woman as the sheriff exited his car, but her sore ankle stopped her. Breathing hard from the pain she replied, "No, someone ordered it for me. Wasn't it you? I had a driver named Nick."

"Good heavens, no," Beth replied. "I didn't even know you were leaving, but now that I think about it, it makes sense that someone other than the family drive you to the airport. But why would you think it was me?"

The deputy sheriff's approach put an end to the questioning. "Good afternoon, Ladies. I'm Deputy Aubrey Jackson. Can you tell me what happened here?" He looked from one woman to the other and back with kind, brown eyes. The deputy was not much taller than Darcy, but he had a quick, reassuring smile and his dark, wiry hair gleamed in the sun. He turned to Beth and said, "Were you the one who phoned this in?"

"Yes. I saw the smoke from a few miles back and called in the fire," she replied.

"That would make you Elizabeth Page, then?" the deputy asked.

"Correct. And this woman on the ground is Darcy Jeffers. She was in the car at the time of the crash." The deputy turned back to Darcy.

"What happened, Ms. Jeffers?" he asked. "Tell me the whole story, please, with as much detail as possible." The smell of the burning car was making Darcy nauseous, so she took only a few minutes to inform the deputy of the situation. "And where is this driver, Nick, you called him?" Deputy Jackson asked. "Did he go for help? Are you sure there was another vehicle involved?"

"As I indicated, Deputy," Darcy said through clenched teeth, "I was asleep when the accident occurred and Nick left the scene. I believe there was another vehicle involved, as I awoke to the sound of metal screeching. I don't know any more than I have told you. May I go now?"

"I'll file this report, Miss, and we'll try to follow up on this Nick person and on the car itself, although there's not much left of it to get an ID," the deputy responded, glancing at the smoldering wreckage. "Where can we reach you?"

"I'm on my way back to Minnesota, but I'll be back here within a week," Darcy replied, now beginning to ache all over from the crash. She pulled a card from her purse that had remained on her arm as she fled the car and gave it to the deputy. "I can be reached at these numbers. Once I am back in Virginia, I can be reached at Winterview in Charles City County. Anything else?"

Deputy Jackson's eyes held speculation. "So, you're the outsider who is going to live at Winterview. Welcome to the neighborhood, Ms. Jeffers. I'll let you know what we find. Right now you are free to go with Mrs. Page."

Accepting a hand up from the deputy, Darcy followed Beth to the car and got in. When she was settled in her seat she said, "I'm glad I saved my purse so I can still get on the plane. Otherwise you'd be stuck with me for another day."

Beth said nothing. She drove quickly and efficiently to the Richmond airport. As they pulled up to the terminal, she turned to Darcy and said, "You had better watch out for yourself. Seems to me someone is after you. I don't like what Mother did in her will, as you know, and there are others around who don't want this situation to go well." She turned to look out the front window. "Let's just call this warning a going away present. And if you're smart you will stay away."

Darcy stared at Beth's profile for a moment, then got out of the car. "No such luck, lady," she said quietly. "I'm coming back in a week and moving into Winterview. A freak car accident isn't going to change that. But thanks for the warning. Now I know which way to look for more trouble." She slammed the car door and went into the terminal.

Six

*My late husband and I took the children to the
Midwest every summer. We splashed in the lakes,
hiked in the woods and played in the long twilight.
We believed it would have been an excellent place to
raise children if we hadn't had Winterview.*

It feels so good to be lying in my own bed again, Darcy
thought, as she pulled the sheet up to her chin. She
tucked her favorite pillow under her head and snuggled
down in the familiar bed. Her foot was now aching unbearably,
but she had taken some ibuprofen and the bed was so comfortable
she hoped she'd be asleep soon. *I wonder if I should take this bed
with me,* she mused as her eyes closed. *That's tomorrow's worry,*
she decided, as she fell into a deep, but fitful, sleep.

The shrieking of the telephone next to her head brought
Darcy straight up out of the bed. Before she could clear her head
and remember where she was, the phone shrieked again. She
grabbed the offending receiver and jerked it to her ear. "Hullo?"
she mumbled into the receiver.

"Darcy, are you OK?" Jane asked anxiously. "I've been waiting
all evening to hear from you! Is everything all right? I was really
worried. I thought you would at least want to see Cairo right
away! I didn't even hear you come in."

Snapping on the bedside lamp, Darcy collected herself. "Jane,
I'm so sorry. I got here so late and all I could think of was to get
into my nice, soft bed. I just fell asleep before I could call downstairs." She yawned loudly to punctuate her statement.

"Oh, that's just like you, Darcy," Jane snapped. "I'm here
waiting for you and you forget me!" She tried to laugh it off. "But
I can understand you being tired after all that's happened. When
am I going to hear the rest of the story?"

"How about lunch tomorrow downtown," her friend suggested. "My treat. I promise to bring you up to date, and you can help me decide what I am going to do with all my stuff. I need to decide what's going with me and what's not. And who better to help than you? You're the best friend I've ever had. Besides, there's no way I'll be up before you leave for work. You leave at the crack of dawn."

Softening, Jane replied, "That sounds great, Darcy. You know I worry about you and I needed to know you got in all right. What am I going to do without you around?" There was a slight whine to her voice as she spoke.

Darcy didn't notice her friend's distress. "Thanks for understanding, Jane." She said. "We'll talk about everything tomorrow at lunch. Right now I need to get to sleep."

"OK. By the way Darcy, how did you get home from the airport? I thought you would call me."

"You won't believe it, but Fran showed up," she responded. "Imagine my sister actually showing up to see me. Must be she heard about my inheritance already and thinks there's more money to be had," Darcy laughed. "It was good to see her, I must admit. But Fran is Fran and nothing will ever change her. Anyway, good night, my friend. Tell Cairo I will walk him in the morning." She hung up the phone.

Before falling back to sleep, Darcy thought about Jane. She was sure her friend would worry about Fran's surprise appearance at the airport. Her sister always had an agenda, and this was a pretty bold move for her. Jane would try to figure out what was happening there before Darcy got too involved again with her older sister. Poor Jane. She lived such a hard life with a family that had been emotionally abusive. She had gotten married just to get out of the house. Once that fell apart, she had been drifting until she and Darcy had found one another again. They had renewed their friendship quickly and easily, and became roommates. Jane had had so little in her life and Darcy was happy to share all that she had with her good friend. It had worked out well for them both, at least until now. Uneasy with her thoughts, Darcy rolled onto her side and fell back to sleep, exhausted.

Robert straightened up and looked to the sky as the first soft rain began to fall. This was just what these fields needed. He picked up a handful of dirt and sifted it through his fingers. He was happy in his life as a farmer. His years in the Marines had been challenging and interesting, but in the end they had proven deadly. Here on the farm he made a difference to his family and to the families who relied on its production and its labor.

The sound of a truck brought him out of his thoughts. The large white pickup was new, and it was getting a coat of mud as it continued past the farm. Robert watched as the truck went past the turn to Winterview and continued down the path toward the slave quarters. Who would be going back there now, he wondered to himself. The only thing he could think of was some kind of survey team from Colonial Williamsburg. If that were so, then Darcy Jeffers had moved very quickly. He'd have to ask George about it next time he went up to the house. The rain soon came down in earnest, so Robert jumped on the tractor and drove back to the barn.

After sleeping in as long as she dared, Darcy gingerly stood up and put weight on her sore ankle. Luckily it didn't seem to be injured too badly, for which she was grateful. Darcy took Cairo outside and they walked around the property in the sunshine, the stiffness of her muscles gradually loosening.

The farm was in Scandia, only 45 minutes from the heart of either St. Paul or Minneapolis, so Darcy had the best of both worlds in this location. The house and the ten acres surrounding it had been her family's home since she was born. She had actually been born in the master bedroom! The white clapboard house was large and neat. As it had been built in 1900, it had beautiful hardwood floors throughout and a built-in buffet and hutch in the dining room. It even had solid oak pocket doors between the dining room and the living room.

The barn was a good distance from the house, with a small pump house and a machine shed in between the two major structures. All of them had been lovingly cared for over the years, and Darcy always felt grounded when she was on the farm. She and Cairo watched the horses run up and down the pasture with their typical spring frolicking. Cairo whined to be allowed to join them, so Darcy set him free. Barking wildly, he caught up to the horses and joined them as they ran.

Darcy and Jane met for lunch in Minneapolis that afternoon and Darcy filled her friend in on all that had happened. That took most of the lunch, so the two went for a walk down the Nicollet Mall while they discussed the future. Darcy felt sure that moving to Virginia was her destiny, no matter how strongly Jane argued that she was getting in over her head. They discussed what should be moved, what to leave and what to give away. By the end of the afternoon Darcy knew what she had to do before returning to Virginia and Jane was close to tears at her friend's departure. Her feelings aside, she would help her housemate get ready and get moved.

When Darcy walked in the door to her house, the telephone was ringing. Thinking that it might be Fran or Jane, she rushed to pick it up before it rolled over to voice mail. Her voice was breathy from running as she said hello.

A deep, male voice responded. "Ms. Jeffers, is that you? This is Jonathan Fulton. I am sorry to bother you in Minnesota, but I needed to talk to you about the Plantation Trust. Do you have a minute?"

"Certainly," Darcy replied, wondering what this was all about. "What's up?"

"You need to set a date for the first board of directors meeting for the Trust," he replied. "I spoke to Grant Hastings, and he said you had made your board selection before you left Virginia. I assume you simply chose those people whom my mother suggested. Have you also made your selection as to who will follow you if for some reason you are not able to be the chair?" he inquired.

A shiver ran down her spine. What was Jonathan up to? Why would he care about who would replace her at the Trust? She replied, "No, Mr. Fulton, I have not made that determination. I have picked the board, though, but why the hurry for a meeting?"

"The Trust needs to start paying the bills on the plantation and needs to decide how to invest the money left to it," he said. "None of this can be done without board approval, so the sooner the better."

"What about the talk of appealing the will?" she asked sweetly. "Don't we have to wait until all of that is settled?"

Jonathan's voice got cold and hard. "No, Graham says the Trust will go on regardless of any challenges to the will or any other course of action, so the board should meet as soon as possible." After a pause he continued, "And you really should have the person who is your successor at the meeting. He or she should know what is happening from the beginning. You never know when something could happen to you."

"Thank you for your call," she replied grimly. "I will be back in Virginia in a week, so you can set the meeting any time after that. I will fax Grant all of the necessary information since he will be helping me with the Trust. I appreciate you taking the time to call. I'll speak to you soon."

Darcy hung up the phone without waiting to hear Jonathan's response. She wondered what his call was really all about. *If he thinks he can coax me into telling him who my replacement will be in case of an emergency, he's underestimated me,* she thought. *He'll find out when I'm good and ready to let him, and everyone else, know.*

The next morning Darcy was awakened again by the telephone. The call was again from Virginia, but this time it was from the Charles City County Sheriff. "Ms. Jeffers, this is Deputy Sheriff Jackson," he began. "I'm calling to follow up on the car accident."

"What can I do for you, Deputy?" Darcy asked. "Were you able to find the driver, Nick, so you know what really happened?"

"Well, that's why I'm calling," the deputy replied. "We can find no record of any driver and the car you were in was stolen earlier in the day from downtown Newport News. We will need you to come back to Virginia as soon as possible so we can look into this matter further."

Darcy was shocked at this news. How could the car have been stolen? Who would do such a thing? What did she have to do with any of this? After a moment, she responded, "Deputy Jackson, I have some matters to take care of here, but I will return to Virginia within the week."

"Sorry, ma'am," he responded. "You have forty-eight hours to show up in the Charles City County court or a warrant will be issued for your arrest."

"Arrest!" Darcy exclaimed. "Why would I be under arrest? I was the victim of this whole situation. What crime have I committed?"

"Ms. Jeffers, you are the only one who can describe the man in the car. We need you to come give your testimony and follow up with this matter. We can only do that if you are here. The court order is only to get you back in the state," he explained. "I'm actually taking a lot of heat for letting you leave."

"Oh, this is so ridiculous," she exclaimed, frustrated at the turn of events. "Well, there's nothing I can do, is there? I will get on the road tomorrow and get to Virginia as soon as I can. Anything else, Deputy?"

"No, ma'am, that's all. If you'll contact me at the telephone number I provided earlier when you get back into town I'll set up your meetings. Thank you for your cooperation."

As she put down the phone once again, Darcy let out a howl of pure frustration. Cairo came running in through his dog door to see what had happened. "Sorry, Boy," she said to him as she absently patted his head. "Looks like we're going to get on the road a lot sooner than we thought." Cairo looked up at her expectantly. "You're right, Boy, first things first. Let's take a walk."

Walking out the door Darcy and Cairo were greeted by the sweet smell of flowers. The garden was finally in bloom after the long winter. It hadn't been particularly cold, but winter had lasted well into April. The soft whinny from the horses had Darcy heading toward the pasture. She was greeted by the sight of her five horses crowding around the fence to get their share of the treats. Laughing, Darcy dutifully pulled out the carrots she had grabbed out of the bag and began to distribute them. The last carrot was for Cassidy, her pride and joy. He looked happy and healthy, and it was a shame there wasn't enough time to ride him before she left again.

"How would you like to live in Virginia?" she asked the horse who was busy nuzzling her for more treats. "I hope you'll like it. You can make new horse friends there." Cassidy moved away to end the discussion.

Calling to Cairo, Darcy continued to walk around the farm. The grass was finally fully green, and she could see the alfalfa just starting to come out of the ground. The sun was warm and welcoming and the sky was a bright blue dotted with puffy, white clouds.

I'll really miss this place, but it's time I leave its security, Darcy thought as she stopped to watch the newborn kittens run around their mother. *It's been my anchor, but this farm has also been my excuse for not getting on with my life. I have a chance to make a difference and I won't blow it,* she promised herself.

Returning from her walk, Darcy spent the rest of the day getting as many things done as she possibly could. She packed all of the belongings she would need immediately, packed up Cairo's things and faxed the Plantation Trust information to Grant Hastings. She followed that up with a phone call to the attorney to tell him about her situation. He told Darcy that he would be available to be with her when she spoke to the Sheriff. Then, she prepared a list of things she hoped Jane would follow up on. She depended too much on Jane's help, but this didn't seem like the time to change. She couldn't ask her older sister—she just wasn't reliable for anything not dealing directly with her own well-being.

The door opened and the preoccupied woman turned around expecting to see Jane. Instead, in walked Fran.

"Well, hello, DJ," Fran said as she made herself at home at the kitchen table. "Bet you didn't think you'd see me again so soon, did you?" she asked. "Since the other night I heard through the grapevine just what a nice little set-up you'll have in Virginia. I knew it was good, but I didn't know it was that good. Way, to go, sis! I didn't think you had it in you."

Darcy stared coldly at her sister. Fran, only two years older than her sister, had blonde hair with a honey-colored accent that she wore long and flowing. That, along with her piercing green eyes and tall, lithe body made her a very beautiful woman. But she is so artificial, Darcy thought to herself. *Under all of that beauty there really is nothing. What you see is what you get. How sad.*

"Going to speak or just stare?" Fran asked. "I know I'm good looking, but it's usually only the men who stare." She giggled at her little joke.

"Hello, Fran," Darcy finally replied. "It's good to see you again so soon. Picking me up at the airport was quite a surprise, but twice in one week is amazing. To what do I owe this privilege? And how did you find out what happened in Virginia? You are awfully well informed."

"Oh, you know me, Honey. I just wanted to stop by the old homestead and say hello. As for knowing about Virginia, you should read the newspaper more often. You're big news. It's not every day a Minnesotan inherits a plantation. You made the front page of the local section today in the St. Paul paper."

"Not likely that you just stopped by to say hello," Darcy replied. "Since you know about my Virginia experience and you didn't pump me about it at the airport, I assume your visit has something to do with that."

"Oh, all right," Fran replied, pouting. "You're no fun. I'll get right down to it, although I really am glad to see you. We don't see nearly enough of each other." Darcy snorted at that and waited for her sister to continue. Seeing no further response forthcoming, Fran continued, "Since you'll be moving to Virginia, you won't be needing this old house any more, right? I was thinking it was time to sell it and take our money out of it."

"Don't you care about anything except money?" Darcy asked, appalled. "This is our home! This is where we spent time with Mom and Dad. This house has been in the family for four generations. I'm not going to sell it," she concluded with a finality that dared Fran to argue.

"Well, seeing as half of it is rightly mine, and as you have someone who is not a family member living here without my permission, I think we'll just take this to the lawyers and see what we can work out," Fran replied forcefully. "I don't care if it's an antique unless it gets me more for my share. You know I don't like to think about the past."

"Still running, Fran?" Darcy asked quietly. Her sister's revelation had cooled her anger. "Someday you're going to have to come to terms with what happened to our parents. I hope you do it before it's too late for you to find any happiness in your life. As for this house, I am not going to sell it, but you can get it appraised and I will buy out your half if the cash is so important to you." She shook her head and walked to the door. "If there's nothing else, I need to get going. I'm leaving for Virginia in the morning."

Fran rose. She was several inches taller than Darcy thanks to very high heels. "Thanks, DJ," she said, avoiding eye contact. "I do need the money, and it really is good to see you. Will you please let me know where you are in Virginia?"

"Why, so you can get more money from me?" Darcy asked.

Recovering from her momentary lapse into sentimentality, Fran said, "Of course, Dear. It doesn't pay to lose sight of one's cash cow, now does it?" With a toss of her golden head Fran walked out the door leaving Darcy looking after her.

Can this day get any worse, she wondered as Cairo appeared in the doorway. His tail was wagging furiously, so he was happy about something. The something turned out to be Jane returning home.

"Hi, there, Roomy," Jane said as she put her purse down on the kitchen table. "How was your day?" Seeing the look on Darcy's face she dropped down into the nearest chair. "Now what's happened? What's been going on today that I don't know about?"

Darcy opened the refrigerator, pulled out a bottle of white wine and poured them each a glass. She sat down next to Jane and filled her in on what had been a long afternoon. Now, she had to tell her friend she was leaving again in the morning.

"Jane, we haven't ever discussed what you'll do when I move to Virginia," Darcy began. "I know this is all so sudden, but what do you want to do? I know I could get you a job at the Plantation Trust if you want it, and heaven knows there's plenty of room at Winterview for you to live."

Jane reached down and rubbed Cairo's sleeping body as she tried to keep her temper in check. "That's a nice offer, Darcy, but don't you think I can make it without you?" She took a deep breath and tried again. "Sorry, I just feel like that was a pity offer and not a real offer for me to move with you. I don't really want to move right now—I love my job and the way I live, but that has always included you and Cairo being around. Besides, you need me to be here to take care of the move and all since you have to leave right away."

"It wasn't a pity offer, but I don't know what life is going to hold for me in Virginia, so I don't really know what I'm offering you. And, I know how much you like your job working at the law firm. You're a whiz at human resources, so you would be very useful to the Trust. Maybe we can take some time to figure it all out and then you can really choose where you want to live. For now, though, I hope you will continue to live right here in the house. I certainly am not going to take a lot of furniture with me, and I want you to feel this will continue to be your home."

"What will Fran say to that?" Jane asked.

Darcy sighed. "I told you she stopped by today for money, but what she really wanted was for us to sell the house. I told her I would buy her half out so she can have the money she craves and I can keep the house in the family." She really wished her sister shared her sentiments about the house, but that was water under the bridge. "So, Fran has no say over whether you stay or go."

"Only you do," Jane commented under her breath. To Darcy she replied, "I want to stay right here and help you get things sorted out and moved. I know you rely on me and it's important to me to be of help."

"Jane, thank you. You continue to be the rock I cling to in my life. I hope you know just how much your support has meant to me over the years. You'll always be my best and truest friend." Darcy got up and gave Jane a hug. "So now I will finish packing, get a little sleep, and hit the road. I'll put all of the information and lists together and you know how to reach me. Jane, take care." She hugged her friend again.

"You're the one who needs to take care, Darcy," Jane replied. "Be careful driving and make sure those southern sheriffs don't gang up on you!"

Darcy waved to Jane in reply as she started up the backstairs.

As soon as the woman and dog were out of sight, Jane gave in to her irritation and sense of loss. Why did Darcy have to make her feel like a servant? Why did she let herself get used this way? No, no, she is my best friend and I love her like a sister, Jane reminded herself, as she held her pounding head in her hands. This just can't be happening. I have nothing of my own. I've shared Darcy's life these past years. How am I supposed to go on with things when she's a thousand miles away? Still holding her head, she got up and headed for bed. Maybe this will all go away if I just go to sleep, she decided. I just don't want her to go, but there's nothing I can do about it.

"Mr. Fulton, telephone call for you on line three," the receptionist said when Jonathan picked up the telephone.

"Thank you Marissa," he replied. "I'll take it in my office." He went into his spacious office, closed the door and picked up the telephone.

"Jonathan Fulton," he said in his rich baritone voice. "How may I help you?"

"Hey, Dad, it's me," Lucas replied. "I was just wondering whether you decided yet about me going to the Blink 182 concert tonight. My friends are holding a ticket for me, and I need to let them know."

Silence followed this request. Finally Jonathan said, "All right, Lucas, you can go tonight. But there are conditions. If you don't agree to them, you don't go and you don't get your allowance."

"Pretty harsh, Dad. What are the conditions? The way you say it I'm sure it's nothing I'm going to like."

Ignoring his son's remark, he continued, "The conditions are: first, you will be home no later than midnight. It's a school night and that's too late as it is." He paused as Lucas made a comment under his breath. "Second, you will go to work for your uncle on the farm. You'll spend weekends there when he needs you and you'll be compensated like any other farm employee."

"You've got to be kidding, Dad!" Lucas shouted. "That's not fair! If Mom were here she wouldn't make me do this."

"Those are the conditions. Take them or leave them, Son. It's up to you."

"Fine. I'll go work for Uncle Rob. How bad can it be? But this is blackmail, Dad. It's just not fair."

"Have a good time at the concert. I'll see you when you get home tonight." Jonathan hung up the phone and pushed back in his chair. He closed his eyes and wondered, not for the first time, where his ex-wife was these days. She had left Lucas and him over two years ago with no other explanation than she was tired of being a Fulton. She wanted a real life of her own. Linda had filed for divorce, negotiated a nice settlement, and walked out of their lives without another word. Lucas had not heard from his mother since that day and he was still suffering over it. Jonathan wondered what would happen to his son who felt abandoned by his mother. Now the whole mess with his own mother and Darcy Jeffers was making things worse. Right at this moment, Jonathan hated women.

Seven

*There is nothing so pleasing as sitting in the shade
of Winterview on a hot summer day, watching the
boats glide along on the mighty James River.
It transports you back in time, makes you feel
a part of the history.*

Darcy and Cairo hit the road the following morning at 5:00 A.M. She had gone into Jane's room to say goodbye, but Jane wanted no part of farewells, so she loaded the dog into the back seat and started out. The woman and dog made good time as they cruised through Wisconsin and into Illinois. Stopping only at rest stops to let Cairo out, she drove through the day and well into the evening before stopping at a motel in Lexington, Kentucky. They could only have a few hours of rest since she had to make her appearance in Charles City County before 5:00 p.m. the next day. As they entered the motel room, Cairo made a beeline for the bed, jumped up, circled three times, plopped down on the soft covers and was asleep before Darcy could shut the door. It was blissfully cool in the room for which both of them were grateful after a warm day on the road.

Darcy tried to call Jane but got no reply. She left a message about where they were staying and tried to go to sleep. All she could think of now was that accident and why this was all happening. Was it really because of Marjorie's will? It seemed strange because the accident had been so soon after the reading of the will. What about the driver who left no fingerprints? The stolen car? Her head hurt thinking about it. It seemed impossible that someone would want to hurt her just because she intended to keep Marjorie's dream alive. Not for the first time, she wished Marjorie were here to talk to about all of this. They had discussed the plantation and its future so often, but they had not spent much time talking about Marjorie and her relationship with her children. Maybe there was more going on than she knew.

Marjorie had always talked about Robert as her one child who had fulfilled his destiny and his mother's hopes. She wanted more for Beth, who had married Andrew at a very young age, against both of their parents' wishes, but she still loved her only daughter. Jonathan was the son who was to carry on the family name and tradition, so he married and had a son, but not many years ago his wife had divorced him and left. Marjorie worried about both Jonathan and Lucas, but she never said a harsh word about them. Not wanting to think anymore about the Fulton family, Darcy finally fell into a deep sleep.

She dreamed, dreamed the terrifying dream of her parents' deaths. Darcy had been 22 and Fran had been 24 when their parents had driven to a dinner party in Minnetonka, a suburb on the west side of Minneapolis. It was June and the weather was unpredictable. On the way home they had run into a terrible storm and the car had run off the road and hit a tree. Her parents had not died instantly, but by the time the police found the car, they were gone, the car an inferno. She could feel herself crying as her neighbor tried to take her in her arms to comfort her. She shook her neighbor off, ran to the barn, threw her arms around her horse, and cried until she had no tears left. Darcy awoke with tears streaming down her face and Cairo beside her trying to lick the tears away.

A few hours later, they were back on the road. Luckily the weather was holding, so they didn't have rain or worse weather to slow them down. They did, however, have to slow down going through the Blue Ridge Mountains. Finally at 3:00 p.m. they pulled into the Charles City County sheriff's office parking lot.

Deciding it was too hot to leave Cairo in the car, Darcy snapped on his leash and headed inside. Her reflection in the glass doorway stopped her cold and she pulled out a comb and some lipstick before continuing in. Deputy Jackson was on duty and seemed surprised to see her walking through the door.

"Well, hello, Ms. Jeffers," he said amiably. "I thought you were going to call when you got to town. Who's this big guy?" He bent over to pet Cairo who, after a cursory sniff, decided to let him.

"We're a little late getting here, and I wanted to make the deadline, so I haven't gone on to Winterview yet," Darcy reported. "You're my first stop. Oh, this is Cairo, and it's too hot for him to be in the car, so you're stuck with both of us."

"Come on back, Ms. Jeffers," the Deputy said. "The judge is in his chambers, and all we need from you right now is to appear before him to satisfy the warrant. After that you're free to go on to Winterview and we'll set up your deposition for later." The Deputy led the way through the back of the office and into the courthouse. They passed a couple of empty courtrooms and, after knocking, entered the judge's chamber.

"Your Honor, this is Ms. Darcy Jeffers," Deputy Jackson said to the judge. "She is making her appearance before you to satisfy the outstanding warrant before heading on down to her home," he continued. The young African American man behind the desk looked up as Deputy Jackson spoke. He had a full head of black hair complimented by a small mustache. He appeared irritated at the interruption until he glanced up and saw Darcy standing before him, tired and ill at ease.

"Miss Darcy Jeffers, I am Judge Ronald Simms," the judge announced. "Please have a seat." Seeing Cairo sniffing around his office, Judge Simms turned to the deputy. "Why is there a dog in my chambers?"

Darcy quickly answered. "Your Honor, it's too hot to leave Cairo in the car, so he is here with me. I haven't been to Winterview yet on my journey from Minnesota."

"Very well, he can stay," the judge granted. "This should only take a few moments. Ms. Jeffers, are you back in Virginia to stay? Do you swear a solemn oath that you will not leave this Commonwealth without the knowledge and consent of this Court again until the investigation of the vehicular accident in which you were involved is completed?"

"Yes, sir," Darcy quietly replied. "I am moving into Winterview today, and I swear not to leave Virginia without the knowledge and consent of this Court."

"Very well," the judge said. "The warrant against you is satisfied. The Deputy will take you out and set up a meeting with the Sheriff," he continued. "Oh, and Ms. Jeffers, I would advise you to get a lawyer just in case one is needed."

After leaving Judge Simms' chambers, Darcy let out a sigh. At least that's over, she thought. She hoped the rest of the day would go as quickly. Deputy Jackson took her back to the office and in a few minutes they had scheduled an appointment for the following morning for the Sheriff to interview her at Winterview. Darcy and Cairo got into the blistering hot car and headed for their new home.

Darcy couldn't believe how relieved she felt when George met her at the car and there was no one else in sight. She had been dreading a scene with one or all of the Fulton family, but luckily not even Molly was at the house. With the help of George and Anita, Darcy unloaded the car, let Cairo run around to get a feel of his new home, then dropped into bed. She chose to sleep in the same room she had always used when visiting, as she just could not bring herself to take over Marjorie's bedroom. That was too final, too soon.

The sound of two dogs yipping and barking awakened Darcy early the next morning. Noticing that Cairo was no longer in the room with her, she hobbled to the window, her injured ankle still stiff from the long journey. The sight that greeted her was charming—a man lying on the ground with two large dogs licking him furiously! Under all that fur Robert laughed until his sides hurt, and he looked up to see Darcy smiling down at them. He succeeded in shifting the dogs to one side and righting himself enough to stand. With a salute to Darcy, he called to the dogs and headed back toward the house.

Darcy threw on her jeans and met them at the door. "Oh, no," she said, wagging her finger at all three of them. "None of you come in until you wipe your feet." She tried to keep from laughing. "You all look like you've had a mud bath!" She reached up and rubbed off some mud lingering on Robert's nose. His hand came up immediately and grabbed her wrist, and the two of them stared at one another for a long moment. It didn't help her equilibrium that her arm tingled where he was touching it, didn't keep the heat from traveling all through her body.

Robert broke the contact first. "Thanks," he acknowledged in a voice not all together steady. He released Darcy's wrist and reached for the towel she was carrying in her other hand. "I'll get to work on these dogs. Any chance there's coffee?"

Darcy watched Robert as he toweled off one dog, then the other, his large hands infinitely gentle as he worked on each animal. She wondered what those hands would feel like toweling off her body, then stopped cold at where her thoughts had led her.

Finally finding her voice, she answered, "You know perfectly well there's always coffee here. What you may not know is that you are welcome to it any time you want it." She glanced at Cairo as she spoke. "And thanks for letting the mutt out this morning," she now changed the subject. "He needed some exercise and he needed to meet Molly. It's great that both things went so well." Robert finished with the dogs and stood holding the towel. "Here, I'll take that," she continued. Regaining her emotional balance, she stepped aside and waved her hand toward the kitchen. "Now, you may all enter," she said in a poor attempt at a British accent. "Even you, Cairo, who seems to have forgotten me for another!" She patted both dogs and followed all three into the kitchen.

An hour later the two were still talking at the kitchen table when George announced the arrival of the Sheriff, as well as Grant Hastings. Darcy looked at both men, noticing the difference between them. Hastings, in his early 30's, had very light skin to compliment his red hair and green eyes. Matthews, who informed her that he had known Robert since they were in school together, was a big, burly man whose thin black hair was sprinkled with gray. Darcy then watched Robert rise from his chair and head toward the door.

The Sheriff stopped his progress. "Mr. Fulton, I will need to speak to you before I leave," Richard Matthews spoke quite formally. "I understand you were the one who ordered the car."

Narrowing his eyes at Matthews, Robert replied, "Rick, we've known each other forever. Are you trying to accuse me of something? If so, you'd better have some evidence. You know I'm not one to fool around with, so you had better be careful how you proceed. I'll be at my house when you want to speak to me." Robert stalked out the back door.

Darcy shivered at the malice in Robert's voice. She had forgotten how mean and nasty he could be. Was Sheriff Matthews right? Had Robert ordered her car? She needed to be more careful around him. Turning back to the men still in the room, she said, "Well, let's get this over with. Grant, do you and I need to talk about anything before I speak to the Sheriff?"

Grant shook his head. "Since you are the victim here and not the criminal, just answer all of the questions as best you can," he replied. "You and I can catch up after the Sheriff has completed his questioning."

"Thank you, Mr. Hastings," Sheriff Matthews said. He had a look of determination about him that reminded Darcy of a bulldog. "Let's get started."

For the better part of an hour Darcy answered all of the Sheriff's questions. As she suspected, he was thorough and pressed Darcy to remember more than she had initially. After that a sketch artist appeared and the two women worked hard to get an accurate sketch of the driver, Nick. Finally Sheriff Matthews was ready to go.

"Thank you for your time, Ms. Jeffers," he said with a slight drawl. "I'll be going to the farm now to talk with Mr. Fulton. I'll let you know when we have any more information. In the mean time, please notify my office if you are thinking of leaving the area." With a nod of his head at Grant, the Sheriff departed.

Darcy collapsed back into her chair. "Well, that was fun," she said sarcastically. "Nothing like being the victim but feeling like the criminal first thing in the morning, is there?" She turned to see Grant standing over her smiling.

"Come on, Darcy," he said as he pulled her from the chair. "Let's go walk in the garden and catch up." His smile was dazzling and Darcy was so disconcerted she let him pull her up. At the back door they were greeted by a symphony of barking. Cairo and Molly wanted to tag along. The pair walked companionably for some minutes before Grant broke the silence.

"So, how are you, really, Darcy? These past days couldn't have been easy for you. And the long drive with a dog in tow, as well. You must be exhausted." He smiled again and took her arm.

Darcy looked up at him, mildly irritated. "Grant, I'm not some shrinking violet that needs to be coddled and kept." Realizing she was taking out her tension from the morning on him, she reined herself in. "But it's sweet of you to ask. Actually, my friend Jane in Minnesota is always so terrific about helping me out, and this time was no exception. And, Cairo's a great companion on long trips. He makes sure I get out of the car often to see to his needs." She laughed as the dog bounded up to her, having heard his name. She scratched him behind the ear and sent him on his way.

"Other than the accident, and the fact that the Fulton family members hate me, everything's grand," Darcy smiled. "How about you? What have you been doing? Have you been able to round up my new board members for the Trust?"

"Actually, I have been hard at work training for a marathon this fall. I'm actually thinking about running in the Twin Cities Marathon up there in Minnesota! It will take a lot of roadwork to get ready and in this heat it's a challenge, but I love to run. As for the Trust stuff, let's not talk business right now, Darcy," Grant said. "I think it would be good for you to have some time to relax before we get into all of that work. There's a lot for you to consider, so you need to be in top form."

This time there was no controlling her temper. Darcy stopped and turned toward Grant. "Let's get something straight right now, Mr. Hastings," she said, her voice like ice. "I am a very capable person and when I want to talk about business we will talk about business. I don't need rest or relaxation in order to make good decisions." She took a deep breath. "Marjorie Fulton wanted me to run her trust, and run it I shall. I hope you will be beside me to provide help as needed, but if you are not comfortable with a woman in charge, now's the time to tell me."

An answering flare of temper lit Grant's eyes, but only for a moment. He bent down, picked off a rose and handed it to Darcy. "Truce," he said with a bow. "You're right. I was being patronizing. Sorry. It won't happen again. Please accept this flower as a token of my esteem."

Darcy choked on that line and smiled. "You pick a rose out of my own garden to give to me as a token? That takes nerve, Grant, I'll give you that." She reached up and patted his cheek just as Robert entered the garden.

The look in Robert's eyes as he watched the two of them together made her shiver. Steering Grant to the gate where Robert was standing, she asked, "How did things go with Sheriff Matthews? He obviously didn't stay too long questioning you."

"Rick's a good man," Robert replied. "He'll get to the bottom of all of this." Looking directly at Darcy he continued, "Just for the record, I did not order your car. If you recall, I showed up the morning you left and told you I would have taken you if you had asked."

"That's right, you did," Darcy replied. "Then who ordered that car? This is getting a little spooky." Realizing she was showing weakness in front of one of her adversaries, she added, "Not enough to run me off, though, if that's what the person had in mind."

Robert's face turned red at the innuendo and Grant tried to placate Darcy. She had had enough of both of them, so she said, "It's been a pleasure to see you both this morning, but I would like to spend some time getting my things out and put into place." They both just stared at her. "I'm kicking you both out—go away!" She laughed and shooed them out the gate with her hands.

Eyeing one another the men went their separate ways leaving Darcy in solitude in her garden.

Her garden, she thought again. Darcy couldn't believe she was the trustee of all of this beautiful land and the regal house. *I wish, however, that it hadn't been because of losing my friend*, she thought. *Marjorie, I promise I will keep your dream alive.*

Calling to the dogs, Darcy decided to complete her tour of the grounds. She had been everywhere except in the old stable, so she headed there now. The dogs went in search of shade, so she was on her own. As she opened the stable door, Darcy was aware of the smell of chlorine. The pool must still be filled, she thought, as she switched on the lights. Most of the original stable walls were completely intact, but the inside of the structure had been gutted and replaced with a beautiful indoor swimming pool.

Mosaic tile lined the bottom and sides of the pool, their green, blue and white colors very much in keeping with the soothing atmosphere of the building. Surrounding the pool itself was a concrete apron upon which sat benches, statues and plants in the Greek style. Zeus, Athena and Apollo all looked on as bathers played in the pool. On one end of the building the wall had been replaced by a set of bay windows so a swimmer could enjoy a view of the dark, cool woods from inside the structure. *It's absolutely enchanting*, Darcy thought. *I feel like Artemis coming for a swim. The thought made her giggle.*

She walked up to the deep end of the pool and peered down to the bottom. The water was clear, but Darcy didn't linger. She loved swimming and this building was a dream, but she had always been afraid of drowning. When she was eight years old she had been swimming with her sister in a watering hole on the family property. As she went under to swim her sister threw a heavy tractor inner tube over where she tried to surface. Darcy was caught under the inner tube and swallowed a large amount of water before being rescued by her father. She had been sure she was going to drown and she still felt that panicky feeling when she was around water. It didn't keep her from enjoying swimming, but it was always present.

Darcy switched off the lights and was about to leave the building when she heard a noise in the far corner of the room. She headed toward the sound, around the far side of the pool, where the water was much closer to the wall than the other side. She sidestepped the narrow walkway next to the water. She heard the noise again, and suddenly, her feet went out from under her and she felt herself falling into the deep water.

Her first reaction was panic and she flailed around until she saw which way was up. She was too far from the bottom to push off, and she had used up too much air with her panic, so she began to claw her way to the surface. She was almost there when she felt something from below tug at her leg! With a gigantic final effort, she broke free of whatever was down there and made it to the surface. She gulped down air and water in equal quantities, causing her to cough and slide back down under the surface. Darcy reached up and hooked her hand on the pool's edge before she went under yet again. Gradually she dragged herself out of the water.

Lying by the pool, still choking, Darcy gave in to tears. This really had been a horrible week, she acknowledged to herself. A car accident and now almost drowning. What was next? Why was this happening to her? Her heart pounding, she put her head down on her arms, spit out a little more water, and sobbed until a hand started rubbing her back.

Startled, Darcy turned her head and found Robert and Lucas standing over her. Robert had bent down and was trying to soothe her while Lucas just looked at her as if she were crazy. "You really should change clothes before you swim, Ms. Jeffers," the teenager said with a sly smile. "Or maybe that's some kind of northern custom we don't share here in Virginia?" The gleam in his eyes was more than Darcy needed to see.

"And how long have you been here, Lucas," she asked through puffy eyes. "I had no idea you were on the property and I don't recall you asking permission to be here," she added. It was gratifying to see the irritation on his face until she realized she was playing down at his level. "Sorry. I'm just not up to your sarcasm right now."

"I'm outa here," Lucas stated. "For the record, Ms. Jeffers, I've been staying on the farm with Rob. We just came over to talk to you. See you back at the house, Uncle Rob." He waved to them both and loped out the door.

"Darcy, what happened?" Robert asked. "Why were you in the pool?"

Looking up at his face, Darcy thought of the contrast between this look of concern and the glacial look of this morning. Robert seemed to be several different people in one body. "I don't know what happened, exactly," she began. "As I was leaving I heard a noise and came to investigate. One minute I was walking next to the pool, the next minute I was in it." The feeling of panic threatened again. "The weirdest thing is that when I was in the water, I could have sworn something or someone grabbed me by the ankle to try to keep me from getting to the surface. Crazy, huh?" Robert didn't answer. He was gazing down at her ankle where there was clearly a bruise. It was now even more colorful than it had been from the other accident. She began to shake as the realization began to hit her: Someone had tried to kill her!

"You should call the Sheriff about this, Darcy," he said quietly. "He should know about this incident."

"Forget it, Robert. I must have just gotten caught on something. This is nothing to worry the authorities over. I can handle myself." She raised her chin as she finished speaking.

"This is no time to let your pride get in the way," he remarked. "Someone has tried to hurt you and you need help."

"Thank you for your advice," Darcy replied sweetly. "However, since you are one of the people who would like to see me long gone from here, I don't think I need to listen to it." She tried to rise but didn't quite succeed. Robert helped her to stand and the two of them went their separate ways in silence.

Damn the woman, Robert thought, as he made his way back to the farm. Damn her for making him feel protective. He didn't want to feel anything about her except contempt. Yet every time he saw Darcy or spent any amount of time with her, he realized what a complex and interesting person she was. That only complicates matters, he reminded himself. Damn her. Damn Jonathan and Beth for putting him in this position and damn his mother for her match making! Mother had always said she'd get Robert interested in a woman of her choosing, and this was her one, final attempt. Well, he couldn't let it work, no matter how much Darcy intrigued him. They all had too much to lose.

"That's strike two," a raspy, hissing voice of indeterminate sex whispered into the telephone. "How hard can it be to get rid of one woman? I want her gone *now*, do you understand? The sooner, the better for all concerned, including you. This time make sure there is no one around to help her."

"It wasn't my fault either time," Nick snarled back at his employer. "How could I possibly know someone would see the smoke? Besides, she was already out of the car. And she was just too strong and slippery in the water to finish the job."

"Just get the job done!" The serpent voice rose to a striking pitch. "I'll give you one more week. If she's not out of the way by then, I'll take care of both of you myself." The line went dead.

Nick sighed as he put down the phone. He had always prided himself on his good judgment in picking jobs. It had kept him out of jail and in good health for years. Now he was wondering if his greed had finally overcome his judgment. Nick thought of his current employer as a snake in the grass. It was clear this person was unstable as well as dangerous. He'd need to get this job done immediately and get out of town before his luck completely left him. Time to do some reconnaissance, Nick decided. He needed to lie low and watch her for a while so the next time he went after Darcy there would be no escape.

Eight

I agree with you completely, Darcy. Colonial Williamsburg is not only a unique piece of American history, but also a splendid tool to teach us about our past and our future. It is also an enjoyable place to spend the day.

Jane looked out the window of her office cubicle to the city below. People were walking down Nicollet Mall to shop at Marshall Field's or to get to their next meeting. From her vantage point on the twentieth floor they all looked like ants moving along the ground. What was Darcy doing now? A spurt of jealousy went through her, but she caught herself before she was consumed by it.

Her job working in a large law firm in the Human Resources department was one she loved. Now and again she even did some paralegal work, so her job was challenging and rewarding. But she missed Darcy, and she missed the sense of being part of a family. Much as she hated to admit it, she thought of Darcy, and even Fran, as her family. With her own family so dysfunctional, this was as close to a real family as she would ever get. It tore at her to have it all gone so suddenly, leaving her once again with nothing.

Jane was also worried about Darcy returning to Virginia after that car accident. Without Jane to remind her, Darcy was always too trusting of those around her. Not for the first time, Jane wished she could be in Virginia with her friend. She had finished up the list of items to be shipped, and now she was working on getting Darcy's horse to Virginia.

At least I'm still needed, Jane thought. But for how much longer?

Darcy decided to stretch her legs. After the final four hours of the first meeting of the Plantation Trust Board of Directors, she was ready for some time outside. The board had met on the campus of the College of William and Mary in Williamsburg, so she decided to walk through the Historic Area of town before heading home. As she walked, she mentally recapped the meeting. It had really gone quite well. The board had agreed on a mission statement and an initial project of restoring the slave quarters on the plantation. Marjorie would be pleased about that. They had also set up one committee to research other plantations across the South that might be in need of preservation and another committee to put together a grant process.

The members of this newly created board ranged from the president of the Colonial Williamsburg Foundation, to Virginia's senior U.S. Senator, to the CEOs of several large corporations. Also included was an expert on restoration and the president of the national preservation group. All of these people were willing to sit on the board because Marjorie Fulton had wanted them, and they respected her choice and her vision. They also respected Marjorie's lifetime commitment of time and resources to historic preservation, especially in the James River area. It was now up to Darcy to convince them they should stay because she could run the Trust and they could all help save the country's past for future generations.

The only rough spot in the meeting had come from Jonathan Fulton and Andrew Page. Jonathan had a seat on the board and had brought Andrew along as his secretary. The two men made the rounds of the room speaking to each board member in turn. Several of the members turned away from the spiteful speeches, but others listened intently. Darcy could only guess at what Jonathan and Andrew were telling the board, but she was sure of two things: one, it wasn't good for the Trust; and two, it wasn't good for her.

The meeting had begun with an air of tension as the board wanted answers about Marjorie's will and whether the Plantation Trust should even be started under these circumstances. Between herself and Grant Hastings, Darcy put everyone at ease about the Trust, and broke the ice with the members by relating stories of Marjorie's e-mails. The board members were still cautious about moving forward, but they saw the sense in getting the Trust up and running and allowing Darcy to hire a staff. The only objections had come from Jonathan, and they were more to create a nuisance than any real substance. The board had adjourned the meeting having completed all of the tasks set out for them, so Darcy felt she had cleared the first hurdle. She would celebrate by visiting the Historic Area.

Since she had first seen it when she was a child, Darcy had been enchanted by Colonial Williamsburg. She had gotten thoroughly hooked on the town, still appearing as it had in the late eighteenth century. It made history come alive for Darcy every time she visited.

Today Darcy was still enchanted with the Historic Area, over 170 acres in size, including 88 original buildings and many other reconstructions made on their original foundations. History became real in the working taverns, at the capitol building, and under the trees behind the governor's palace where Patrick Henry and others made impassioned speeches daily. Darcy would always have a soft spot in her heart for Colonial Williamsburg.

Walking down Duke of Gloucester Street, a main thoroughfare through the Historic Area, Darcy decided to stop in the historic Bruton Church. Figures from history such as George Washington and Thomas Jefferson had worshipped in this church, and she always felt the peace and strength of these figures when she was in the timeless structure. She waited in one of the pews to have a moment's reflection without other tourists around. Head bowed, Darcy sat quietly in the straight-backed pew. She lifted her head to admire the exquisitely restored structure with its painted wooden pews and the red cushions that gave color to the otherwise cream and brown painted church.

Each pew had a door that could be closed to stop the cold winter drafts, but in summer it remained open for more air circulation. She looked at the hand-carved, raised pulpit, which seemed as if it hadn't aged a day. The brass candle chandelier, the miniature chandeliers on either side of the church, the cross and sconces gleamed even in the low, filtered light. The whitewashed walls towered above with rounded arches leading the way to twelve-foot windows, all multi-paned.

Darcy bowed her head once more. A hand came down softly and rested on her shoulder causing her to start in surprise. Her head shot up, and she stared, wide-eyed, into the handsome face she was beginning to know well. Immediately relieved that it was Robert and not someone chasing her, Darcy realized she still didn't know what his intentions were. He was always around the plantation and had been in the area when she had fallen into the pool, so he, as well as anyone else in his family, could be responsible for her mishaps.

Realizing she was still staring, she asked, "What are you doing in the Historic Area? It's not as if you're a tourist."

"I was in town doing some shopping and saw you walking down the street, so I came to say hello," came Robert's easy reply.

"Shopping? Where were you shopping? This is the Historic Area. The shops are back the other way." She pointed toward William & Mary College.

"Actually, I come to the nursery here to pick up some of my plants. They grow excellent specimens and I find they are heartier than those I get at regular nurseries," he continued. "In fact, I buy all of my plants for my house garden from here."

Intrigued by this bit of information, Darcy decided to try to get more out of Robert. He was never forthcoming with information about himself and his family, but maybe here in the relaxing and magical world of Colonial Williamsburg she could get him to open up.

"Are you finished with your shopping?" she asked. "I'm taking a walk to stretch my sore legs after the board meeting, and I would love some company. You'll be happy to know my ankle is almost completely healed." She looked straight into Robert's eyes as she spoke and was gratified to see surprise at her offer.

"I'm never one to turn down an invitation from a lady," he replied as he gave Darcy a slight bow. "Shall we go?" He held out his hand, and after a moment's hesitation, she placed her hand in his. His palm was rough and calloused from his work, but his long fingers had a grace Darcy admired.

Leaving the church, the couple headed farther into the Historic Area. The air was full of sweet flower scents, including her favorite, hyacinth, and the musky scent of boxwood. The many variations of tulips were planted into a carpet with the ever-present boxwood as its trim. Ivy made ground and tree cover, and the air was heavy with humidity.

In companionable silence, they strolled down the street and into the gardens of the Governor's Palace. "Down here," Darcy pointed. "Let's go along the pond."

They sauntered along, enjoying the beautiful day and the relative peace of the area. The path was made of crushed shells, and the small pond was lined with water lilies and other plants growing next to the trees. The sound of a small waterfall splashed in the distance. The couple paused several times to admire the plants.

"Let's stop here a minute," Robert motioned to the green wooden bench. "I think it's time we talked."

Darcy immediately came to attention at his tone and she sat down, her back ramrod straight. "What do you want to talk about? If it's Winterview again, I'd just as soon skip the whole conversation."

"No, it's not that, Darcy," Robert assured her. "It's just that I'm worried about you. You've had two nasty incidents since you have inherited the plantation and I'm concerned you are not taking this seriously enough."

"Oh, Robert, that's rich coming from you! The biggest threat to me right now is you, your brother and sister. Not to mention your cuddly nephew! How do I know you're not the one behind what's happened? I know you still want me gone."

"You're right, of course," he conceded. "We are still looking into our options where you and the Trust are concerned. But you need to believe that I would never want to physically harm you in any way, Darcy."

"Only mentally? A few scares here and there?" She was getting angry. "Because that's all that has really happened, isn't it? I got out of the car and out of the pool, and you were there for one incident and your sister the other! What am I supposed to think?" She took a deep breath and tried to contain her anger.

"Darcy, look at me," Robert ordered. "I promise you here and now that I am not trying to hurt you. I want you to believe that. If you can't right now, will you at least accept a truce for the rest of the afternoon?"

Surprised by his request, she asked, "What do you mean? What kind of truce?"

"You enjoy the Historical Area, right? Then let's make a pact that while we are here today we are just two people, maybe on the verge of being friends, enjoying the beauty and history of the area. We can go back to being adversaries when we leave. Deal?"

Darcy studied the handsome man in front of her and felt reckless. After all that had happened in the last couple of weeks she wanted a few hours to just be normal, to be a woman with a man. "Deal," she said, standing and extending her hand. Robert caught it with his, stood up, and the truce was under way.

After walking through the streets, with their eighteenth century houses and taverns and visiting the windmill as well as the capitol, the couple stopped along the street to watch young men in uniform march by playing their fife and drums. It was a fantastic sight and the music lifted everyone's spirits. The couple then stopped by an outdoor souvenir stand near the Magazine where the gunpowder used to be stored. The stand sold everything from toys to ginger bread, and the straw hats for sale enchanted Darcy. Robert wandered off to look at the courthouse, so Darcy took her time shopping.

She was still looking at the hats when Robert returned. He came up beside her and offered his help. It seemed such an intimate thing to do, choosing a hat with a man she barely knew and didn't really trust. But, it also felt very right to ask his opinion and share the moment, smiling when he tried to be diplomatic. The straw hat she finally chose had a deep headpiece and no tie ribbons. It was, however, adorned with purple and white ribbons around the brim that trailed behind as she walked. The wind caught the strands and played with them as she moved along. Darcy had to keep one hand free so she could catch the hat before the wind could take it. She was now ready to face the heat of the afternoon, with a man next to her giving off another kind of heat.

The sun was low in the sky when they both decided it was time to leave. Walking slowly back up Duke of Gloucester Street toward their cars, Robert draped his arm around Darcy and pulled her close. She stopped their forward progress and turned to him. Without giving it any thought, she reached up her hand to his head and pulled it down toward her. There was only a second to see the glimmer of surprise in his eyes before their lips met and they were both lost in the moment. Robert's left hand came up to caress her face while his right hand pulled her even closer.

As their lips melded the emotional rush was staggering. Darcy moved even closer to its source and put her arms around his neck. How long they would have stayed that way she didn't know, but the sound of a car horn honking close by brought Darcy back to reality. With a sigh of regret, she stepped back from Robert. Regaining the use of her voice, she said, "That was really nice, Robert. I wish I could tell if it was real."

He blew out his frustration and replied, "I guess you'll just have to trust your feelings. This was a truce and I think we took full advantage of it." He kissed her again quickly before taking her hand. They walked on to the parking lot. "Darcy, it has truly been a pleasure to spend the afternoon with you." With that, Robert turned away and the truce was over.

Grant Hastings watched as Darcy Jeffers got into her car and drove off toward Winterview. Such an interesting woman, he thought. He needed to spend more time with her. That scene with Robert Fulton was a little irritating, but he knew Fulton was still the enemy, so he had the better chance of becoming friendly with the intriguing Darcy. He considered himself to be something of a ladies man, so he would wait for his opportunity. Then, he would make a play for her. She was such a mix of fire and naiveté that he found himself drawn to her more than he had ever expected to be. He probably was playing with fire, but he would enjoy the danger.

Robert replayed the afternoon's events as he drove home. Darcy was just too perceptive for her own good. He did want her gone from Winterview, but he was also concerned about what was happening to her. They all wanted her out of the way, but not literally. There was not supposed to be any violence. The one thing he had learned in the military was that violence was a last resort, not something one used casually or as a mere scare tactic.

Again Robert thought about their kiss and Darcy's comment. He was surprised to feel a stab of hurt. He knew she was right—there was no reason she should trust him, or him her. What a web has been created, he thought again. How will it ever get all untangled?

"Jane, I must be out of my mind!" Darcy exclaimed. She had called her friend as soon as she hit the house. Even Cairo had to wait for his walk until she had spoken to Jane. "Can you believe I kissed him? It wasn't him kissing me! I'm so embarrassed and so confused."

"There's nothing to be confused about," Jane replied. "That man is trying to soften you up so he can move in for the kill.

Mark my words, he and his siblings are up to something and you're the one who's going to pay the price. You have to be more careful, Darcy," she was almost shouting. "You always let your emotions rule your head."

"I know you're absolutely right. I got caught up in the moment. I promise I won't let it happen again. Oh, I miss having you here to talk to. Why don't you come down and visit soon?"

"I'm still trying to get things in order for you here, but it's almost done. After that you couldn't stop me from visiting. Oh, by the way, Cassidy will be on his way down tomorrow. They are picking him up at daybreak and they think it will take a little over two days to get there, so you'd better have his stall ready."

"Terrific. It will be great to get out and ride again. I miss the big guy. And I promise that he'll be the only guy in my life once he gets here."

"I'll hold you to that, Darcy. Hey, I've got to run. Take care of yourself."

"Thanks yet again, Jane. I hope I'll see you soon." Darcy put down the phone and looked up to find two dogs staring at her. "OK, OK, I give up! Let's go for a walk." The three of them headed out the door and into the velvety dark evening. "Stick to the road, OK guys?" she called to the dogs. "There are snakes and other animals out at night and I'm not going into the woods to find you." She laughed as both dogs bolted off the road and into the night.

Down the road the farmhouse was full of people. Robert had returned home to find the whole family there waiting for him. As he walked in the door he was hit with all kinds of questions and remarks.

"Hold on a minute!" Robert shouted. "I've just walked in the door. Let me at least get a drink and sit down before we get this meeting going. Anyone else want a drink?"

Andrew Page stood and said, "I'll do the honors. You know this is something I'm good at," he added with a smirk. "Who wants what?" Drink orders were taken and drinks delivered. Everyone sat down in the cozy parlor of the eighteenth century farmhouse. Jonathan started the meeting.

"As you know, things are progressing with the Trust and with Ms. Jeffers moving into Winterview. If we are really going to act on this, we need to do it soon otherwise there will be no stopping her. Andrew and I made a good start today at the Trust meeting by talking to all of the board members. However," he added gloomily, "they still feel Darcy deserves a chance, so things are proceeding as she wants them to. Since the meeting today, Andrew learned some new information that we can use to plant real doubt."

All eyes pivoted to Andrew. He squirmed under the scrutiny. "Why don't you tell them what you've learned, Andrew?" Jonathan coaxed. "I'm sure they are all anxious to hear about it."

Realizing he had no choice but to comply, Andrew rose from his seat next to Beth and cleared his throat. "Ah, it's just a little thing, really," he began. "Ah, I was doing a little research on Ms. Jeffers' history through some contacts in Minnesota, and I found out about her parents' deaths. Seems that at first there was some thought that she was responsible for the accident." He paused to take in everyone's reaction. Beth smiled up at him and urged him on. "It seems that our friend Darcy was driving the car earlier in the day and had had a little fender bender. She rear-ended another car that was stopped, and her car sustained damage to the front end, but not so much that you could really notice it. Darcy didn't tell her parents about the accident, and they took the car out later that night, never to come back." He smiled a sly smile.

A gasp arose from Beth and even Robert felt startled. "Why do you think one had anything to do with the other?" Robert asked.

"Well, it seems there was more front end damage than any-one knew. It came out at the coroner's inquest. Seems they were never too sure if the explosion came so quickly after the accident because of damage to the gas line sustained in the earlier accident." Andrew paused again for dramatic effect, his earlier nervousness forgotten. "Darcy's parents were both still alive when the car went up in flames," he finished triumphantly and looked at Jonathan.

Lucas jumped to his feet. "How can we let someone who helped kill her own parents take over our lives?" he cried. "She's got to go. I want my house!"

Jonathan put a hand on his son's arm. "Calm down, Lucas. All of this takes time and it takes patience. We have to work together if we want to get rid of Ms. Darcy Jeffers."

Robert unwound his long legs and stood, facing Jonathan, Lucas and Andrew who were now standing side by side in front of the fireplace. "Just how far are you going to go to get rid of Darcy? And why is this so important to all of you?" He looked at Beth to include her in the question. "I agreed to be part of this because you were going to find a legal way to get Darcy out of Winterview. I did not sign up for a smear campaign, nor did I sign up for attempted murder. I've had enough killing to last a lifetime."

"What are you talking about, Rob?" his sister finally spoke. "Who is trying to kill Darcy? Or, why do you think someone is trying to kill her?"

"There have been two attempts on her life in the last couple of weeks," Robert replied. "The first was with that car accident that you ran into, Beth. Someone hired that driver, Nick, and sent him to wreck the car with her in it."

"You can't be serious, Rob," she snapped. "Why do you think the driver was hired by anyone other than you?"

"Because I didn't hire any driver, and certainly not someone who would steal a car, drive Darcy toward Richmond, then trash the car with her in it. That's what happened. The Sheriff and his men have been investigating the accident since it happened, and I am the prime suspect because I was the only one who knew when Darcy was planning to leave since I made her return plane reservation."

"Well, I certainly didn't hire anyone named Nick, did you Jonathan?" Beth asked. "How about you, Andrew?" She glared at her husband who was helping himself to yet another drink. Both men turned to Beth and shook their heads in the negative. "Well, Rob, maybe there's someone else after that woman, ever think of that? But maybe we can use this to our advantage."

Lucas turned toward the group and said, "Yeah. No one's going to trust someone who was so stupid as to help get her parents killed in a car accident, then almost got killed herself. Maybe she hired this guy herself, how about that?"

"We are getting way out of control here," Robert said quietly. "Are we all so sure that Darcy is a bad thing? Does she deserve to have her past grief used against her so coldly? Does this mean there is no legal way to get her out of our lives?"

Jonathan answered him. "No, Rob, it doesn't look as if there is any legal way to stop the will, the Trust or Ms. Jeffers occupying Winterview. Our only option is to try to persuade those around her that she's not up to the job Mother left for her. That will get her out of the Trust and maybe out of the house. If not, we'll have to keep working at her until she's tired of it all."

Robert sighed and rubbed his eyes. This was wrong and he knew it. He also knew he was getting too involved with Darcy for his own good. If he kept this up he'd have to choose between his family and her. God, what was he thinking? One kiss during a truce didn't make them any closer. He needed time to sort things out.

"Come on everyone," Beth said. "Let's let Rob have his house back. Seems like we know in which direction we have to move. I'm still not convinced that Darcy isn't some gold-digger anyway, so we may be actually saving Mother's project, not hurting it." She got off the couch and headed for Andrew.

"One more thing before you go," Rob said quietly. "These attacks on Darcy have to stop if you want me to continue to be involved in this campaign. No one deserves to be threatened or die over this."

"You're getting friendly with her, aren't you Uncle Rob?" Lucas accused. "Next thing you know you'll be sleeping at Winterview with her! Man, you need to get a grip." Jonathan tugged his son toward the door.

Beth turned as she was leaving. "I know you don't like how we're doing things, but it's really for the best. What should have been ours will be ours. But I do promise not to make any attempt to physically harm Darcy, and I swear I wasn't the one to hire the driver."

The dogs were happy to be out and taking full advantage of their mistress' lack of supervision. Even after her order, the two dogs dodged in and out of the trees on the edge of the woods. Darcy was still deep in thought when she had to quickly move out of the way as a car came rapidly out of the woods. It did not even slow down as it passed, and all Darcy could see was a dark colored sedan with tinted windows. It looked as if a man was driving, but she couldn't see much else in the fading light. What would someone be doing in my woods, she wondered. Probably just some tourists who got lost, she decided. Didn't Andrew have a car like that? No, there would be no reason for him to be out in the woods. That's why they were going so fast. They didn't want to get caught trespassing, I'm sure.

After walking the dogs, Darcy decided it was time to look through more of the house. She had kept to the main floor and her bedroom, not wanting to deal with her sadness by entering Marjorie's room. She hadn't even explored any of the other bedrooms on the second floor, so tonight she would make the time to do it. Both dogs in tow, she headed up the stairs.

The first room on the left side of the hall, next to her bedroom, was a small but charming room that had obviously once been a nursery. There was no dark paneling in this room, as the woodwork had all been painted a cheery pale yellow. A border of suns and moons had been placed chair-rail height, and a single bed sat next to a very old cradle. The smoothly polished wood of the cradle was mellow brown in color and it swung effortlessly when Darcy brushed it. Hanging above the cradle was mosquito netting, and for a moment she was again carried back to the eighteenth century. She could picture the nanny making the bed as a soft little baby lay cooing in its lovingly made cradle. The whole room was warm and soothing. For now she'd leave it exactly as it was.

On the right side of the hall was another bedroom, and from the looks of the décor, it had been Robert's room. The walls of the room had dark oak paneling from the floor to the chair rail, then plaster walls painted blue all the way to the ceiling. The colored walls were a perfect backdrop for all of the posters and models of helicopters and airplanes scattered throughout the room. Robert's obvious love of aviation was a surprise to Darcy, as she had never heard him mention flying. Above the desk was a set of newspaper articles she imagined Marjorie had put there. The articles detailed the career of Robert James Fulton who had flown combat missions in the Gulf War, then had been part of special operations in the drug war in Columbia. There was also an article about his being shot down and injured during a conflict, then about his resignation from the Marines and his return to life in Virginia.

Darcy was floored. Never once did she think of Robert as a military man, much less a pilot! But now that she thought about it, his short hair, upright bearing and follow-through style were all indicative of a person who had been in the service. She wondered why he gave up his career. A puzzle for another day, she decided.

Bypassing the other bedrooms, Darcy went straight to the master bedroom. Similar to Mount Vernon, this master bedroom was on the second floor, but not very accessible from the rest of the house. It was its own suite situated at the far end of the floor, between the second and third stories, with a staircase built into the wall that led to its entrance. She took a deep breath and opened the door.

Turning on the light, Darcy was greeted by the sight of one of the most elegant rooms she had ever seen. Large and airy with windows on two sides, the room was dominated at one end by a huge four-poster bed, complete with steps up to the high mattress. Covered with curtains of white and red floral design, the bed looked fit for royalty. Its frame, as well as the highboy dresser and armoire on the opposite side of the room were obviously antique and had been kept in perfect condition. A spinning wheel had been placed as decoration on one wall, next to the desk where it was obvious Marjorie had done her correspondence. A laptop computer lay unobtrusively on a shelf below the desk's main writing surface.

Although the room looked as if it came right out of the eighteenth century, Marjorie had added up-to-date touches to make it a functional room as well. A large alcove had been transformed into a bathroom, its entrance cleverly hidden by a full-length mirror. There was also a telephone and even a television hidden in the armoire. The warm and charming room beckoned to Darcy. She would love to stay here, but it would have to wait until she had cleaned out Marjorie's belongings.

She wandered over to the desk. It was obvious that someone kept the room clean, as there was no trace of dust on the papers or wooden surfaces that hadn't been used since Marjorie's death. Darcy suspected Anita took this job on herself, as she and Marjorie had been close. Idly flipping through some papers, she found a stack of letters around which had been placed a bright yellow ribbon. The letters were from her! Marjorie had kept all of her correspondence. Tears formed in Darcy's eyes, as she again felt the pain of losing her friend.

Under the letters was a leather book, Marjorie's diary. Not wanting to intrude on her late friend's privacy warred with her desire to learn more, and she finally flipped open the book. On this page Marjorie was swearing at her computer and cursing technology. The woman had a flare for writing and Darcy was laughing out loud reading about her friend's exploits. She decided not to intrude further and put the book back on the desk. Moving to the door, she wiped away her tears and turned out the lights.

Nine

The plantations in Virginia were run with slave labor. Many of the slaves were master craftsmen and farmers. You can still see their skill and artistry throughout the plantation buildings. It is time they receive credit for their work in running the plantations.

"**Jump!** Jump! You've got to get out now!" Robert could hear the hysteria in his voice, but he couldn't see whether his men had gotten out of the helicopter. He could barely see the water of the river coming up quickly to meet him through the thick jungle brush, so after jamming the stick in place, he unbuckled his harness, ran though the aircraft and jumped into the waiting jungle river. Not far from him, the copter hit the water with a mighty roar and exploded one final time. A piece of debris hit his head as he looked for his men.

Hardly able to keep his head above water, the debris had knocked him nearly senseless. Still, he swam toward shore. Behind him he heard the call of two men, so he knew Dave and Jesse had made it to shore. But where was Jorge? He couldn't see him anywhere.

Suddenly, the water next to him erupted and Jorge popped to the surface. "Rob, help me! I can't get a breath. Something's got hold of me." He disappeared beneath the murky water as fast as he had appeared. Robert was knocked over as something else swam by—a huge snake! It had Jorge in its coils and was moving downstream. The reptile felt like a tree trunk as it hit him. He tried to swim after the man and snake, but he couldn't move, couldn't scream. He reached out for the snake's tail as it passed, but it was too strong and Robert's grip too weak after bailing out of the copter. "No!" he screamed. "Help Jorge, someone. Help him!"

Robert sat up quickly in bed and wiped his brow. It had been a long time since he had had the nightmare about Jorge. He wondered why he was having it again now. It must have something to do with the conversation tonight, he thought. I couldn't do right by Jorge—am I not doing right by Darcy? Is that the message? Hell of a way for my subconscious to tell me, Robert thought. He got out of bed. His t-shirt was soaked through and his hair was slicked back from his exertion. Would he ever be able to think about that incident without the pain? It had been over six years ago, and he still felt responsible for the helicopter going down and Jorge not making it out. There must have been something he could have done.

Shaking his head to clear out those haunting thoughts, Robert changed his clothes and went back to bed. It took him a long time to fall asleep, and when he did, he was thinking of a beautiful woman with blonde hair and hazel eyes standing in the garden at Winterview.

"Ms. Jeffers, please wake up," a voice implored from the other side of Darcy's door. "Ms. Jeffers, there are people here to see you already. Are you awake?" Another knock, more firm than the first, sounded on her door.

"Anita, is that you? What time is it? What's going on?" Darcy got out of bed and opened the door.

"There are two women downstairs waiting for you who say they are friends," Anita responded. "They don't seem like friends, though, as they're constantly sniping at one another. They also have a trailer with them they say belongs to you. What shall I tell them?"

"You don't need to tell us anything," a silky voice said behind Anita. "I'm sure my sister wants to see us right away, right DJ?" She looked at the surprise on Darcy's face. "Guess you really didn't know we were coming, did you?" She smiled like a cat that had just feasted on an innocent bird.

"Lord, Fran, can't you wait for anything?" Jane demanded as she came up to the group. "Maybe Darcy wanted to wake up before we invaded her privacy."

"Oh, poor little Jane, always protecting DJ. She's not made of glass, you know, and I am her sister, her flesh and blood." Anger flooded Jane's face, but she made no response.

"Enough!" Darcy yelled, getting the attention of all three women. She stifled a yawn and turned to Anita. "Thanks for waking me, Anita. This is my sister Fran and my best friend Jane. Do you think you could get us some coffee or juice? We'll be down in a few minutes."

"No problem, Ms. Jeffers," Anita replied, glowering at Fran. "Come down any time. I was just making some muffins to go with the coffee." Her back rigid at the rudeness of the new guests, Anita departed.

"Well, you've got yourself a couple of real watchdogs, haven't you, Sis? I mean that woman's husband tried to stop us from driving in and then she tried to keep us from coming upstairs. After all, we're your family, right? Why do we need to stand on ceremony?"

It was now Darcy's turn to glower. "Because, Fran, the rest of the civilized world actually calls ahead to let people know they are coming, and they certainly don't barge into their houses at 7:30 A.M. As long as you're both here, come on in while I get dressed." She pulled on her jeans and a clean shirt. "It's a wonderful surprise to see you, Jane! I'm so glad you could come down. But why are you here now?"

Jane didn't have a chance to answer. Instead Fran replied, "Because we've brought your precious nag down. He's waiting out in the trailer."

"Boy, Jane, I could swear your voice is starting to sound like Fran's," she joked. "OK, you two, let's go see my baby."

"What about the coffee and muffins?" Fran whined. "I've been with that horse for days now. I want a nice, quiet breakfast."

Leaving Fran in the kitchen with Anita still glowering at her, Jane and Darcy headed out to the trailer. "Oh, Jane, as usual you're a wonder," Darcy said as she gave her friend a big hug. "Thanks for coming down with Cassidy. I know it cost you dearly since you obviously had an unwanted rider. How did you manage to get away from work?"

"Fran wasn't too bad except when she was bored and wanted to bug me. But it's great to see you, too, Darcy," Jane added. "I actually have quite a bit of vacation stored up, so it was no problem to get away. This is the slow time for me. "She looked around at the house and the grounds. "This place is unbelievable. Even from your descriptions I never expected this. I'm so glad you've found your slice of heaven. Maybe someday I'll find someplace as wonderful as this." Turning back toward the trailer she continued, "Now, what about saying hello to the big guy?"

As Darcy rounded the side of the trailer, she was greeted by a soft whinny. Cassidy had his head out the window and his ears perked up at the sound of Darcy's voice. "Oh, you beautiful thing. How are you, boy? It's so great to see you." She rubbed his soft muzzle and gave him a piece of the carrot she'd grabbed from the kitchen on her way out. "Let's get him out of here. We can walk him over to the farm so he can stretch out and I can say hello."

There was no problem getting the horse out of the trailer, and once out in the sunlight, Cassidy's chestnut coat turned to glimmering copper. His blue leg wraps made his walk a bit stiff, but for a nineteen-year old horse, he looked wonderful. Still over sixteen hands, the gelding stood tall and proud, but bent his head to nuzzle Darcy when she came near. As she and Jane walked Cassidy down the road to the farm, they caught up on what had been happening in each other's lives. The horse was content to walk slowly and eat grass as the women talked.

"The truck with the rest of your belongings should be here tomorrow," Jane commented. "As you requested, most of the furniture and decorations were left in the Minnesota house and I only sent the things on the list. It was hard to part with some of your things, Darcy, as it seems as if I'm losing you forever," Jane admitted with tears in her eyes. "But we're here together now, and that's what counts, right?"

Darcy gave Jane's shoulders a squeeze. "I've told you before, you're welcome to move here and stay with me. It would be fun to have a roommate."

Just then, Cassidy swung his head up and stood stiffly in place, his ears cocked, his lower lip quivering. Robert and Lucas were approaching. Darcy blushed when she found Robert staring at her. Turning to Jane she said, "Well, looks like you get to meet two of the people who sincerely wish me gone from here. How's that for a way to start the day?" She smiled at her friend as Jane turned to the newcomers.

"Hello, Robert, Lucas," Darcy said, pinning a smile to her face. "I'd like you to meet my best friend, Jane Marshall. Jane, this is Robert Fulton, and his nephew Lucas Fulton." Turning to the horse she continued, "And this beauty is Cassidy. Cassidy, meet the man who is going to stable you."

Robert moved up alongside Cassidy and began to talk to him quietly and stroke his neck. Cassidy held himself aloof for a moment, but as soon as he spied a treat sticking out of Robert's pocket, the horse gave him a gentle nudge. "He's a beauty, all right, Darcy. And there are plenty of trails around here for you to ride. I think he's going to be happy here. Let's show him his new home."

"It won't be inside will it? He hates to be in a stall unless it's bad or cold weather. He likes to look around, see what's going on."

"No problem. We'll put him in with the other horses. It's a small herd so he shouldn't have too much trouble. We only bring them in at night or in bad weather. Lucas," Robert called as he started to walk toward the farm, "Go get the trailer and bring it to the farm." To Darcy he said, "I assume you have things to put in the tack room."

"Yes, that would be great. Is that all right with you, Lucas?"

The teenager stared at her for a moment, then gave in. "Sure," he said. "I'm here to work for Uncle Rob, so if he says for me to do it, I'll do it. No charge, either," he added for her benefit.

"Jane, you must have gotten here early," Robert said as he fell in step with her. Darcy and Cassidy followed behind. "Have you had breakfast yet?"

"Uh, no, actually, I haven't," she replied. "Darcy was so excited to see Cassidy that we came right out. After we dropped off her sister, of course."

"Darcy's sister is here as well? Well, I hope you both get the chance to meet all of my family. In the mean time, would you like some breakfast? I'm a great short order cook," he laughed.

Jane was bumped aside before she got to answer. Running up next to Robert, Fran answered for Jane. "I'm sure Jane would love some breakfast. I would, too, since Anita wouldn't give me enough to eat," she pouted. "Where are my manners? I'm Fran Jeffers, Darcy's sister. And you must be Robert. I've heard lots about you."

Robert peeled Fran's hand off his arm and replied, "It's nice to meet you, Fran. However, I have to say I haven't heard anything about you. You are, however, most welcome to join us. What about you, Darcy?"

"Oh, I wouldn't dream of interfering with you getting to know my sister and my friend," she replied sweetly. "I'll just get my baby settled and then join you for a cup of coffee." With that she led the horse toward the barn. She glanced over her shoulder and chuckled at the look on Robert's face. He clearly didn't know what to do with his guests.

Darcy joined the threesome half an hour later. They were all sitting on the porch outside enjoying the view. Fran, her blonde hair blowing in the breeze, was hanging on every word that Robert uttered. Jane's compact body was wound tightly, and she looked as if she wanted to get out of there as fast as she could. The man laughed at Fran's joke, and the sight of him so at ease with her sister made Darcy see green. Joining the group she said, "So, Fran, what brings you down here? Or can I guess?"

"Now DJ," Fran said in her sweetest voice, "Why do you think there's a reason I'm here other than to see my baby sister? You know I've wanted to see you and this beautiful place since you told me about it."

"Knock it off, Fran," Darcy said coldly. "The last time you came to see just me was about 11 years ago. What gives?"

Trying to pout and look seductive at the same time, Fran said, "Oh, it's just family business. It can wait. I'm sure the others wouldn't be interested. I don't want to be a bore." She smiled again at Robert who smiled back.

Darcy had had enough. "Well, then, let's get back to the house. You've imposed on Robert long enough. He has work to do and so do I." Turning to their host she said, "Thanks for letting Cassidy stay here. He looks good so far, and Lucas brought over the tack and put it away. And thanks for entertaining my guests!" She was rewarded by a smile of her own from Robert, but Darcy didn't pay much attention as she was still fuming about her sister as they left.

Nick watched the scene from behind the woodshed as the women returned to Winterview. He was running out of time, but he knew what his next, and final, move would be. Having a horse around always made for accidents, didn't it? He just needed to make some adjustments and he would have his plan in place within twenty-four hours. That should make his boss happy. Much as he didn't go in for hurting or killing women, he was looking forward to taking care of the Jeffers woman since she wouldn't seem to take the hint. Nick stepped into the shadows, then into the barn and into the tack room.

When they arrived back at Winterview it was to find Grant Hastings waiting. Darcy again made the introductions and was gratified to see that Grant didn't fall all over her sister as Robert had. He was polite but distant and he only wanted to talk to Darcy.

She and Grant walked through the house to Marjorie's study, which had originally been the plantation office. Grant admired the collection of horse paintings. "These are great, aren't they? The horse is such a majestic animal and makes such a good subject for the paintings. Speaking of horses, how is yours? I heard he just arrived."

"Word travels fast," Darcy acknowledged. "Cassidy is fine. He's getting to know his new place and the new herd. I am really looking forward to riding as soon as he is settled."

"Do you like horse racing?" Grant asked. "I go up to the Richmond track regularly when it's open and I very much enjoy the excitement of the races as well as the gambling spirit. We should go together some time. I have to admit to a weakness for the horses, and I love to see if I can figure out which one will be the winner." He laughed. "I guess that's why they have horse racing."

"Actually, I love going to the races," she admitted. "It would be very nice to get out and go one night. If we can find a free night, I'll take you up on your offer."

"Great. I'll keep pestering you until you find that free night." Grant ran his hand through his curly red hair. "Now, down to business. I have some Trust papers for you to sign, and I am wondering if you have made a determination of whom you will have as your replacement in the event one is needed. It's the only action you have not yet taken."

Looking the lawyer directly in the eye, she said, "Yes, I have made my decision. This is something I can change at any time, right? I mean this decision doesn't have to be forever, does it?"

"No, it doesn't. You can change the person at any time, as long as you are still in control of the Trust. Now, who will be your replacement?"

"You will be, Grant."

The lawyer appeared floored by this announcement. He gathered his wits together and finally found the voice to respond. "I'm a lawyer, Darcy. Why would you want me in that position?"

"Because the only other people who I would want to appoint would be a member of the Fulton family, and until I can find one

I trust enough I need to have someone in place who knows the business of the Trust and will follow through with the wishes of Marjorie Fulton and myself. Do you have a problem with this?"

"No, I'm just surprised by it, and I have to admit a bit flattered," Grant admitted. "Thank you, Darcy for placing such faith in me."

She laughed. "Well, I don't want to burst your bubble, but I hope I never find out whether my faith was justified. Thanks for coming out, Grant." She rose from her chair and held out her hand. "I have to get back to my guests now, but I will be in touch soon."

Jane and Darcy flung themselves down on Darcy's bed. It had been a tiring day, to say the least, but a lot had been accomplished. The two women had finally gotten away from Fran, but only because Robert had come to take her out. Darcy knew it shouldn't matter that her sister was stepping between Robert and herself, but it did, and she hated both of them at this point. To make things worse, Jonathan was also joining them. Who knows what the three of them would plot, Darcy thought.

"A penny for them," her friend said.

"What? Oh, sorry, Jane. I was just thinking about Fran with Robert and Jonathan Fulton. That seems like a lethal combination. I wonder what they're up to."

"Don't you think the junior Mr. Fulton likes Fran the way every other man does? Why would you think there's anything else going on?"

"First, because Fran doesn't do anything without a selfish reason. The only reason she's here now is because the papers on the buy-out of her half of the Minnesota house are ready to sign. She wants her money. Second, Jonathan Fulton doesn't do anything without a reason. I'm sure he's not looking at any sister of mine for a date. No, this feels like a setup. They're probably all trying to figure out how to get me out of the house and out of my money. I hate this, I really do!"

"Much as I agree that people are sometimes out for your money, I think you may be wrong about Fran. We had some really good talks on the way down here, and she seemed sincerely worried about you when I told her about those incidents."

"You, what? You told Fran about the car and the swimming pool?" She jumped up and paced the length of the room. "Now I know she's up to something. She'll use that knowledge some way, maybe to get a piece of the action if they can all get rid of me. Why did you tell her?"

Jane's whole body stiffened at the rebuke. "Because she is your sister so she has a right to know, Darcy. I would have thought you'd want her to know. Pardon me if I overstepped my boundaries. I can never keep straight exactly where they are." She too got up off the bed and stood looking out the window. "In the future if there's something I am not supposed to tell your only living relative, let me know, please. That way we can avoid this kind of unpleasantness."

"If you'll take that stick out of your back, I'll apologize. It's just that you know Fran and you know she goes out of her way to hurt me. I don't know why, or maybe I do and I just can't accept it, but she does. You're closer to me than Fran will ever be."

"Closer, but not flesh and blood, right?" Sighing, she faced Darcy. "All right, let's just let it drop. I'm sorry if it's a problem I told Fran, but the damage is done, so let's just move on. I'm going to bed. Oh, and I have an appointment in Williamsburg in the morning to get my hair done. Fran is taking me as a thank you for putting up with her on the drive down. So, we'll see you sometime in the afternoon."

Beth Page stopped the exercise bike as she finished up her forty-minute workout. It was still early and the gym was only now starting to fill with people. She looked up to see her best friend, Patty McCloud, walking toward her.

"Hey, Beth, how are you?" Patty asked. "I've barely seen you at all these past few weeks. I wanted to tell you again how sorry I am about your mother's death."

"Thank you," Beth responded. "I'm sorry about not returning your phone calls, but I've been so upset about Mother and now about this Jeffers woman that I can hardly function." Seeing her friend's sympathetic smile, she continued. "My brothers and I are trying to get Winterview back, but so far we can't find a legal way to do it." She hit the bike handle hard and got off.

"Come on, Beth," the other woman said gently, as she noticed other gym patrons looking at them. "Let's go get some juice and you can tell me all about it."

Beth picked up her towel and followed her friend to the juice bar. With glasses of orange juice, they sat down at one of the tables and continued their conversation.

"What does Andrew think of all of this?" Patty asked.

"Andrew is actually very involved with our effort, and it's good to see. I worry about his drinking, and I know he tries all of these get rich quick schemes to make his mark on the world, but he never makes them work, so he's unhappy most of the time. I think he is trying to catch up to my brothers, and it's really taking a toll on our marriage. However, his work may make a dent in our efforts to get Darcy Jeffers back to Minnesota. I will have to be content with that."

"Oh, Hon, I didn't know things had gotten so bad for you," her friend replied. "If I'd known I would have been there for you. Let me know if there is anything I can do from now on to help. In the meantime, let me fill you in on the latest gossip. That will take your mind off Winterview, at least for a little while!"

The morning turned cloudy and cooler. Darcy decided to take a ride on Cassidy to work out her frustration with her sister. She fretted about Fran and Robert all night, and had stewed some more over Jane going with Fran that morning. She was clearly getting paranoid. *Everyone can't be out to get me*, she thought. *I just need to clear my head.*

Cassidy seemed eager for a ride. She quickly groomed him and threw on the saddle. Horse and rider headed out toward the slave quarters. She saw some movement by the farmhouse, but she didn't want to see or talk to anyone. She just wanted to ride. After letting Cassidy get used to the trail, she gave the horse his head and worked into a gallop. It was exhilarating! She felt light as a feather as she and the horse became one and flew over the trail. He might be an old horse, but Cassidy still has some speed, and it felt wonderful.

As she came up to the neglected village, Darcy slowed the horse and entered at a walk. In the gloom of the overcast sky, the dilapidated buildings looked even more run down and a little scary. Fearing Cassidy would step on a nail or some other bit of hardware, Darcy dismounted. Leaving her horse to graze, she took her camera off the saddle and began a thorough investigation of the structures.

Picking her way through the entrance to the largest of the structures, Darcy studied the construction. The building was made with weathered wooden slats side by side topped with a roof also made of old wood planks. Now the structures were weathered gray, most slats long rotted, like missing teeth. Daub, probably of Virginia clay, still hung between the pieces of wood. The structures were all small in size and constructed around an open courtyard. Inside one of the huts there were pieces of wood and rope strewn in the corner where there may have been a makeshift bed. Another of the structures had two rooms, probably for two families. In the courtyard there was a pit that had obviously been the fire pit for communal cooking. The slaves had made themselves a home even under the tyranny of the slave owner.

It was a miracle any of this survived the weather, Darcy thought. She had recently read that there were no surviving slave quarters, yet here stood this village at Winterview. There were even holes to show where a fence had stood, probably to hold in livestock. Darcy tried to capture some of the sad, neglected scene on film, and she said a little prayer of thanks to Marjorie for giving her the opportunity to be involved in this project.

She remembered how her friend had spoken of the old village with the excitement of a child. She felt guilty about its neglect, and wanted to make it all better. But most of all, she wanted the public to be able to share in the history of the African American slaves and to learn just how integral a part of plantation life they were. The slave quarters was a significant piece of that story and she wanted what remained preserved and the rest recreated. Darcy would make sure that would be done.

Away from the main village was a small cabin that had obviously belonged to the foreman. It was more sturdily built, and Darcy could imagine how it must have looked when it had been in use—a broom made of twigs to sweep the dirt floor, a bed with rope for holding the mattress, a chest for belongings at the foot of the bed and clothing hung on pegs on the walls. There wouldn't have been room for much more. The fireplace had remnants of shelves beside it for food and cooking utensils and maybe a personal item or two. Still, it was a far cry above the sheds where the slave families lived together and shared the cooking and other duties.

Hearing a noise from outside of the cabin, Darcy emerged to find Cassidy moving restlessly. "What is it, Boy?" She tried soothing the horse with her voice and hands. "Do you hear something, or do you just want to go?" Cassidy quivered under her hand, so she decided it was time to leave.

Gathering the reins she stepped up into the saddle. As soon as she did, Cassidy took off through the woods at a hysterical gallop. Trying to collect the horse while staying on was impossible. Cassidy seemed possessed, and each time Darcy tried to sit back and control him, he would swerve and go crazy. Tree branches hit her face and ripped her clothing as they tore through the woods. Cassidy ran right up to a huge tree that had come down in an earlier storm and stopped short, launching Darcy over his right shoulder and onto the ground. Cassidy stood still, puffing and nickering, his eyes darting back and forth in terror, his sides heaving from the run, his bottom lip quivering from physical distress.

Darcy lay still on the ground, trying to figure out how badly she was hurt. She could barely breathe, but that was just from the wind being knocked out of her. She could still move her legs and her neck, but her right arm was twisted beneath her. Great, she thought. I have no idea where I am, my arm is injured and I can't ride my horse. What else can happen? At that moment the gray skies opened up and the rain poured down. Darcy lay back on the ground and added her tears to the pounding rain.

Damn! Why didn't it work right? Why didn't she get thrown into that log? She would never have survived that. But it had been fun to watch her try to control her spooked horse while making the problem worse. He heard the sound of other hoof beats and decided to get out of the area. No use getting caught. That was the best part—they'd blame someone else for his fun. Giggling, he took off at a run.

Ten

Dearest Darcy, Robert is not usually so gruff with people. He is a compassionate man who would give the shirt off his back to help a stranger. It is therefore more puzzling that he has such a strong reaction to you. Do not judge him harshly.

"**Grant,** you have a visitor," Graham Hastings announced to his son. "He's a client of mine, so whatever you two talk about it had better not be business. This whole matter with Darcy Jeffers and the Fulton family has put us all out on a limb with our firm representing both sides. It is a conflict of interest of sorts, so we are walking a fine line here. Don't do anything foolish."

The younger man, followed immediately by his father, went out to the lobby to find Andrew Page pacing. "Well, Andrew, this is a surprise. What can I do for you?"

Looking much steadier than usual, Andrew's eyes were clear and his voice calm. "Actually, Grant, it's what I can do for you. I have something to discuss with you."

Graham turned to his client. "You and your family are represented in all matters by me, Mr. Page. Is there something I can do for you now? My son, as you know, represents Ms. Jeffers."

"Oh, I can assure you this has nothing to do with that squabble, Graham," he said to the older man. "This is just something I thought would amuse Grant. A little something with which I need his expertise." He laughed when he saw Graham's face cloud over. "Come on, Grant. You're going to love this!" The older man turned away from his client and walked through the side door into his own office.

When they were alone in his office, Grant hissed, "Why do you have to bait my father? You know that only makes him suspicious of me. Do you want him looking into this little arrangement of yours?"

"Calm down, it's not a big deal," Andrew replied. "He thinks we're talking about another one of my schemes or else you betting on the horses. Didn't you see the way he looked? That was priceless." Sitting down across the table from the lawyer he continued. "Now, let's get down to business. I have some of the information you need to help your clients get their project underway."

"Darcy? Can you hear me? Darcy, open your eyes!" Robert's face swam into view as she complied with his order. The rain was still coming down, but the brim of Robert's hat now shielded her face. His face was full of concern, and she wondered if this was all a dream. Opening her eyes, she reached up and touched his wet face. He took her hand and kissed it, then held it to his cheek. "Are you all right? My heart nearly stopped when I found you lying here!"

Darcy tried to sit up, but moving her arm caused her to cry out in pain. "Robert," she cried as he helped her sit up against the felled tree. "It's my shoulder. I think I've dislocated it."

Robert looked at her right arm that was hanging by her side. "You sure did, and now I'm going to pop it back into place." He stared into her face. "This is going to hurt both of us, but once it's over you'll feel much better. Ready?"

Darcy had no time to think. Robert was immediately at her right side, and with a swift movement put the shoulder back in place. Darcy howled in pain as the shoulder went back together. She felt faint but managed to stay upright.

At last turning toward Robert she said, "I hope never to experience that kind of pain again." She winced as she moved her sore arm. "Thank you for taking care of that. I never would have made it home in that condition." She heard the horses shift restlessly. "How's Cassidy?" She tried to turn toward her horse.

"He seems fine. What happened? How did you get so far away from home?"

"I was in the slave quarters when I heard Cassidy getting uneasy," Darcy tried to remember the sequence of events over the throbbing of her arm. "I decided we should go home, but as soon as I got into the saddle he took off at a run. He seemed spooked, and no matter what I did, he only got crazier. He stopped short at the tree and luckily I was leaning to the right so I fell off that way. What's the matter with him? He's never been like that before! Oh, I hope nothing has happened to my baby!"

Grabbing Darcy's chin, Robert turned her face toward him. "What about you? You could have been killed. You could have been killed!" He punctuated his statement with a bruising kiss to her lips. He tasted of rain and fear. Darcy put her good arm around his neck and kissed him back for all she was worth. When he reached for her, Robert hit her injured arm and she cried out, breaking the kiss.

"We've got to get you back to the house before you add pneumonia to your injuries. I want you to ride Prince home." Robert pointed to his big bay gelding standing patiently behind him. He held up his hand to forestall her argument. "I know, before you'll get on I need to see that Cassidy's all right. I will, then you'll ride back and I'll lead the horses." He got up from her side and began speaking softly to Cassidy who had calmed down now that there was no longer anyone on his back.

"Would you look at this," Robert whistled as he lifted the saddle from Cassidy's back. "There's a huge knot of nails under this saddle! They dug into Cassidy's back as soon as you got on, and I suppose it got worse as you moved around trying to stop him." Seeing her stricken look, he continued, "There's no way you could have known about this, Darcy. This was done deliberately and cruelly. It's a lucky thing that it wasn't placed quite right, or it would have really been bad for the horse. As it is, it looks as if he'll just need some stitches and some loving care and he'll be just fine."

"How could anyone be so cruel to an animal? If they wanted to hurt me they could have done it a million ways," she cried, "but did they have to hurt Cassidy? What's going on, Robert? Who is doing this to me?" She looked back at the horse's back, which was covered with blood.

"I honestly don't know, but when I find out someone is going to pay," he promised. "This has all gone way too far. Come on; let's get you both home. Whoa!" He jumped, swinging his foot over the object in front of him. Sheepishly he smiled and said, "Sorry about that. The stick looked like a snake, and I'm a little nervous around those guys. Let's get going."

"Thank you for coming, ladies," the receptionist smiled as she handed Fran her credit card and showed them to the door. "I hope ya'll enjoy your stay in Williamsburg. If you need anything else, we're open seven days a week, so come back soon."

Fran waved goodbye and turned to Jane. "Now, wasn't that refreshing as well as relaxing? I always feel so much better after a facial and a manicure."

"I don't usually agree with you, but you're right about this. Although I couldn't relax as much as I wanted to with all of that gossip everyone was spreading. No one ever quit talking."

"That's true, Jane, but that is the best way to learn about a place," Fran replied. "I learned a lot about the Colonial Williamsburg Foundation that DJ's always talking about, as well as what people think about her taking over Winterview. They were also talking about some new, fancy development that's going up by the James River. It's always worth a trip to the beauty parlor, not only for the treatments, but for that very enlightening gossip."

"You never change, do you Fran?" Jane stated pointedly. "Always interested in what other people have to say, living on your looks and your reputation. Isn't it time you get a life?"

"Oh, that's a hoot coming from you. You've lived in DJ's shadow for ten years now. Of course now you have no choice but to get a new life since she's thrown you out of hers."

"You can be such a bitch, Fran. Darcy hasn't thrown me out of her life. As a matter of fact, she's invited me to move here if that's what I want. I'm sure you haven't received such an invitation, have you?" Jane got into the car and started the engine. The two women were silent during the drive back to the plantation.

Jane came quietly into the darkened bedroom, a tray of tea and pastries in hand, compliments of Anita. "Darcy, are you awake? I have a treat for you." She was pleased to see her friend smile up at her.

"No pain, no problem, Jane. Whatever the doctor gave me is really making me float. Ah, tea and yummy pastries. A perfect complement for a dislocated shoulder." Her medication was making her loopy. "Good thing I'm left-handed so this injury won't get in the way."

"I'm so sorry we weren't here for you, Darcy," Jane said contritely. "Here we were getting pampered and you were out in the woods all alone. It's horrible. I never should have gone with your sister in the first place. She's just so persuasive and I didn't think it could hurt to get a little pampering. I'm so, so sorry!"

"Take it easy, Jane," Darcy said as she sat up to drink her tea. "It's not as if you could have stopped this from happening. Some psycho is out there trying to hurt me and you being here wouldn't have made a difference. Besides, I got a kiss from a handsome prince in exchange for my injuries." She smiled as she thought about the bruising kiss she had received. Robert cared, no matter what he said.

"What do you mean you got a kiss? What's going on with you? You can't mean Robert, can you? Last night you were sure he was in league with Fran and his brother and today you're kissing him. Have you lost your mind?" she shouted.

"You have a point, Jane. I really don't know what's going on. I have never had control of this situation and things are only getting worse. I really need to do some thinking and planning. I guess my injured arm will give me that opportunity." She paused, hearing noises downstairs. "What's going on down there, Jane? Do you know?"

"Oh, that's the other thing I'm supposed to tell you. Deputy Jackson and Sheriff Matthews will be over shortly. Plus, Grant Hastings is downstairs demanding to see you. He's very worried, and very cute, Darcy." She moved toward the door.

Darcy groaned. "What is with Grant? He acts like I am Juliet to his Romeo. His act gets old fast. Well, I guess I had better try to take a shower so I at least look presentable." She tried to throw back the covers with her right hand and giggled at the result. She finally made it to her feet. "It's not a bad thing to have Grant here in his capacity as my lawyer when the police arrive. Will you ask him to stay? Will you send someone up to let me know when the police arrive?"

"Everything will be taken care of—no need to worry. Just take it easy. As always, I'll take care of you." She bowed low in Darcy's direction.

"Cut it out, Jane. I can't deal with you feeling used by me right now. You know I love you like a sister, I don't mean mine, and I appreciate all you do. I feel like a truck has run over me and now I have to face the police, so I would appreciate a little tolerance."

"I'll be up soon." Jane responded, closing the door sharply.

Darcy spent an agonizing half hour trying to get a shower and wash her hair. Every inch of her body ached or was on fire, and she didn't know how she would manage getting dressed. After gazing at the gash on her face in the mirror, Darcy looked for other cuts and bruises on her body. She heard a knock on the door and absently called for Jane to come in while continuing her search.

When her friend didn't come into the bathroom, Darcy looked up into the mirror and saw not Jane's reflection, but Robert's! What was he doing here? His face was hard and cold, and he was looking over every inch of her backside, and what he could see in the mirror of her front! Whipping the towel back into place, Darcy tried to whirl around to face him, but her wounded body wouldn't cooperate and she ended up launching herself at him.

Quickly moving to keep her from falling again, Robert caught Darcy in his arms and they both ended up dropping onto the bed. The breath was knocked out of him as she landed against his chest, and Darcy was stunned at the turn of events and at the desire blossoming as she lay across Robert. He was heaving from the exertion of breaking her fall. Propping herself up on her left arm, she stared down into Robert's amber eyes which glowed with anticipation. She had such a desire to kiss those eyes shut and go from there. The amber was no longer cold and brittle as it had been a few moments ago—now it was warm and inviting.

The pressure was too much for her good arm, so Darcy unceremoniously dropped to Robert's waiting chest. It felt good to be there and even better when he moved his hands down her injured body. Despite the calluses on his hands, his touch on her shoulders, back and buttocks was soft and soothing. His cotton shirt gently rubbed against her cheek, and she could hear a rumble of contentment run through his chest. Finally, he broke the silence. "Sorry about startling you, but I wanted to see for myself how badly you were injured."

"I bet you got more than you bargained for," Darcy tried to make light of the situation. "Quite an eyeful of bruises, aren't I?"

"You're an eyeful, all right," he agreed. "You're also very beautiful and very brave, and I have to tell you I'm not exactly unhappy you ended up right here." He kissed her forehead, then her eyes, nose and finally her waiting lips as Darcy rose up to meet him halfway. Then it was her turn to kiss Robert's nose, his ears and down his neck until he could hardly stand it. He began to wriggle beneath her, his need for her mounting.

Pulling back, she looked down at Robert once more. "You know this isn't a good idea. Things are so messed up right now, and I don't know where I go from here, but I want you to know this feels good to me, too. Maybe we can try it again some time when I'm not playing damsel in distress to your white knight. It only seems to complicate things further."

"You're right, Darcy. We need to stay focused on keeping you alive and well." He punctuated his statement by running his hands down her legs and back up her arms.

"Why would you want to do that? I know you're as unhappy as your brother and sister about me being here."

"I was at first," Robert admitted. "But I never was a part of trying to hurt you. I was willing to be involved in a legal termination of your rights, with a little intimidation, but I have no part in all of these so-called accidents. Do you at least believe that?"

"I do believe that, Robert, or I wouldn't have stayed in this position with you." She once again bent down and met his lips, this time more forcefully. She reached down and unbuttoned his shirt so she could feel his flesh against hers. He began tugging at the towel, her only covering, when a knock on the door sent them both off the bed.

"The Sheriff and his deputy—I forgot all about them! You have to help me get dressed and then come out of the room after me." She got off Robert and the bed slowly, savoring each inch of exposed flesh. He looked fabulous with his shirt unbuttoned, lying on her bed. Darcy gingerly walked toward the clothing hanging on the chair. "Is that you, Jane? Are the police here?"

"Yes, Darcy, it's me, and everyone is downstairs. Do you need any help?"

"I'm almost ready. It would be the most help if you can keep everyone from getting too restless downstairs. I'll be there in a minute." Turning back to Robert she motioned for him to stand beside her. "I need help getting this shirt on. I can't lift my arms enough to do it."

Robert helped get the shirt over Darcy's head, then slid his hands down her bare torso. Her shirt settled on her skin after his hands stilled. They were both breathing heavily by the time Darcy was dressed and out the door. "See you in a few minutes," she whispered as she placed a quick kiss on his lips. "Thanks."

Robert didn't move immediately. What had just happened to him? He didn't know whether he was angrier from seeing all of the damage that had been done to Darcy or more turned on from seeing every round inch of her. She was all woman, that's for sure, not too thin and bony, not too young, just right. Her skin still looked smooth and pink having just finished her shower. He could hear his mother chuckling at his current situation. Robert was afraid he knew the answer to his question and decided now was not the time to deal with it. Gathering his emotions behind a mask of indifference, he headed down the backstairs to join the assembled group.

Darcy felt as if she'd walked into the lion's den. Seated in the parlor were Deputy Jackson, looking official and rigid, Sheriff Matthews, trying to look at ease while still being in charge, Jane, completely uncomfortable in the surroundings, Fran purring at Grant, Grant looking anxious and worried, and the two dogs who were working the room for food and attention. This should be quite an event, she thought, as she saw Robert slip in from the kitchen.

Upon seeing Darcy enter the room, Sheriff Matthews took control. Deputy Jackson helped maintain order, as Fran and Grant leaped to their feet to go to Darcy's side, and for the next hour Darcy went over the incident and Robert filled in what he could, including producing the knot of nails in a plastic bag. Finally, having all of the information they needed or could get, the two officers ended the interrogation.

"We are going to need to sit down and discuss this matter privately," Sheriff Matthews said to Darcy. "Someone is succeeding at doing you bodily harm, and you are going to need protection until he is caught. I'll be in touch tomorrow after we've gone out to the scene to let you know what we find. Good night, Ms. Jeffers, and I suggest you keep your doors locked."

As the officers left, Fran and Grant finally got to Darcy. Grant immediately put his arm around her and tried to get her to sit down. The day was bad enough without his hovering, Darcy thought, as she pushed his hand away. "Grant, I hate that," she said sharply. Seeing Grant's face drop into a pout, she softened. "It's very nice of you to think of me and come see how I am. I'm also grateful you could be here in your capacity as my attorney. However, what I need most is to go to bed."

"Absolutely right, Sis," Fran chimed in, stepping between Grant and Darcy. "It's been a pleasure to meet you, Mr. Hastings, and I hope you'll stop by again soon. Darcy needs her rest now, so Jane will see you to the door." With that, she turned Darcy around and pulled her toward the stairway.

"Good night, Darcy," Grant called as he followed a seething Jane to the back door. "I'll call you tomorrow."

"What's this all about, Fran?" Darcy asked as she painfully wrenched her arm free of her sister's grip. "Getting a conscience all of a sudden, or just afraid of losing your meal ticket? You'll have to start being nicer to Jane, you know. She's the executor of my estate!" Darcy got perverse pleasure from seeing the color drain from her sister's face.

Composing herself, Fran countered, "You know, DJ, you haven't given me much of a chance to be a sister, either. I know I constantly live down to your low expectations of me, but it seems like the only way to get your attention. I may not be the best person in the world, but I do care a lot for you—you're my sister and my only relative. So, please don't shut me out of your life completely, and believe me when I say how truly sorry I am that all of this has happened to you."

Stunned by the speech, Darcy stared at her sister. "I do believe you, Fran. I'm not sure what that means, but I believe you. Just now, though, I need Anita to help me to bed and I need about twenty-four hours of sleep. Good night."

"Good night, Sister Dear," Fran whispered as Darcy slowly climbed the stairs.

Eleven

The James River plantations vary greatly in size, style and preservation. A person needs to visit both sides of the river to appreciate the work that went into making this area so outstanding. Preserving its rich heritage should be a priority for everyone.

Nick watched the police leave the house, then the rest of the crowd. This was getting way too complicated. Who stole his idea about the horse? Whoever had pulled off that stunt this afternoon had put everyone on alert for another attempt on Darcy Jeffers' life. Nick wiped his brow as he realized how little time he had left to take care of this matter. If he didn't do it soon, he'd be the one in trouble instead of that woman. He wondered, not for the first time, just how many people were trying to get rid of Darcy Jeffers. He had found several areas where he could make a move, but with the Sheriff watching things more closely he was going to have to be very good at his next attack. He rocked back on his heels and looked up at the clouds parting. Lucky for him the weather was improving. He'd take that as a good omen.

Andrew Page staggered into his bedroom at 2:00 A.M. Beth immediately turned on the bedside lamp and glared at him. "Where have you been this time, Andrew? Off on another one of your wild schemes, or just out drinking?" she asked nastily. "Why can't you ever just stay at home with me?" She tried to reach for his arm but he jerked away. "You know, I think we still make a pretty good team."

"Don't try to play nice, my dear," he purred. "It doesn't suit you. I know you think I am a lush and a loser, but I'm not either. How about the way I found that information on the Jeffers woman? I also helped your brother at the board meeting. One of these days you're going to realize I'm a great guy." He lurched toward the bathroom. "Don't wait up," he said as he slammed the door shut.

Beth leaned back on her pillows and willed the tears away. She would not cry over Andrew. She might cry for her lost marriage, her lack of children, but she would not cry over him. They had been so happy when they had first married, but Andrew just could not get used to Beth having the money in the family. Once he had started to drink their relationship had gone downhill until now it was almost non-existent. At least he's sticking with the business of getting rid of Darcy, she acknowledged. Maybe that would help his self-esteem enough so they could try again. She turned the light off and tried to sleep.

Darcy made it to the kitchen by mid-morning. Scolding her immediately for being out of bed, Anita sat her down and made her a huge breakfast. Everything on Darcy's body hurt, even her teeth, but she was hungry and ate all she was given. After finishing her second cup of coffee she asked for a rundown on where everyone was and what she had missed.

"One thing I'm sure of this morning is that Lucas is not around," Anita began. "That boy drives me crazy even when he is over at the farm with Mr. Robert. He, by the way, went off with the sheriff this morning into the woods. Your sister, I believe is still in bed. Ms. Marshall took the dogs out for a run and here you are." She smiled at her employer. "There have also been several phone calls, but before I tell you about them, I just want to say something to you." Darcy sat up and looked straight at Anita.

"What I want to tell you is that Marjorie Fulton was not only my employer but my friend. She and I were together too many years to count. I know her dreams for this place as well as she did." She paused, weighing her words carefully. "And I also know how fond she was of you and why Marjorie thought you should be the one to fulfill her dreams. I agree with her choice."

Darcy waited for more, but the older woman had said what she wanted to say. "Well, thank you for that, Anita," she responded. "It means more than you know to hear that, especially from you. I appreciate you letting me know today. I needed some good news for a change."

"I know you do, that's why I wanted to tell you that before I gave you your messages." She looked a little sheepish at the admission. "You're not going to like what I have to tell you now. First, Mr. Hastings called twice to see how you were doing. I assured him you would call first chance you get. Second, you got a call from Deputy Jackson letting you know they are going to be around today to check on things. Third, you got a call from the folks at Colonial Williamsburg about the slave quarters, and last, you got a call from a Trust board member, Mr. Clay Chambers. He needs you to call him. Seems he and the other board members have been hearing rumors about you and they want to meet immediately to settle the matter."

"Oh, what now?" Darcy moaned. "Can't I even catch a break when I'm injured?" She tried to rein in her self-pity. "Sorry, Anita. I was just hoping for a quiet day. Did they say they wanted to meet today?" Anita nodded in the affirmative. "Too bad. Last I checked I was still in charge of the Trust. Could you please dial the number for Mr. Chambers? I'm going to clear this up right now."

"I'll make the call. Hang on." Anita punched in the number and spoke to Mr. Chambers' secretary. The conversation didn't last long. Anita handed the phone to Darcy. "Mr. Chambers is coming on the line for you."

"Clay, this is Darcy Jeffers. You called about setting up a meeting? What is going on? This must be serious for you to try to set up a meeting without my consent today. You know that's not possible since people have to come from out of town."

"Actually, Ms. Jeffers, I hadn't thought of that. You are right. I know you are supposed to call the meetings, but the other board members and I have some concerns that won't wait. So, we are using our prerogative to call an extra meeting for tomorrow afternoon in Williamsburg. Does that suit?"

"That will be fine," she replied. "But can you tell me what this is all about? How can I prepare for a meeting when I don't know the subject matter?"

"The subject matter, as you put it, Ms. Jeffers, is your conduct and your ability to lead this organization. I will see you tomorrow." He hung up the phone before Darcy could even attempt to find out more.

Robert stood to the side as Deputy Jackson and Sheriff Matthews looked over the scene where Darcy had fallen off the horse. It was obvious that a crude path to the fallen tree had been made, deliberately setting up the fall. He took all of this in from a distance, as he was still reeling from yesterday.

How could he have said any of those things to Darcy? Maybe it had something to do with the naked body under my hands, he thought wryly. But it hadn't really been that, it was his uneasiness about these accidents. This last one seemed much more malicious and cruel, as well as dangerous. Either the perpetrator was getting desperate, or there was more than one person after Darcy. *What a situation I've gotten myself into this time,* Robert acknowledged to himself. *Now, if the line has been drawn in the sand I'll be forced to side with Darcy and against my family. I'm a military man, I know about honor and loyalty, but I'm not going to let anyone else around me die. Once was enough. I couldn't save Jorge, but I can save Darcy.*

Glancing back to the men at work, Robert wondered about Deputy Jackson. He had known him since childhood, and he had never before seen such passionate interest on Aubrey's face as he had when they were walking through the slave quarters earlier. He wondered if the deputy's family had been slaves on this very plantation. It had never occurred to him until now. He'd tell Darcy about it and perhaps she could include Aubrey in the preservation work there. He thought Aubrey would very much enjoy being part of such a project.

After her phone call with Mr. Chambers, Darcy was ready for time away from all of the nasty business in her life. Jane came in with the dogs and announced that it was a gorgeous day outside, so when Fran came down for breakfast, Darcy suggested the three of them go explore some of the other plantations on the James River.

"What a good idea, Sis," Fran said. "I think getting away from all of this would be great, and I know I would love to explore the area. Jane, are you coming, dear?"

"Cut it out, Fran," Jane grumbled. "Of course I'm coming. I think that's a great idea. Let me just change clothes and I'll be right down."

"Darcy," a voice called from the doorway, "I have a better idea." The startled women turned to find Grant standing in the kitchen door. He continued, "It would be my pleasure if you would allow me to drive you all to the plantations today. That way we can be together and you won't have to try to drive with your injuries. Would that work for you?"

Thinking it over for only a moment Darcy replied, "Grant, you're a sweetheart. That's a great idea. Thanks."

In less than an hour the three women and their chauffeur for the day were on their way up the James River toward Richmond. "Let's start at Shirley Plantation and work our way back," Darcy suggested. The drive to Shirley took very little time, and soon the three women stood in front of the brick plantation house and outbuildings sitting on the bank of the James River.

"This plantation is still a working farm as the fields surrounding it attest," the tour guide stated. "The ninth and tenth generations of the family still live in the house today. This plantation is the oldest continuously run family business in the country. The carriage entrance is actually the back door, as the front door faces the James River. The other buildings are called dependencies. Servants would have lived upstairs and field workers lived in wooden structures away from the house."

Continuing into the house, the guide gave a history of the family as well as the building itself. "Shirley started out as an eight thousand acre land grant. The first wooden plantation home was built on the site in sixteen thirty-eight. The present house took fifteen years to build. The railings are black walnut and were milled on the property. The present house was occupied in seventeen thirty-eight.

"The real wonder of this house is the staircase. It is a square-rigged flying staircase, the only one in North America. There is no visible means of support to the stairs, and they do give when you walk on them, but they are sturdy, as metal is put under the paneling. Isn't it wonderful?" The guide stepped back so everyone could get a look at this marvel.

"Boy, that's really something," Jane whispered to Darcy. "But this house seems so small in comparison to Winterview, don't you think?"

"This one has three full floors, I think, Jane. Winterview has three floors but the top one is only attic space and some old servant quarters. Plus, you have to remember that the original Winterview house didn't include those wings, so it was just the house minus the ballroom and office."

"Yeah, that would make it about the same size then, I guess," Jane said. "I can't believe how old things are in this part of the country."

Her friend laughed out loud at that and earned a stare from the guide. The woman continued with the story of Ann Hill Carter. "Ann Hill Carter married Lighthorse Harry Lee, and they were the parents of Robert E. Lee. She is a Carter, born and married here at Shirley Plantation."

After the tour Fran and Jane took a quick look at the dependencies while Grant assisted Darcy back to the car where she rested.

When the women returned she announced that it was time for lunch. "Let's eat at the Coach House Tavern at Berkely Plantation. Grant, the next stop, please." Darcy felt relaxed and was enjoying the late spring day. She could see that Fran and Jane were, too.

Darcy felt that Grant was happy to be spending time with her. She knew he had hoped to be alone with her, but seemed content to be with all three women. She wondered whether it was wise to be enjoying his company and leaning on him for support. He might get the wrong impression.

They arrived at Berkely and Grant dropped the women off at the door of the restaurant. The room was crowded with people enjoying their lunch. Grant joined their table after he had parked the car.

"I'm starved," Fran complained. "Let's order soon. And can we get some wine? I would so like a decent wine for a change."

"Order what you want, Sister," Darcy replied, "But count me out on the wine. I have enough chemicals running through my system without adding that. I'm sure Jane and Grant would enjoy some, though."

"Yes, I would, thank you," Jane said. "This place is charming. It used to be the coach house? How ingenious to turn it into a restaurant. There aren't many places to eat around here, are there?"

"No, there are not," Darcy answered. "That's one of the charms of this area. People like to see things the way they were and not have everything taken over by fast food and strip malls. There are enough of those in Williamsburg."

"But won't that all change with the new development?" Fran inquired. "From what I hear it's supposed to be a luxurious place."

"What development?" Darcy cried out. "Where did you hear about a development in this area? Nothing has been said to me about it. Where would they find the land to do it?" she wondered out loud. "I can't imagine any of the landowners around here wanting to let in a development and all of those people."

"Oh, it's probably nothing, DJ," Fran replied. "I just heard some talk in the beauty salon about it yesterday. You know how those things go. It's probably just someone's big dream."

"Still, I think I'll look into it. Something like that would jeopardize our plans for Winterview." Darcy smiled at her sister. "Thanks for telling me about it."

Grant quickly cut in. "Don't you think it would be good for the economy of Charles City County to have a development out here? There are lots of people who would benefit from such a project."

"No, I don't, Grant," Darcy said emphatically. "The charm of the plantations and this part of the James River is that it isn't spoiled with the crush of development. Isn't it bad enough to have that big plant right across the river from Shirley Plantation? No, I would fight any such project." Looking around at her companions, then to the neighboring tables, she realized she had gotten a little loud with her tirade. "Oops. Sorry about that. Let's eat."

All four people decided on a meal of absolutely fabulous oyster stew and an order of crab cakes. The excellent food hit the spot, and they then worked off the lunch by touring the plantation house and walking out into the extended Berkely gardens.

"This plantation was the home of Benjamin Harrison, a signer of the Declaration of Independence," Darcy announced, acting as the tour guide. "It was also home to William Henry Harrison, President of the United States. His grandson, Benjamin Harrison, was also President. It has quite a history, as this plantation dates back to sixteen nineteen." Looking around at all of the flowers she added, "Aren't these gardens wonderful?"

Berkeley's ten acres of formal terraced boxwood gardens and lawn extend a quarter-mile from the front door to the James River. White, yellow and blue flowers blossomed all around under a clear, blue sky, giving the tourists a taste of the serenity of the gardens. The scent of boxwood reminded both sisters of their visits to the area as children, and they stopped to enjoy their memories in silence.

"It's all so beautiful here," Fran commented. "After looking at these places I can see why you're so stuck on history, DJ. The students in your seminars must have gone nuts when you got going on the colonial era," she teased.

Darcy stuck out her tongue at her older sister and walked on. "Oh, here is my favorite part of the grounds," she cried and started up a path away from the garden. "This is where it is said that the song 'Taps' was composed in eighteen sixty-two," she recited breathlessly. "The Union forces were camped here and the bugler blew 'Taps' for the first time. The story goes on to say that a bugler from the Confederate troops on the other side of the river heard the song and played it back, so the haunting melody was heard from both sides of the river. It makes me want to cry listening to it," she said as she pushed the button. The song began to play.

"Does anyone want to go down to the river?" Jane asked when the song had finished. "They have a replica of an old sailing ship moored down there." She glanced at Darcy. "No, we had better leave. I think we're all getting a bit tired."

"I'll second that," Darcy said, smiling at the other woman. "I'm still feeling a bit like a punching bag, and a little rest would be great."

Back in the car Grant asked quietly, "Do you want to go home, or would you like to take your friends to see the gardens at Westover? I know we are wearing you out. You should be home resting."

"Thanks for your concern," Darcy replied, putting her hand on his, "But we're so close, let's stop. Westover is such an impressive house and the gardens there are as lovely as those at Winterview. We can only visit the garden and the outbuildings, so it won't take up too much time."

The women got out of the car and strolled around the grounds of this magnificent plantation. "Westover has this row of tulip poplars, over one hundred fifty years old," Jane read from the brochure. "There's also a secret passage. Hey, isn't there one of those at Winterview, too?"

"Yes, there is one on the grounds, very similar to this one from the description," Darcy replied. "But the one at Winterview cannot even be seen these days without someone to point it out to you. Maybe we'll have to fix that, as well." Turning back to the Westover brochure, she said, "This home was built by William Byrd II, the founder of Richmond. I didn't realize that."

"Oh, and there's the famous Westover doorway!" Jane cried, running up to the house. "I've seen this on television several times. Wow, this place is really nice. Let's go check out the garden." She ran off behind the house to the enclosed garden while Darcy and Grant rested on a nearby bench. Fran had wandered to the other side of the house.

"There you are," Fran grouched as she found Darcy and Grant. "You can get lost in this place if you're not careful. Did you know there is even a vegetable garden tucked in the back? It really has everything. I wish I could have seen it all in bloom. I bet it was stunning."

"You'll have to come back for Garden Week," Darcy commented. "Every spring, gardens in the area are opened to visitors so they can see all of the wonderful plants blossoming and see the fruits of so many people's labors."

"Is that an invitation, DJ?" her sister inquired. "Are you going to let me come back again for a visit?"

"As if I could stop you," Darcy mumbled. To her sister she said, "Fran, you are always welcome at Winterview as long as you call *before* you show up!" As she tried to stand up she hit her sore arm against the trellis and swore. Grant was immediately at her side to help. "Guess it's time for me to get back home. I think a nap is in order."

On the way back to Winterview, Jane said, "Thanks for the outing, Darcy. This was loads of fun. Plus, your knowledge of the history of the area really makes it come alive for us. Maybe you should keep on teaching. You really have a gift."

"I am hoping to do both with the work at the Plantation Trust, but thanks for the compliment. I'm glad you enjoyed it."

Twelve

My dear friend, I know a strong woman when I see one. You only need to believe in yourself as much as I do. There is nothing you cannot do if you put your mind to it and have the courage to follow your dream.

Jonathan walked down the hall to Andrew's office. "Come on. It's time for the Plantation Trust meeting. Do you have all of the information straight? We need to get to the board members before Darcy arrives. That way they will be primed and ready to go after her."

Coming around his desk Andrew replied, "Yes, I think I have all we need. I went ahead and made out a fact sheet for everyone. I think we have finally found a way to get rid of Ms. Jeffers. The fact that she's injured and not up to full strength can only help." He looked at his brother-in-law and smiled. "Jonathan, I believe today is going to be a wonderful day!"

Startled by the hand on her shoulder, Jane looked up to see Lucas standing over her. "Where did you come from?" she asked the teenager. She settled back into her lounge chair on the balcony where she was enjoying the morning sun.

"I saw you from down below and thought I'd come up and scare you," Lucas replied. "I did a pretty good job, I'd say." He started to laugh when he saw the irritation on Jane's face, a strange laugh that made her wonder if he was on something. His behavior certainly changed from one meeting to the next, and she didn't like his manner.

Getting control of her temper, Jane thought this would be a good time to learn more about this young man and the family. "Don't go yet, Lucas," she said as he had moved to the doorway. "Pull up a chair and stay if you want to. I can always use the company. It gets pretty quiet around here when everyone leaves."

Suspicious but curious, Lucas plopped down in the other lounger. "Can't stay long. I have to help Uncle Robert in the south field this morning. But, I'll stay for a few minutes." He leaned back and closed his eyes against the sun's glare.

"Why don't you tell me about yourself, Lucas," Jane prodded gently. "We haven't had a chance to get to know one another and I would like to know more about you."

Lucas opened his eyes and stared at Jane. He must have decided that she was all right as far as adults went, for the two stayed talking for over an hour. Robert finally came looking for his nephew. Before he left Lucas said, "You know, Jane, it's been fun talking to you. Maybe we can do it again some time." With a huge smile, he jumped over the railing onto the ground one story below.

Back to reality, Darcy thought as she hauled herself out of the car, walking as if she were eighty-two instead of thirty-two. With even more aches and pains than yesterday she did not feel up to what she knew was going to be an ugly meeting. The sight of Jonathan and Andrew waiting for her didn't help. Resigned, she walked toward the two men. After curt greetings, the three-some walked into the Wren Building on the College of William and Mary.

The board members of the Plantation Trust were all seated when they entered. Darcy took her place at the opposite end of the table from Mr. Chambers. "Well, ladies and gentlemen,"

Darcy began. "Would you please tell me what this impromptu meeting is all about?" She looked at each person in turn.

Mr. Chambers rose. "Ms. Jeffers, this meeting has been called because we have received very disturbing information about you, and we are all concerned about your involvement in this Trust. I know Marjorie Fulton thought you were the right person for the job, but I do not believe she had all of the facts."

"Just what information do you have that is so damning, Clay?" Darcy asked, beginning to get angry. "I believe I have the right of rebuttal."

Clearing his throat, Clay Chambers looked straight at her. "We understand that the cause of your parents' deaths ten years ago is still unclear and that there is evidence to point to your negligence in the matter. Further, you are under investigation for another car accident here in Virginia, unable to produce a mysterious driver. The police have no leads there, either. We, the board members, feel that until these matters are cleared up to our satisfaction, you should no longer be in charge of the Trust." He sat quickly down in his chair.

To say that Darcy was stunned was a mild description. How could these people so blithely accuse her of being the cause of her parents' deaths? The horror of that time in her life threatened to swamp her where she sat. Yet, she realized everyone was waiting for her reply. Glancing around she saw the smug faces of Jonathan and Andrew and her grief and guilt were immediately replaced by fury. Gathering herself, Darcy stood to face her accusers.

"Fellow board members." Her anger radiated around her like a shield. "I know that we have not gotten to know one another well enough yet for you to have faith in me, but this is outrageous. What I have been subjected to since my good friend Marjorie Fulton's death is nothing compared to this abuse. I have a good idea of who told you these things," she paused to look at Jonathan and Andrew who squirmed under her gaze, "and I can understand why you might want to believe them, as you have known them longer than you have known me. So, I will answer your accusations this time. I hope from now on you will have more faith in me than to even listen to such nonsense.

"As to the matter of the accident here in Virginia, the police have made it clear that I am not a suspect, but a victim. After someone also tried to drown me and yesterday tried to kill me by sabotaging my horse," she held up her arm in its sling for all to see, "the police have determined that someone is trying to kill me. Does that answer that charge?" Darcy asked, glancing down the table. Shocked by the news, several heads nodded in the affirmative.

"As to the matter of my parents' deaths ten years ago, this charge is so low as to be slanderous. I loved my parents, and I still feel guilty about my role in their death. I had driven the car earlier in the day and gotten into a fender bender. I had a friend pound out the fender, then I drove home. I didn't tell my parents about the accident—I was twenty-two years old and didn't want to cause my parents further irritation—and then they took the car out that night and lost control. They were killed not by the impact but by the immediate explosion of the gas tank. For a long time I thought I was to blame because the earlier accident must have broken something I hadn't seen and caused the explosion." She paused, trying to keep the tears from falling. "At the inquest it was proven that my accident had nothing to do with the explosion. The only reason the case is still open is that it is part of a class action suit against the car manufacturer. We believe the explosion was caused by faulty manufacturing."

With the tears of rage and grief still standing in her eyes, Darcy glared at Jonathan and Andrew before making her final statement. "I assume I have cleared up these matters to everyone's satisfaction. As I stated earlier, I hope from now on you will take the things you hear with a grain of salt. I am willing to prove myself to you in the area of historic preservation and administration of the Trust, but this kind of petty personal slander will not be tolerated." She paused, looking around the table then said, "Now, if there is no further business, I am going to use this unexpected time in Williamsburg to check on the schedule for the platting and excavation of the slave quarters. Meeting adjourned."

Darcy sagged against the door once she had left the meeting room. This abominable treatment was going to stop and stop now. *I've been playing the victim, but now I'm going to be on the attack. I'm going to stop all of this nonsense and get on with my life!*

As she turned to leave the building, Darcy heard the sound of an organ coming from the chapel. She quietly opened the door. Tourists sat in rapt attention as a man dressed in eighteenth century garb played a pump organ, which sat high above them.

Finding a chair near the door and leaning back against the darkly paneled wall, Darcy closed her eyes and let the music wash over her. It was just what she needed. The piece was over too soon, and the audience clapped, bringing her eyes quickly open. The musician introduced the next selection, Fugue in B flat, by Morris Green, composer and organist at St. Paul's Cathedral. Bach, she knew, was unknown in England and the Colonies until the 1800's.

Darcy assessed the people present. Most were tourists with their Colonial Williamsburg passes hanging around their necks, but there looked to be a few music students as well. A young girl, listening to the organ concert, played along with the organist on her imaginary keyboard on top of the pew. She looked about eleven years old and had dark hair in a ponytail; olive-skin, and a dominant, rounded nose. Her actions and her pink tank top seemed so normal. *My life has got to get some kind of normality into it, soon, so I can come back and enjoy a concert like this.*

Darcy left as the organist played his final song, the most popular tune of the eighteenth century. It was *Rule Britannia*. The song was originally part of a masque and an essential part of any celebration. Darcy left the Wren building in a lighter mood.

Waiting for her by the car was Jane. "Where did you come from"? Darcy asked.

"I had George drop me off," Jane replied. "I thought you probably wouldn't want to be driving, so I thought I could chauffeur you home. How did the meeting go? Anita told me it came up suddenly."

Darcy explained to Jane what had happened as she steered her toward the Colonial Williamsburg offices. The two women walked side by side in the heat, oblivious to their surroundings. Jane's face was suffused with color as she listened to the story.

"That's appalling, Darcy!" she cried. "How could anyone be so mean? I warned you something like this might happen. But you wouldn't listen, wouldn't stay in Minnesota on the farm with me. Now you're paying the price. Have you considered giving this up and just coming home? Someone is out to kill you."

"I think that's over dramatizing things a bit, Jane." Darcy tried to calm her friend. "It will all settle down as soon as everyone realizes I'm not going anywhere."

"I hate to mention this, but have you thought that Fran might be involved? She did go out with the Fulton men the other night, right before you had that accident with Cassidy. She's gone off again this afternoon with Robert and Lucas. I just don't think you can trust her, not to mention either of them."

"There is enough happening around here without thinking Fran is in the middle of it. Thanks for the concern, but I think Fran is just being Fran. I'll talk to her about her involvement with the Fulton family when this all gets closer to being solved, but I don't think she's out to hurt me. Ah, here we are," she said as they neared their destination. "I need to talk to some of the Colonial Williamsburg Foundation people, Jane. It shouldn't take long, and you're welcome to stay, or we can meet in an hour back by the car."

"I'm not leaving your side, Darcy. All of this is really getting to me. Why aren't you more upset?"

"Because I'm past upset," she responded heatedly. "Now I'm angry and I'm going to take action." With that Darcy walked up to the receptionist.

Jane sat down in a comfortable chair as the receptionist led Darcy to her destination. She was now more worried than before. Darcy was going to take action? That was just inviting trouble and with all that was happening in this crazy place, she knew the invitation would be accepted. Something needed to happen soon to bring this matter to a conclusion. She yearned to be back on the farm in Scandia watching spring come up after the long winter. There it truly was peaceful and their life had been so quiet, so routine.

Jane remembered seeing Darcy again at her parents' funeral ten years earlier. It had been so good to see her friend again, even under such terrible circumstances. So much had happened since they had left for college. Jane had gotten married the spring after she entered college, and a year later it had ended. Not only was she devastated emotionally, but she had also lost all of her savings to the man. So, when Darcy asked her to stay at the farm with her, it was what she needed as well.

In the ten years they had shared the same house, she and Darcy had built a new relationship as adults. Jane had even been able to take some of her hard earned money and put it in the stock market to build up her savings, only to lose it all in a swift downturn of the economy. Ten years later she was no better off than when she had moved to Scandia, yet there was Darcy increasing her wealth and her holdings. *Obviously Darcy had the golden touch, and I had the black touch. Here I am, still taking care of things for her while my life goes nowhere. Where's the justice in that?*

Jane pulled out of the dark thoughts and concentrated on the present. Someone was out to get Darcy, and Jane would put her envy aside to help her stay safe.

An hour later Darcy walked into the reception area followed by an elderly man and Grant Hastings. "Thank you, Dr. Rhodes. This information will be invaluable in getting the Winterview slave quarters protected. If we can get the temporary designation, that will buy us enough time to do the paperwork needed for not only Virginia designation but also the national designation.

Then, nothing can touch it except our preservation efforts. You have made my day."

"A pleasure to see you again, Ms. Jeffers." Dr. Rhodes replied. "I have always enjoyed talking with you at the Colonial Williamsburg Foundation functions, and I am thrilled to be able to help you with this project. Good day."

Darcy turned to Grant. "I'm glad you were able to come over on such short notice. As you can tell from all of this paper," she pointed to the file she had set on the table, "I am going to need a great deal of legal help."

"As your lawyer, I am here to serve," Grant replied. "However, I am not convinced you want to go with the historic designation. I think we need to talk more about this. How about over dinner?"

"That's a terrific idea, but I can't do it tonight, Grant," she replied apologetically. "According to my doctor and to Jane here," she turned to include the other woman in the conversation, "I am supposed to be in bed and resting if I am not at some official function. We'll get together soon, I promise."

Grant picked up her hand and gently kissed it. "I'll hold you to that, Darcy. I would very much like to get to know you better. And, we can talk about business, if we must." He laughed as he lowered her hand. "Goodbye, Jane. Take good care of our girl."

That afternoon, another meeting of the Fulton family took place at the farmhouse. Fran had participated in the previous meeting and had been invited back for this one. Fran looked from Robert to Lucas to Beth. She joined the group at the farmhouse late, and noticed the rest of the group seemed very upbeat. Except for Robert. He appeared tense and irritable.

"What are you all so happy about?" Fran asked. "You seem in an awfully good mood."

Beth looked at the other woman and smiled. "Oh, we're happy because it's a beautiful day and my husband did something right, for once. That always calls for a celebration." She and Lucas clinked iced tea glasses.

Fran knew there was something they weren't telling her. These people were spoiled and downright evil, and she'd thought so since she had met them. Except for Robert. Somehow he had changed recently, and he certainly was not celebrating. Maybe she could get more out of him. "Hey, Rob, how about taking a walk with me?" she asked in her sweetest, flirtiest voice. "It's so beautiful here and you promised to show me around."

Robert got up and headed for the door. "Let's go, Fran." He looked back at his relatives. "I need some fresh air." The two headed out the back door.

"Robert, what's wrong?" Fran asked when they were a distance down the road. "Why are you so upset and everyone else so happy? You look like you're about to explode."

He stopped to stare directly at Fran. "Just which side are you on in all of this, Fran? I can't figure you out. You're Darcy's sister and yet you're hanging around with my family, plotting her downfall. Do you dislike your sister so much? What's between you two?"

Fran sighed. She tried to size up this man and his motives and decided she needed to be fairly honest before he would talk. "Robert, despite appearances I love my sister. We lost touch after our parents were killed, and I'm afraid I'm to blame. I blamed DJ for the accident and for taking away my parents who were my life. I did everything I could to make her as miserable as I was. It got to be a habit, I guess, but I do love her and don't want anything bad to happen to her."

"So she can continue to support you?" Robert asked snidely. "You sure seem to be sincere with all of my family in your distrust and dislike of her despite her being your meal ticket. Why should I believe this story?"

"Because I think you and I are now in the same position. Look, I wanted to know what was going on with the Fulton family, so I got in on the plotting." She could tell he was confused. "You know, when you, Jonathan and I went out, I made sure to let you both know that I was on your side. But now that DJ has been seriously hurt, I want to do what I can to stop this. Isn't that how you feel?"

Robert glared at her. "Why would you say that? Oh, hell, I give up. Yes, that's how I feel about the situation now. I was all for getting rid of Darcy when she first inherited, as I really thought she was a gold digger. Now that I have gotten to know her and to see her strength and convictions, I think Mother probably made the best choice for Winterview and probably for our family, as well. I don't want to see her hurt." He sighed. "I can hear my mother chuckling at me from beyond."

"Then what's going on with your family? Why are they celebrating?"

"Apparently Andrew found information about your parents' accident that implicates Darcy. He and Jonathan are at the meeting right now trying to use that against her. They think that will get rid of her once and for all."

"Oh, my gosh, they're going to blame DJ for the accident? They can't do that! It wasn't her fault. She doesn't need this on top of everything else. Rob, what can we do? I feel responsible for this. I mentioned something about the accident to Andrew, but I never implicated Darcy. He must have found out some other way, but I gave him the ammunition!"

"There's nothing to do," Robert replied, glancing at his watch. "The damage is done. The meeting should be over by now. But, Fran, don't sell your sister short. She's stronger than any of us gives her credit for and I think she'll weather this storm, too. I just don't know how to end this. I'm caught in the middle of a dangerous game, and my mother put me here. Not only did she leave me, she also left me with this mess."

"Robert, this is all mixed up. Maybe we need to sit down and talk to DJ about it all and come clean. Together we might be able to make this all work out. How about it?" She smiled at him.

"Yeah, that's probably the best plan, but it will also depend on what happened at the meeting today. I have to admit I'm still wary of you and where your allegiance really lies, but any ally who was willing to help me stop this madness would be welcome."

"My pleasure. I can tell you care deeply for my sister, don't you? Don't look so surprised. I can tell when a man is interested. Don't worry, I'll keep your secret." Laughing at his surprised look, Fran reached up and gave Robert a big hug.

A car came to a halt next to the couple. Darcy got out as quickly as her injuries would allow. "Well, isn't this a cozy little scene? Planning more trouble for me or just enjoying one another?" Ignoring their shocked faces, Darcy continued, "Well, here's a news flash for you—I am still in charge of the Plantation Trust and everything is going full speed ahead. All of your little plans and accidents have failed, and I will never, ever let anyone undermine me! And, I can see I was right in not trusting either of you. Let's go, Jane."

Fran and Robert stared in shock as Darcy got into the car and drove up to the house with Jane. Her anger and jealousy was not lost on either of them. Robert spoke first. "About talking to Darcy...I think we're going to have to put that off for a while. She doesn't seem to be in the best frame of mind to hear what we have to say."

"That's putting it mildly. Damn, this just makes things worse. Now she thinks we're not only against her, but thinks we're together. It will take a miracle for us to get out of this one. I've been down this road with DJ before, stealing her boyfriend to make her mad. She can hold a grudge a long time."

"Fran, I have no idea whether to laugh or yell. I hope you're being honest with me. If not, you're going to find out just how angry I can get. We'd better get working on sorting this out so we can get some closure to the whole mess. I'm afraid things are going to get worse before they get better."

Lucas smiled at his aunt again. "Aunt Beth, do you really think Winterview will be ours again soon? I hate someone else living there. It should be in the Fulton family and since I am the next generation, it should be mine. My mother always said I should keep my heritage at Winterview."

Lovingly, Beth watched her nephew as he paced the room. Not having children of her own she tried to be a mother to Lucas whenever she could. "I think your mother was right about that. Your heritage is something no one can take away even if Darcy Jeffers continues to live at Winterview. You are a Fulton and always will be. And, I am always here for you, Lucas, if you need someone to talk to."

"Thanks. When do you think we'll hear from Uncle Andrew?"

Darcy was fuming as she got out of the car and slammed the door. The jarring of the slam hurt her all over, but she barely noticed. How could Fran act like this? How could Robert be kissing her one day and in Fran's arms the next? Ooooh, this was just all so frustrating!

"Darcy, earth to Darcy," Jane called, trying to slow her friend's progress. "Wait up. We need to talk." Jane grabbed her friend's handbag and pulled her to a stop.

Darcy glared at her friend. "Not now, Jane. I'm so mad I can't control it and I don't want to take it out on you. Just let me go."

"No, not this time. You need to face the facts of your situation. I know I'm taking my life in my hands, but we need to talk things through. I told you this might lead you to more grief, and I'm sorry to say I'm right."

"This is a great time for 'I told you so', Jane. That's just about the last thing I need. Give me a break."

Her friend didn't let go. "Please, Darcy. You know I care a lot about you. Let's talk about this."

Darcy sighed. "Ok, Jane, let's go in and talk. I give up. I give up on everything."

The two women walked into the kitchen and sat down. "Anita, can you give us a few minutes alone?" Darcy asked. "Jane and I need to talk."

"No problem, Miss Darcy," Anita replied. "I'll be upstairs. Let me know when I can get back to the dinner preparation." She smiled at Darcy and left the room.

"I'm sorry about this, all of this," Jane soothed. "I know you have been through so much recently, and today has made it worse. I really wish I could make it all go away for you. I've tried to do that for the last ten years, but this time you need to face facts." She studied her friend and continued on.

"Someone is trying to hurt you, Darcy. Not only are they trying to get you back to Minnesota, now they want to actually see you harmed or dead. Do you understand that? You know all of the Fulton children are plotting against you, and I know you thought maybe Robert was going to be an ally, but it's pretty clear he's not. Why would he be with Fran if he were your friend? As for your sister, well, she's always been jealous of you and she's obviously made the most of this situation for herself."

Darcy finally looked up at Jane. "Fran, jealous? She's not jealous; she's just always wanted me to hurt as much as she hurts. I've always known that. She too thinks I'm to blame for Mom and Dad's accident. And as for Robert, I just can't talk about him. I know you're trying to help, Jane, as you always do. You are my rock, but I have to go this path alone. Thanks for caring and for being my friend. I'm going to rest until dinner."

From outside of the kitchen window, Nick watched the two women part. He had heard most of the discussion between the two of them, and now he was ready to make his final move. Once darkness was complete, he'd get this done once and for all. That woman has had too many lives already. This time she won't be able to escape.

Jane wandered down the road and ran into Lucas bringing in a tractor from the field. He stopped, and she strolled over to the idling machine.

"Hey, Lucas, how's it going? Do you drive these big tractors all the time?"

"Yeah, Uncle Rob's really great about letting me do the big jobs as well as the crappy stuff. But being a farmer is not for me. As soon as I can, I'm going to get a job in town, maybe start playing some of my music." He scowled at Jane.

"How can you be friends with Darcy? You're so good about listening and not judging anybody. She's so uptight and greedy. She makes me so mad!" He pounded his fist on the steering wheel.

"She's not a bad person, Lucas, she's just in a bad situation. I think if you got to know her you might even like her."

"I doubt it, but you have to say that since she's your friend."

"Want to give me a ride down to the farm?" Jane asked. "Then we can talk more when you walk me back to the house." Lucas gave her a hand up, then put the tractor into gear.

Thirteen

You have lost some of your family, Darcy, so you too know how important it is to stay connected to them. I have not been a strong communicator with my children, and you appear far removed from your sister. Let us both work to bring our families back together.

The shadows lengthened across the lawn bringing some much needed coolness to the hour and signaling the end of the day. Darcy sighed heavily as she plopped into the garden chair. How had she gotten into this position? Her mother had always warned her that making friends so easily was bound to get her into trouble. Her father and sister had always laughed at Darcy's frustration when her mother was proved right. She thought back to the days when she had a complete family. She and Fran had been so close, plotting their revenges, playing make-believe, sharing the love and affection of two wonderful parents.

They always seemed larger than life. Her father, a hard working man who became Governor of Minnesota, fought hard for the citizens who had the least; and her mother, editor of the St. Paul daily newspaper, had worked her way up to that position in a time when women didn't hold that kind of power. These people were successful in their careers but still managed to teach their girls right from wrong and how to make their way in the world. They also managed to be around for their joys and sorrows.

Darcy was glad she could still remember things her parents had told her, and she felt fortunate to have such good memories. If they were still alive, her parents would encourage her to fight for what she believed was right, as she had been doing so far. They had taught both daughters to stand up for themselves, and also to respect all ways of looking at a situation. If only Fran were still her ally and not her enemy, she could weather this storm much more easily. Little chance of that after today, she decided. Calling to Cairo and Molly, Darcy headed into the house.

As Darcy entered the kitchen, she again found Anita working on dinner. "Anita, are there linens in Marjorie's room?"

The woman looked up in surprise. "You look like a different person, Miss Darcy. You're still dead on your feet, but you look determined about something." Receiving no reply from Darcy, she answered her question. "Yes, there are linens up there, Miss Darcy. Will someone be staying in there tonight?"

"Yes. I will. I think it's about time I took control of this whole situation, don't you?" she asked with more bravado than she felt. "This is the first step—moving from the guest bedroom into the master bedroom." After a moment's pause she asked, "You don't think Marjorie would mind, do you?"

Anita smiled deeply and sent a prayer up to her departed friend. "No, I don't think she'd mind at all. In fact, I think she's been waiting for this! You go upstairs and start packing and I'll get the bedroom open and aired out. Give a holler when you're done and I'll send George up for the moving. And, I'll send supper up on a tray so you don't have to worry about that." Darcy still hadn't moved, so Anita continued, "Get going, child. This is the right thing to do, so let's do it now." She gently pushed Darcy to the door.

"What a mire this has turned into, Robert," Fran said as they arrived back at the farmhouse. "I'm sorry to have made it worse. DJ looked furious, didn't she? I'm sure she'll get over it soon. Oh, it looks as if the rest of your family has arrived. Let's see what they have to say."

Robert eyed the Lincoln Town Car parked in front of the house. He really didn't want to deal with Jonathan and Andrew right now, but Fran left him little choice. He was still trying to figure out how to straighten things out with Darcy as he walked in the door. He could hear shouting from the front parlor.

"Damn those people," Jonathan thundered. "Why couldn't they just realize what a manipulator Ms. Jeffers really is? They bought her story with amazing ease; especially after all of the trouble we took to tell them about her background. I do have to admit she's a good actress, and they are sure buying what she's selling."

"You mean she's still in charge, Dad?" Lucas asked, disbelief in his voice. He had just returned from the barn. "After all you and Uncle Andrew have done, she's still here, still in charge? Man, this reeks. Can't you grownups do anything right?"

"You have to have patience, Lucas," his father admonished. "We thought this was going to work, but it didn't, at least for now. We have planted even more reason to doubt Darcy's character, so with a little more time I am sure we can get the board to see things our way." He watched his brother-in-law pouring himself another drink. "We'll just have to keep Andrew doing research on this subject, right? If anyone can come up with more dirt, I'm sure you can. That and drinking are what you do best."

"Enough," Beth commanded. "Just because this plan failed is no reason to go after Andrew. After all, he is the one who obtained this current information. He's been working hard for you, Jonathan. No reason to tee off on him."

Robert finally spoke. "So, your smear campaign was a bust, huh? I'm not surprised. You two don't give anyone credit for having common sense and some compassion. It was bound to go her way if she had a credible response. I assume she did, so now what?"

"It's not clear we should include you in these meetings any more, Brother," Beth said. "Seems as if you spend most of your time consorting with the enemy and her family." She looked pointedly at Fran. "Maybe we should take our meetings elsewhere while we let Robert decide where his loyalty lies."

"Maybe you should," Robert responded quietly. "You know how I feel about violence and destroying people's lives for no reason other than greed. I'm sure you can keep Fran in your group, though. She seems as bent on destroying her sister as you are, and she does have the inside track."

Fran gave Robert a hard look but made no reply. She looked around the cozy room to the other participants and just gave a shrug. It would be up to them if she stayed, and she didn't really care all that much what Robert thought. Someone had to know what was going on.

"Let's go," Lucas cried, getting up from his chair and charging toward the door. "There's no action here, and I think Uncle Rob's gone soft. Let's go and take some action of our own." The house shook as he slammed the door.

"That boy needs a strong hand, Jonathan. He's a hard worker when he's out here on the farm, but some of the things he says are downright scary," Robert told his brother. "I wonder about him using drugs when he gets so wild."

"It's just teenage stuff, Rob. You know he says things he doesn't mean and talks about actions he never takes. Let me worry about Lucas. You have bigger problems." He turned to the others. "We should leave. Rob has a lot of thinking to do and we need to come up with another plan. Rob, if you decide to become Darcy Jeffers' ally, you know you will be going up against your whole family. I think that is something to consider very seriously. Good night."

Darcy and George completed her move to Marjorie's room. *No, I am moving to the master bedroom, now my room.* "Thanks for all of your help, and please thank Anita for the wonderful supper. I'm going to settle in and go to bed. If anyone is looking for me, would you please tell them I am not to be disturbed?"

"As you wish, Miss," George replied. "I hope you have a restful night's sleep. After all you have been through, you deserve it."

"Thanks. I can't wait to get to bed. It looks so soft and fluffy that I'll probably get lost in it. A perfect place to sleep for days."

George stopped off at Darcy's old room where he met Anita taking the linens off the bed. "Do you think this is the right move for the Miss?" he asked.

"Oh, yes," his wife replied. "She's finally decided to take control of the house and, I think, of her situation. I wouldn't be surprised to find it all settled very soon."

"Good. There have been too many accidents and too much hostility in this family. I know Marjorie meant well, but I cannot imagine what she was thinking when she made these arrangements. Someone is going to end up seriously injured or dead."

"Let's hope not, George. Here, give me a hand with putting the comforter back on the bed. No, never mind. This can be done in the morning. Just leave it." Together the couple closed the door to the guest room and went downstairs.

Nick saw the lights go out in the Jeffers' woman's room and breathed a sigh of relief. Now all he had to do was wait for George to put out the garbage and his plan could be put into motion. There was no moon, and the night was humid. Nick broke into a sweat as he waited. Soon, George came out the back door with the trash bag in hand, and Nick, dressed completely in black, slipped silently through the open door. He got through undetected, surprised to find the kitchen also empty. Seizing his chance, he snuck up the back stairway and headed for Darcy's room.

The upstairs hallway was illuminated by one small wall lamp. Nick extinguished it with a quick turn of the bulb. He crept down the dark hallway wall, avoiding any squeaks and moans from the old floorboards. At Darcy's door, he carefully gripped the handle and soundlessly turned the knob. Upon entering the room he stopped and held his breath as he looked toward the bed. In the dim moonlight all he could see was a tangle of sheets in the middle of the bed. Nick pulled out his knife and cautiously made his way over to where she lay.

Quietly taking another deep breath, he raised the knife into the air and brought it down on the pile in the bed. The air whooshed out of him when the blade hit nothing but sheets! She wasn't in the bed! Where was she? He peeked around the corner and found the bathroom empty as well. Nick was beside himself with anger. This was his last chance to get her. Now she had sentenced him to dealing with his mysterious boss' wrath. What was he going to do? He didn't have time to search the whole house.

Anger and frustration overwhelmed him, and he began to slash everything in the room. He slashed the sheets, the comforter, and the pillows. He gashed the headboard and the dresser and he took several mighty swings at the curtains. Anywhere he could leave a mark, he did. Nick didn't stop to wonder about the noise he was making. He wanted to destroy this room as second choice to destroying Darcy. It was fear for his own life making him this crazy, but he couldn't, didn't, stop until the whole room was in tatters.

He stood in the center of the room trying to control his breathing when he heard a noise in the hallway. He had to get out of there fast or be caught. He slipped out of the room and made it to the back staircase before realizing someone was coming up those stairs toward him. A light came on and Nick was staring down the barrel of a shotgun held by George. Anita was still on the first floor. He could hear her footsteps running toward the stairs as she called out for help. Nick thought about bringing out his knife, but being in jail was preferable to his employer's wrath. He stood where he was.

"Oh, my gosh, what's happened?" Jane asked as she got to the stairs. She looked down at Nick, then at the shotgun. "Has everyone lost their mind? What's going on? What was all the noise?"

Fran came up behind Jane. "Get a grip, girl. This man's obviously been after Darcy. Looks like you didn't find her, though, did you?" She turned to the others. "I called nine-one-one when I heard the noises. The Sheriff should be on his way."

A flurry of thuds heralded the arrival of Darcy and the two dogs. She looked at Fran and Jane, and then peered down the stairs at the man who was being held. "Well, well. It's nice to see you again, Nick. I haven't seen you since my wild ride to Richmond. I guess now the Sheriff has no choice but to believe you're real."

Nick didn't move or in any way acknowledge Darcy's speech. His head was down against his chest, but the sound of sirens brought him upright. The dogs were whining at the sirens and uneasy about the intruder, but everyone stood their ground until Deputy Jackson arrived with two other officers.

"Deputy, this is Nick," said Darcy. "You know, the man the sheriff thought I was making up. He apparently got into the house and was coming after me again."

"Put him in cuffs and read him his rights," the deputy ordered.

"Ms. Jeffers, did he hurt you? Is there any damage?" Deputy Jackson asked as everyone moved up to the hallway.

Before she could reply Fran did. "Yes, there's damage, and lots of it. Our uninvited guest did quite a number on DJ's old room before trying to get away. Seems he didn't know she changed rooms tonight and must have gotten pretty mad about it from the way the room looks."

George had put away his shotgun when the officers took the prisoner away. He joined the rest of the group upstairs. When they got to the door of Darcy's room, Jackson issued a warning not to go in or to touch anything. With that said, he put on a pair of gloves and opened the door. The onlookers were startled by the complete destruction of the room.

"Wow," Jane commented. "He must have been out of his mind to do so much damage in such a short amount of time. Darcy, now do you believe you've been in danger? Good thing you decided to change rooms tonight or we'd all be attending another funeral. Where did you go tonight?"

"I moved to the master suite," Darcy replied, shivering at the fury shown in the room. "I wanted to take control of my situation and that seemed like a good way to start. Now, more than ever, I'm glad I did."

Deputy Jackson stepped into the room but held the others back. As he began his investigation, voices could be heard coming up the main staircase. Three more people joined the group—Sheriff Matthews, Grant and Robert.

"What are you doing here, Robert?" Darcy snapped. "Haven't you had enough fun at my expense today? Thinking you were going to find me in a pool of blood? Well, I am happy to say that your family's plan for me was thwarted. As you can see, I am still alive and kicking. Too bad for all of you." She gave him a look of contempt and walked past both men, heading for the stairs.

"I heard the sirens," Robert replied, "and I did fear the worst, that's for sure. Look at this room. The guy who did this was obviously in a rage."

"George caught him, Robert," Fran informed him. "The deputies have him in custody, so the accidents should now be over. It's only a matter of time before they find out why all of this happened."

Sheriff Matthews addressed the group. "This is now a crime scene. I need everyone to go downstairs and give your statements to the deputies. Then you can go back to bed. This room will be sealed and nothing more will happen tonight."

Grant ran after Darcy. Catching up with her at the bottom of the stairs, he pulled her into his arms and hugged her tightly. His hands were hot and moist where he gripped her. "I thought something terrible had happened when the Sheriff called, and I was right. I am so relieved that you're not hurt. I would feel terrible if anything had happened to you." He rested his chin against the top of her head.

Darcy tore out of his embrace. "What's with you Grant? You're acting as if we are lovers or something. I'm flattered you were concerned for my welfare, but you need to get some control. After everything that's happened, this is nothing. Now, sit in that chair, across the room, and tell me why the sheriff called you."

Grant did as he was told, taking a seat in one of the overstuffed chairs in the family room. "They called me because something was happening out here and since you are a client of our firm, they thought it prudent for either my father or me to be here. I came because I wanted to know you were all right."

"As you can see, I am. Thanks for your concern, both professionally and personally. But you've got to stop acting as if I'm some doll you can just pick up and squeeze any time you feel like it."

Taking a deep breath, Grant replied, "You're right, of course. I act like a total ninny when I'm around you. The truth is that I care very deeply for you, as you suspect. When I thought you might be hurt again, or even dead, I was overcome, hence the greeting when I found you were safe and unharmed. I am sorry. It is inappropriate because you are my client."

"It is also inappropriate because you've never talked to me about your feelings or tried to find out about my feelings. I hardly know you, and I only seem to see you in these crisis situations which doesn't help me get to know you any better. You are my attorney and I try very hard not to mix business and pleasure."

"I understand. You're right on all counts. Perhaps you will finally let me take you to dinner sometime to make up for this, and we can get to know one another. In the meantime, I will pull myself together and be your attorney. As such, I do have one question for you. Neither my father nor I know anything about your estate. Do you even have a will? Who is in charge should something happen to you?"

There was a motion behind her, and Darcy turned to find Robert lounging by the door to the kitchen. Despite his casual stance he appeared upset. "This is none of your business, Robert," she said. "But maybe it will help everyone to know this information so there is no confusion or thought that they might get any of my estate.

"I do, in fact, have a will, and I guess that needs to be updated with all of this change. But, as it stands now, I have left a lump sum to Fran, lump sums to several organizations, and the remainder is left in the will to be put into a trust which will be left in Jane's care. Jane is also my executor and will be in charge of making all of the arrangements. Obviously, none of what was in Marjorie's will and testament really affects my will, as the

Plantation Trust is its own entity and I only live in this house. Any questions?"

"So, if you had died tonight your sister and Jane and a bunch of organizations would have benefited, right?" Robert asked. "Just so we're clear," he added.

Darcy stared at him a good long time before answering. He looked tired and worn out, and she couldn't find even a trace of the snide, sneering man she had seen at other times. She wished things were different for them both. "Yes, that is correct."

Turning to Grant she continued, "I haven't had time to talk to Jane about having you and your father take over my estate, but I'm sure she will be thrilled not to be the only one carrying this burden. Not that I plan to make anyone happy with my death any time soon. Now that Nick has been caught I should be all right." As she left the room, Darcy noticed Robert and Grant exchange a worried look as they watched her progress.

Fourteen

The slave quarters at Winterview must be
preserved, no matter the cost. I am impressed with
your dedication to preservation efforts. I hope you
will consider joining me in Virginia when I finally
get the project underway. What fun we will have!

Jane

had finished breakfast when Anita brought in the newspaper. She handed it to the younger woman without a word, and Jane started reading about last night's exploits. How dare Darcy take such chances with her life, she wondered. Didn't she know how many people loved her and depended on her? Jane remembered how happy she had been to give up her job and home when her friend had needed help. She had gladly given up everything to live with Darcy and help her through the trauma of her parents' deaths. She did everything the woman asked of her and yet Darcy would not, in this situation, do as Jane asked and return to Minnesota. It was unfair. The whole situation was so confusing and frustrating. She hated to think of losing her friend to death, but it was just as bad losing her to Virginia. Jane knew she was being irrational, but she couldn't help wonder how this would turn out for all of them.

"Earth to Jane," Darcy laughed as she came into the kitchen. "Isn't it a glorious day? The sun is out and Nick is in jail. What more could a person want?"

"I don't see what you're so happy about. I've been reading the newspaper and they say the Sheriff believes Nick was hired by someone to go after you. He hasn't named names yet, and until they do you're not safe."

"Do you have to take the joy out of this moment? I know it's not over yet, but last night was a turning point in many ways.

Today is a beautiful day and I am going to spend it in Colonial Williamsburg with the Raleigh Tavern Society." At Jane's blank look, she explained. "The Raleigh Tavern Society (RTS) is one of the donor societies of the Colonial Williamsburg Foundation. They are a group of people who have committed their resources to keeping this important piece of history alive for everyone. It's the society's semi-annual meeting this weekend, and I am looking forward to seeing some acquaintances and friends I only see on these occasions. So, cheer up. I know what's going on. What are your plans for the day?"

Jane studied her friend's face. There were lines around her eyes that showed her lack of sleep, and the bruises from her fall were faintly visible up the arm of her blouse. She decided that Darcy did indeed know the score. "Oh, I just thought I would wander around. I have no plans unless Fran wants to go shopping or something."

"If you spend time with Fran, maybe you want to help her see it's time for her to go home," Darcy said darkly. "I think I have had just about all I can take of my beautiful sister. She and Robert deserve each other. They both lie and cheat at will." She stopped. "Sorry, Jane. I was just telling you to lighten up and here I am ranting and raving. I hope you have a nice, restful day."

Sheriff Matthews sat down at his desk hugging his mug of coffee. He had been up all night interrogating the prisoner, and he was frustrated with the lack of results. True, he could now pin Nick to the car incident, as well as the swimming pool incident, as he had confessed to his role in both of those events, but Nicholas Bradley Martine had an alibi for the time of the horse accident. Was there someone else involved in all of this? The worst part was that Nick had been hired to do these jobs but he said he couldn't identify his employer. He had only spoken to this person on the telephone and they had always used a voice scrambler so Nick could not even positively identify the person as male or female.

Still, he could be lying, the sheriff thought, and it will only take time to get to the name. But even if that were true, Ms. Jeffers was still in danger. This whole mess was not yet over.

The sheriff went out into the main office. "Jackson, you need to go home and get some rest. That's where I'm headed. Neither one of us will be able to do any more until we've gotten some sleep." He turned to address the other deputies. "In the meantime, I want regular patrols of the Winterview area and I want someone on Darcy Jeffers at all times. Get on it!"

Fran found Jane still brooding in the kitchen. "Hey, Girl. Time to get out and go."

The other woman just glared at her. "How come everyone is so cheery this morning? Nothing has been solved. Not only that, but I am losing my friend to this place. I just hate this whole situation."

"I know what will cheer you up," Fran said, pulling Jane by the arm. "There's nothing like shopping at the outlet mall to bring a smile to a woman's face. Let's go!"

It didn't take long for the women to reach the mall. The only problem they faced was where to start their shopping expedition. Deciding on a plan of attack, the women went their separate ways, agreeing to meet for lunch.

Fran made her way into the Dana Buchman store and started a conversation with the clerk who was a native of Williamsburg. The two women chatted about everything from the clothing in the store to the happenings in and around the area. Fran found some of the information unsettling but useful. Her purchases made, she headed for the Coach store to see what else she could learn.

"Grant, what is the meaning of this memo?" Graham Hastings asked his son as he entered the younger man's office. "Why haven't the motions been filed in the King trial? Without those motions, we may lose the whole case." His stern look caused his son to squirm.

"Sorry, Dad," Grant said, scrambling to take the file from his father's hand. "With my secretary deserting me, I just can't keep track of everything. Plus, all of these problems at Winterview have kept me pretty busy. I'll get right on it. Anything else?" He tried to usher his father out the door.

"Not so fast, Son," Graham replied. "I need to talk to you. You may have the problems you just outlined, but I think you forgot the biggest one—not being in the office. How many times have you been out of the office either all or part of the day this week?"

Grant didn't answer. He didn't have to, as his father obviously knew the answer. Quickly deciding on the best course of action, he took the offensive. "I'm trying to do what you want me to do, Dad. I am out there every day trying to get new clients, get younger clients. I am helping the firm's image and keeping things in the black."

Graham studied his son for a few moments before replying. "If that's true, son, I owe you an apology. However, getting new clients should not involve daily visits to the Richmond racetrack. I have had reports of you being there regularly. Be careful, Grant, or you'll find yourself in a very tough position, one from which you cannot get out."

As she entered the lower level of the DeWitt Wallace Museum, Darcy saw several familiar faces. She loved coming to the Raleigh Tavern Society meetings, as she got a chance to learn more about Colonial Williamsburg, life in the eighteenth century, preservation efforts, and the program most near and dear to her heart, the Teacher Institute. All of these areas were of interest to her, but as a teacher of history with a focus on preservation, the Teacher Institute was something she followed closely. This year Raleigh members were going to get the chance to learn more about the virtual tours of Colonial Williamsburg as well as the other programs available via the Internet. Darcy didn't want to miss any of it.

Relieved that none of the Fulton family was attending today's meeting, she settled into her seat in the auditorium. The first exhibition was woodcarving. Darcy was mesmerized by Williamsburg's Master Carpenter's hands as he carved a table leg out of a piece of wood. A special video camera was used to enhance the presentation and to allow those watching to get a close-up view of the work being done. The twenty-first century craftsman worked in the manner of an eighteenth century craftsman, creating beauty and elegance out of a piece of wood using only hand tools. The whole group got involved with the presentation by asking questions of the carpenter which he answered as he continued to work. Darcy decided she'd like to attend one of the weeklong institutes offered by the Colonial Williamsburg Foundation on furniture or clothing. It would be a unique experience.

Following the demonstration, the president of the Foundation, Randolph Caine, gave a State of the Foundation report. Darcy paid close attention to this, as she knew within a year she would have to give a similar speech to the members of the Plantation Trust. It was good to hear that the foundation had purchased more land adjoining the Historic Area for further preservation, despite the downturn in the economy. They were still making progress, and to that end Mr. Caine's speech was followed by opportunities to become more involved in the fundraising efforts.

Darcy's thoughts wandered during the other presentations. She tried to piece together all of the accidents and events that had happened since Marjorie's death. How could she make some sense of it all? She hoped the sheriff would have good news for her when they talked later in the evening. She was still confused about Grant and his behavior, and she was still furious about Robert and Fran. She shoved those feelings aside and tried to pull together all of the facts.

Her reverie was broken when she heard Amanda Blake, a Vice President of the Foundation, saying, "With us today is a RTS member who is involved in her own preservation project. The Plantation Trust is utilizing some of the Foundation's assets to make one person's dream a reality in which we all can share. Darcy Jeffers, where are you?" Darcy raised her hand, and Amanda continued, "Can we ask you to come up and say a few words about your project, Ms. Jeffers?"

There was applause from the members, so Darcy made her way to the platform. "This is an unexpected opportunity for me. I didn't think I'd get to make a pitch for the Plantation Trust to a group here to support another Foundation!" The audience laughed. "The Plantation Trust has much in common with the Colonial Williamsburg Foundation and I am happy that we will be working closely to make Marjorie Fulton's dream a reality.

"As you know Marjorie passed away recently, and at her request the Trust is going to fully restore the slave community at Winterview and open it to the public. This restoration will include interpreters on site as well as many other opportunities to learn how slaves lived and worked on the plantation. There are buildings still standing, although all of them need a great deal of restoration work. It is a project close to my heart, as well as a living reminder of Marjorie Fulton, and I hope all of you will take the time to visit. Perhaps during another RTS meeting we can incorporate a visit to see things as they progress. The Plantation Trust looks forward to working with the Foundation on this wonderful project. Thank you."

Anita was in the kitchen garden when Robert found her. "Who are you looking for Mr. Robert? None of the women are at home right now." She stood up cradling newly picked tomatoes in her apron.

"Darcy's not here? Has the Sheriff talked to her yet?" he demanded.

"She's in Williamsburg. Some society meeting or something, she said. She's been gone since this morning, so I'm sure she hasn't talked to anyone. She was so happy when she left." She noticed how worried Robert seemed. "What's wrong?"

"You know as well as I do that she's still in danger. Why can't that woman ever stay put?" He combed his fingers roughly through his hair. "I don't want her out and about unprotected."

"Seems like that's none of your business, Mr. Robert," Anita said harshly. "Any hope you had of working things out with Darcy seems to have vanished when you and Fran started getting friendly. You should be more careful."

"Anita, it's not like you to talk this way." He glared at the older woman. "You don't have all of the facts, and my relationship with Darcy is no one's business but my own. Thank you for the information." He stalked out of the garden leaving Anita wondering exactly what was going on with him.

Lunch at the RTS meeting relaxed Darcy as nothing else could. Seated at the table with Randolph and Lois Caine, she had the chance to get caught up on their lives and reminisce about their last trip together. They had had a great time traveling in and around the English countryside visiting beautiful homes and gardens, and seeing the restoration efforts in England. Darcy was grateful for the couple's continued kindness toward her.

The setting for lunch could not have been more magnificent. The meal was set up outside under a large awning in front of the Carter's Grove Plantation house, overlooking the James River. The day was warm and muggy, but nothing could dim the beauty of their surroundings. The lawn stretched out from the plantation house to the river, and a garden area had been planted in vegetables, as it would have been in earlier times. The green plants made the garden pleasing to the eye as well as functional.

The RTS members enjoyed a hearty lunch and then were treated to a real craft fair, where artisans from the Historic Area showed members their skills. The weavers demonstrated how to spin wool into yarn, then into cloth; the gunsmiths shared how they made the guns; farmers showed their crops; and many more craftspeople exhibited their eighteenth century techniques. Since the exhibits were outside, the group all enjoyed the glorious spring day.

As Darcy wandered down the path to the archaeological museum of Wolstenholme Towne, the seventeenth century town which disappeared after an Indian raid and was not rediscovered until excavations in the twentieth century, she felt a hand close around her wrist. Whirling around in panic, she confronted Robert.

"What on earth are you doing here? Oh, I suppose you're a Society member, aren't you? You're probably here to look at more plants. Well, I'm off to the museum, so I won't be in your way."

"Stop it, Darcy," Robert growled. "You know perfectly well I came here to find you. Why isn't there someone with you?"

"I came by myself because I wanted to see my friends and be free of your family for a day. Apparently I'm just not that lucky."

"I thought the Sheriff was going to give you protection, that's why I asked about someone with you. Isn't there a deputy here?"

Stopping their forward progress, Darcy faced Robert. "Why would I need any protection? Hasn't Sheriff Matthews gotten what he needed from Nick?" Seeing him hesitate she commanded, "Tell me the truth, Robert. You know I'll find out soon anyway."

As directed, the man conveyed the information he had learned from the Sheriff that morning. As Robert outlined the reason she was still in danger, Darcy felt a small flicker of fear. She wanted the truth, so he gave it to her.

"Well, that certainly puts a damper on things, doesn't it? I suppose I will have to have one of the deputies accompany me to the formal dinner tomorrow night. I'm skipping tonight's event, as I want to be home to work through some of these questions. The Sheriff promised to stop by tonight, as well."

"Do you mean the Society dinner tomorrow night? If you would prefer, I can accompany you to the dinner and then the deputy can stay around the perimeter." Darcy choked, wondering why she should trust him. Robert continued, "Look, Darcy, I know you think something is going on between Fran and me, but it isn't. Believe me or not, it's you I care about and you I worry about. Please let me accompany you to the dinner."

"How can you say these things to me? I saw you and Fran hugging yesterday! And it's so like Fran. Any man I have ever been interested in, she's right there to take him away. I'm so sick of feeling second best to my own sister." Struggling to regain her composure, she sat down on a bench beneath a large oak tree. The shade helped to cool her off physically as she reigned in her emotions.

Robert sat down beside her. "Do you really care about me? I couldn't tell if it was just my mind playing tricks on me, or if I actually mean something to you."

"Oh, I care more than I should, and I certainly shouldn't admit that to you. For all I know, you really are the one who has been after me all this time. You are always there when I get into trouble, you've treated me poorly since the day we met, and it's no secret that you and your family want me gone. So, is there any reason I should believe that you care?"

Darcy looked straight into those amber eyes and saw a reflection of her own turmoil there. Before he could think better of it, Robert pulled her close, at the same time kissed her with all of the emotion he felt. After a moment's hesitation, she reached up to put her good arm around his neck and returned his kiss. They broke apart and she laid her head on his shoulder. He sat quietly, as well, rubbing his hands up and down her back in a gentle motion that both soothed and aroused. They might have gone on that way for some time, but a musical voice directly above them had the couple springing apart.

"Well, Miss Jeffers, it seems you have found something more than crafts on the banks of the James River," Lois Caine laughed. "I thought you two were bitter enemies. It just proves the adage that love and hate are part of the same emotion." Seeing their embarrassment, Mrs. Caine waved and moved on.

"Does this mean I get to accompany you to dinner tomorrow night?" Robert asked, striving to get back on an even keel, still holding Darcy's hand.

"Uh, yes, that would be wonderful. Will you pick me up about six o'clock?" She squirmed under the pressure of the moment, uncomfortable about her feelings for this man coming out in the open.

"I'll be there. I'll always be there for you." Kissing her lips one last time Robert got up from the bench, waved at Mr. Caine who was coming up the path toward Darcy, and headed back to his car.

Fifteen

I do not understand my children's lack of support or enthusiasm for my preservation projects at Winterview. Do they not want to protect their heritage and share it with others? I am saddened by their attitude.

Fran cautiously entered the barn. She looked around to see if the workers were there, but found no one except Cassidy. He nickered softly as she entered his stall. "Feeling better, boy?" she crooned as she stroked the horse's nose. He began to seek out her pockets looking for treats.

"Stop that," Fran said laughing. "It tickles! OK, OK, here's your treat." She pulled a plastic bag from her back pocket, opened it and fed Cassidy his favorite apple slices. When she finished she took a look at the injury on his back. It was healing nicely, but it would still be some time before he could have a saddle on his back.

It looked like such an amateur job, Fran thought. She decided to take the time alone to look around the barn for any clues as to who would be able to do something like this. In the tack room she found a couple boxes of nails and a hammer, but she was sure she could find those in the house and in the other buildings, too. It didn't prove a thing.

"Looking for a roll in the hay Babe?" a young voice questioned. "I'm here to oblige, especially a good looking woman like you. I don't care how old you are. I bet you're a real fighter." He laughed.

Fran turned around to face Lucas. She studied his unruly hair and his unshaven face, but it was his wild eyes that really caught her attention. "Are you on something? You look a little out of it. Maybe you'd better go lie down for a while until you feel better."

"Just what I had in mind, but with you next to me. You're the bomb, Babe, and I really would like a piece of your action." He walked toward her, each step slow and deliberate.

"Keep your distance, Lucas," she ordered nervously. "I am not going to bed with you. You're just a boy and you are obviously high on something. Stay back or I'll have to hurt you," she warned.

"I knew you were a fighter. Well, I like it rough too, so let's get to it." He lunged in her direction. Fran managed to evade his outstretched arms, but she fell over his foot as she tried to escape. For someone high on something, he was quick to recover and throw himself on top of her.

"Stop it!" she screamed as the teenager tried to pin down her arms and kissed her. As she struggled he began to bite her where he could and she roared out in pain. Fran closed her eyes and continued to struggle against his advances until all of a sudden there was no one against whom she needed to fight. Opening her eyes she saw Jonathan standing over her and Lucas sitting in the corner sobbing.

"What have you done to him?" she asked as she dusted off her clothing and tried to stand. "He's a boy in trouble and he needs help. All you've done is subdue him."

"I did what needed to be done to stop him from hurting you," Jonathan answered quietly, his anger radiating around him. "That boy has no sense. Ever since his mother went away he's hated women and has tried to do whatever he could to hurt them. When Marjorie changed her will, it was like the last straw for him. I honestly don't know what to do any more." He helped Fran up. She moved toward Lucas.

"Keep away from me, Bitch! And take your sister with you. You've ruined our lives. Why couldn't you just have stayed away?" The boy began sobbing, his body shuddering.

"Jonathan, you need to get your son to a hospital right now. He's in real trouble." When he made no move to help, she cried, "Look at him! Really look at your son. He is pale, sweating, shaking and delusional. He needs medical attention followed by a treatment program. Jonathan, snap out of it. You're the only one who can help him. Lucas needs his father, NOW!"

Fran was kneeling in front of his nephew as Robert entered the barn. It was clear he was unwell. Jonathan was still frozen to the spot. Sizing up the situation as best as she could, Fran walked up to Robert and suggested he see to his nephew. Then, she went to Jonathan and laid a hand on his shoulder.

Swallowing his own feelings of distress and anger as he looked at Fran's tear-streaked faced, Robert gently addressed his brother, "Hey, Jon, you need to pull yourself together. It looks as if we need to help out your son." He turned to look at the boy on the ground. "Come on. Let's get Lucas on his feet, then I'll go with you both to the hospital. We'll take care of this as a family." Jonathan finally broke free of his paralysis and joined him in helping his son to stand.

"Up we go, Lucas," Robert said as he none too gently pulled his nephew to his feet. "Your father and I are going to see that you get some help." Each man took one arm and led the boy out toward the waiting cars. Fran watched the men shuffle toward the exit.

As they passed Cassidy's stall, the horse reared up and pranced to the back of his stall. The men didn't notice, but it caught Fran's attention. She wondered to which of those three men the horse was reacting. Could one of them have been the culprit who hurt him? Her sleuthing would have to wait. Getting Lucas some help and getting herself home and cleaned up were her first priorities.

Darcy, upon arriving home, found a message from Grant. Deciding he deserved another chance with her, she picked up the phone and returned his call. He answered on the second ring.

"No secretary, Grant?" she kidded. "Things bad in the lawyer business or are you just more client-friendly today?"

"That's not funny, Darcy," he replied grumpily. "My secretary quit a week ago and I hate having to answer my own calls. She didn't like dealing with some of my business associates. Enough about my problems. It is very nice to hear from you. Thank you for calling me back. I just wanted to apologize for my behavior last night. I should not have said half of the things I did. The last thing you need is for me to add my affections to the list of things with which you're dealing. You need to remain focused on your current situation."

"You apologized enough last night," Darcy cut in feeling irritated anew. "I was just puzzled by your actions. I thought we were friends and you threw me for a loop with your declaration of affection."

"I am your friend, Darcy, but I'd like to be more. I have to say I was extremely jealous to find Robert already at the scene. He's around you too much for my liking."

"There's no reason for you to be jealous. After all, I had no idea about your feelings." She didn't like having to deal with this kind of situation, but it was better now than later. Gathering her courage, she continued, "Grant, I am never going to be any more than a friend to you. I'm flattered by your attentions and affections, but I just do not feel the same way. It would be unfair of me to let you believe differently. And as for Robert always being on the scene, I could say the same thing of you, couldn't I? I don't know how you find out about my troubles so fast, but you are always right there. Should I be worried about that?"

There was silence on the other end of the line for so long that Darcy wondered if he had hung up. Finally, Grant replied, "No. I don't want you to think, even for a moment, that I could be capable of harming you. That is the last thing on this planet I would do." He paused, then asked, "Are you seeing Robert romantically?"

She didn't like the petulance in his voice. Quietly Darcy responded, "That is no one's business but mine. I'm sorry I do not return your affection, but now that you know, you need to stay out of my personal life or I will have to find myself another attorney. Good day, Grant." As she hung up the phone she felt the hairs on the back of her neck stand up. There were so many people around her with hidden agendas. It was time to find out what else people were hiding.

Andrew picked up his cell phone and made his call. "Why haven't you been answering my calls?" he whined when he finally reached the other party. "I have important information for you, and it's about Winterview."

"What could you possibly know that I don't?" the bored voice asked. "I really am on top of things, Andrew. You just need to keep calm."

"Did you know Ms. Jeffers is going to the Raleigh Tavern Society dinner tomorrow night with Robert?" he asked in triumph. "She agreed to be his date this afternoon and they were seen kissing in public. Things are getting serious for those two, and that could really mess this deal up for us."

"It does present an obstacle, I'll give you that," the voice replied. "We'll have to think of a way around it. There is still plenty of time. Andrew, please don't call me again until the plan is in full swing." The connection ended.

Grant changed clothes and hit the streets. Soon he was cruising in the zone, his breathing and running in rhythm with the music coming through the headphones. A long run was exactly what he needed after his conversation with Darcy. He knew he had taken the wrong tack with her, but she usually managed to make him feel like an idiot. And, damn it, Fulton was always around complicating things. Soon his mind also got into the zone. He'd run twelve miles tonight and worry about his relationship, or lack thereof, with Darcy Jeffers tomorrow.

Sheriff Matthews arrived at Winterview at seven o'clock, right on time. Darcy met him in the old plantation office, located in the wing opposite the ballroom. This room was not where guests had been received but where the business of the plantation had been handled. It was situated away from the receiving rooms that faced the James River. Here the plantation overseer was instructed, contracts signed. Heavy green tapestries hung over the windows and still smelled faintly of tobacco. The whole room was masculine in character but Darcy somehow felt at home sitting behind the giant oak desk.

"Sheriff, thank you for coming here tonight. I think we need to discuss what happens now and move ahead."

The Sheriff sat down in one of the green leather wingback chairs in front of the desk. "I think you're right about that. Let me go over what we know to this point." He proceeded to outline the case. Most of what he told Darcy she had already heard from Robert. His last comment, however, was new to her.

"I really think whoever hired Martine is not going to stop. Nick was a successful criminal until he hooked up with this employer. Now he's going to jail for a number of previously unsolved petty crimes in the area. If he knew who had hired him, I think he would have told us. So, in a way, we are no better off than we were before. You need to be even more cautious. What's your schedule tomorrow?"

Darcy sat back in her chair and mentally reviewed her calendar. She finally replied, "I have some Trust work to do in the morning, but I plan to work on it from here. Tomorrow night I will be going into Williamsburg for the Raleigh Tavern Society dinner, and Robert Fulton will be accompanying me."

Frowning, he said, "Are you sure that's smart? He is still a suspect and could be involved with these incidents, Ms. Jeffers. I would hate to see you in trouble of your own making. There's enough without that."

"I appreciate your concern, Sheriff. Believe me when I tell you that I am still wary of Robert, but I think he may actually be on my side. Still, I am hoping you will have a deputy present at the Governor's Palace during the event. Maybe they could follow us home as well?"

"Will do. I am going to station a deputy here tomorrow. Wherever you go, he goes. Tomorrow night I will have a deputy on duty at the dinner, so you know who to look for if there's trouble." The sheriff stood up and moved to the window. Pulling back the curtains he stared out into the night. "I hope you'll get your dinner party in before the storm they're predicting hits. It's early for hurricanes, but they say this one's supposed to be almost as bad." He turned toward the door. "I'll say good night, Ms. Jeffers. Please be careful whatever you do. This case isn't solved yet."

Darcy walked the sheriff out just as Fran was coming in. "Fran, where have you been? You look like you've been in a fight."

"In a way I have. Let me grab a shower and some other clothes and then we can talk. I really need some time with you."

"Fine by me. I have a few things to say to you myself, Sister Dear. When you're ready I'll be in the office."

Fran had ended up accompanying the men to the hospital to make sure Lucas got the care he needed. She was still in her soiled clothing with a bruise running up one arm. She glanced in the mirror and shuddered at her reflection.

Fran took her time in the shower looking at her bruises from Lucas. She was still trying to make sense of that whole encounter. Maybe if she and DJ put their heads together they could figure it out. They had been good at solving puzzles together when they were kids, had in fact been champions in school when they had held competitions. She gingerly toweled off her sore and bruised body and put on worn, comfortable sweats before heading back downstairs.

She passed Jane as she headed for the office. The other woman gave her a hostile look when she realized that Fran was going to talk with Darcy. It seemed to Fran that Jane was trying to get between her and her sister, and she was getting tired of it. She knew Jane was envious of her being Darcy's flesh and blood.

Restless, Darcy looked out the office window. Molly and Cairo were running in and out of the sprinklers under the spotlights. The two dogs chased one another around the yard and through the water. Darcy laughed out loud as they slipped and slid on the mud they had created. She thought about sharing the moment with her sister but decided this was a time for business, not pleasure. She saw the reflection of Fran entering the room in the window glass.

"Where have you been, Fran? No one knew what had happened to you this afternoon. Were you out planning your next revenge on me with your new best friends?"

"I guess I deserve that, DJ, but I hope you'll at least give me a chance to explain, to really explain everything that has happened since I've arrived in Virginia."

"You want to play true confessions? Don't you think it's a little late in the game for that? I'm only interested in what you've been up to today."

"I'll start with that, but only if you promise to hear me out. DJ, you're my sister. I think you at least owe me that."

"Owe you? You think I owe you anything? You've spent the last ten years punishing me for Mom and Dad's deaths. Every chance you got you made my life a living hell and now you think I owe you anything? That's carrying familial loyalty a little too far, Fran."

"You may think that, but I'm not giving you any information unless you promise to listen to everything I have to say. Take it or leave it."

"That sounds much more like the sister I've come to know. All right. I promise to listen to everything you have to say. Now, what happened today?"

For the next half hour Fran told Darcy about her encounter with Lucas in the barn and the subsequent arrival of Jonathan and Robert. She ended with the information about Cassidy's reaction when the men had walked past his stall. "What do you think it means, DJ? Did one of them put that horrible thing under his saddle? Or am I just grasping at straws?"

Darcy turned back to the window to consider what Fran had told her. The dogs were finished with their play and were now sitting on the front porch waiting to come into the house. She wondered if they would dry off enough to come in at all tonight. She turned back to Fran. "I think it has to be one of them. Horses are very attuned to the emotions of people around them, and they also fear anyone or anything that has harmed them. The question now is which one?"

"I can't believe it was Robert, although he is the one who found you, so he was obviously not too far away."

"No, I don't think so. I've been around when Robert has been in Cassidy's stall since the incident, and the horse was perfectly calm, nuzzling him for treats. He wouldn't be friendly one time and freaked out the next, so I think we can at least acquit Robert of this incident.

"As for the other two, I think it could be either one. They both wanted me gone. Now that I think about it, Jonathan doesn't know much about horses, does he? He only comes out to the farm to see his brother or drop off his son. And whoever did this would have to be able to saddle a horse. Lucas could do that—he's been working with Robert at the farm for most of the past year. With your description of his behavior, I think Lucas has to be the one. We'd better call the sheriff."

"Do you think we should do that, DJ? I mean, they'll arrest Lucas and he may have to go to prison. He's 17 years old, so he could go through the system as an adult. Do you really want to do that to him?"

"Maybe I should think this through more thoroughly before doing anything. You're right about it affecting the rest of Lucas' life. I want to see him get the help he needs, but I don't want him to be ruined for life." Darcy sat back down at the desk, away from Fran. "At least we've figured this much out. Thanks for the help, Fran. I need to bring the dogs in."

Fran came around the desk and put her hand on her sister's shoulder keeping her from getting up. "Oh, no, DJ. You promised to listen to me, so sit down. I have some things to say to you."

Surrendering, Darcy sat back down in her chair. She didn't want to have this conversation, now or ever, but she had given her word, so she sat back, ready to listen. "Fire away, Sister Dear. I can hardly wait to hear what you have to say."

Fran started to speak but was interrupted by the flurry of fur as Molly and Cairo found Darcy. George came running after them, a towel in hand. "Sorry, Miss Darcy," he puffed. "I was just drying them off when they got away."

"It's fine, George," she replied. "They are here now so let's just leave them. I'll finish toweling them off later." With a nod the older man dropped the towel on the floor and left the room.

The dogs made their way around the room to each of the women before settling down on the floor on either side of the desk. "Sorry, Fran. Go ahead."

Slowly Fran drew her long blonde hair back from her face, then began to pace around the room. "Look, DJ, this is darn hard for me. I know these past ten years have been hell for us both, and I want you to know I realize I've done my best to keep you feeling miserable." She looked at her sister's face and laughed. "I wish you could see your face. It's priceless and worth the apology. I am sorry to have been such a bad sister these past years. I know the accident was no more your fault than mine, but it was so much easier to blame you and take out all of my grief on you. I also wanted to keep you my little sister so I wouldn't have to grow up. As you know, I've tried my best on that score and have been relatively successful until recently."

"Fran, why are you saying these things? You look and sound

so sincere, but only a couple of days ago you were consorting with the Fulton family over my demise. How can I believe any of this? You can't change so quickly. I just cannot accept that. Why should I? It only sets me up for more heartache than I already have about you."

"DJ, I know this seems like a quick about-face, but it has been happening for quite a while. Every time I felt like getting closer to you, something inside me rebelled, or you would say something to set me off again. Like when I picked you up at the airport in Minneapolis. I really was just trying to be nice, but when you assumed I wanted something, I perversely decided you must be right, so I went for the house. I was also scared that you would just send me away and out of your life for good. I know neither of us knows each other in our real lives any more, but if you believe nothing else about what I say, I hope you believe that I would never want you harmed in any way. Regardless of everything," she added quietly, "you are my sister and I love you."

Darcy was stunned and touched, once more, by her sister's words. She paused a few moments before replying, "That's why you went after Robert when you thought I was interested in him, right? Jeez, Fran, how can you love someone and be so mean to them?"

"It was another programmed response. And, for your information, Robert wouldn't take the bait. He was rather brutal in his rejection, if you want the truth. He's apparently only interested in one Jeffers sister and it's not me. DJ, please cut me some slack. I really am only interested in your safety and your happiness."

The dogs began to whine when they heard someone coming down the hall. "I guess we'd better end this little chat, Fran. I will certainly take this all under consideration, but right now I need to try to resolve these other pressing problems. I wish I could really trust you. I could use an ally, but that's still only a wish."

Sixteen

I could never tell Robert this, but I was approached again today by a group of men who want to purchase part of Winterview. I am not unclear as to what they are planning. They were assured there would be no sale. It is so hard to have to be on my guard all of the time.

Nick's boss was furious. That idiot not only bumbled his attempts on the Jeffers woman, but he had gotten caught in the process. Now there was only time for one more attempt before everything would fall apart. Action needed to be taken immediately so that woman didn't interfere with the plans. Tomorrow would be the end of this whole situation, the boss would see to that. Then Nick would get what he deserved as well. Being in jail wouldn't be enough to keep him safe.

Andrew Page prowled around his living room. He had failed in his attempt to help the Fulton family rid themselves of Darcy Jeffers, but he had tried. He reached for the vodka bottle and poured the remaining liquor into his glass. He wished he could still get a buzz from the stuff, but all he got was the need for more booze. Beth had warned him that she would throw him out if he didn't straighten up soon, and he had hoped that helping Jonathan would make the difference. She still looked at him as if he was gum on her shoe, and he hated the feeling. He also held it against her that he didn't have a real life. If she hadn't been a Fulton and hadn't listened to her mother at all times, he would have been the breadwinner in the family. It was Beth's fault he was a lush, or actually it was Marjorie Fulton's fault. Her last act of leaving him nothing in her will made Andrew feel so mad he could hardly think about it without losing his cool.

His new business venture would change everything. He would see to that. Then he would have the pleasure of seeing all three Fulton siblings in debt to him. That was something to which he eagerly looked forward.

Darcy awoke feeling physically better than she had in days. She decided to start the morning with a jog, as her ankle had finally healed enough to start being active again. Her arm, now out of the sling, moved fairly well, so she was ready to try it out. After donning a sleeveless t-shirt and jogging shorts and getting the dogs up and out, she jogged down the road past the farm. The sun was rising under a thin layer of clouds, and the temperature was still warm. It felt as though the humidity was on the rise, and she wondered about the storm the sheriff had mentioned. It had been quite a while since there had been a real rainstorm. Today might be the day.

With the dogs running in and out of the fields next to the road, Darcy kept a steady pace. With each step her body unkinked and she felt better and better. She enjoyed the feel of the breeze on her face as she ran, the smell of the alfalfa on one side of the road, and the vista of wheat fields on the other. She waved to some of the farm workers who were also out early, then turned to take the road that wound back through the woods to the slave quarters.

Darcy hadn't been back to the village since the incident with Cassidy, and as she came to the dilapidated buildings she was reminded of the film she had taken that day. She wondered where it was. Surely it would help when the Trust people started working toward the restoration. She wished she had had photos to send in with the application she had prepared for the Virginia Historical Society for temporary designation as a historical landmark. Oh, well, she could still send them with the application for permanent status. Darcy made a mental note to look for the film when she got home.

Darcy felt no unease at being in the slave quarters again, but she did notice a large, white pickup truck parked behind one of the structures. There didn't seem to be anyone in the vehicle, and she didn't want to stop her run to look around, so she continued back to the house. She'd ask about it when she got home. Maybe the Colonial Williamsburg people were already on the job. That was a pleasant thought.

Back at the plantation house Darcy ran directly down to the edge of the river and watched as the dogs leaped into the now placid waters. She was as hot as they were, and in a moment of madness jumped into the river with them. The James River wasn't the ideal swimming hole, but it felt so good. She paddled around with the dogs, then lay on her back and watched the birds soaring, then diving, then soaring again as they flew on the wind. The sky was blue, but the thin cloud layer kept the sun from being too hot. The current carried them down to the other end of the property.

After cooling off, Darcy pulled herself up on the dock and sat looking at the house. How majestic it looked sitting at the top of the rise, the lush, green lawn rolled out like a carpet in front of it. The huge magnolia trees with their waxy leaves sat sentry on either side of the house, and the tall, old oak trees provided shade. The house itself was symmetrical—the same number of windows on either side of the huge front door, connecting pieces between the house and the ballroom on one side and the house and office on the other side. Even the chimneys were symmetrical—four on each side of a slate roof.

Darcy allowed herself a moment of happiness thinking that she was queen of all she surveyed. It was certainly a prize worth fighting for, and she knew Marjorie would want her to do so. She just wished the fight wasn't with Marjorie's family. She would see this through, and in the end she would make sure that her friend's dreams were fulfilled and her family satisfied as best she could. Feeling hunger pangs, she resolved that after a good breakfast she'd get down to her work for the Trust.

Jane joined Darcy as she was finishing breakfast on the front lawn. "You look soaked! Did you fall into the river?"

"No, I jumped in, actually. The dogs looked so cool and happy I just had to join them. It was quite a nice swim and I feel great having gotten in a run already this morning. How are you?"

"Obviously more in tune with reality than you are, Darcy. Nothing's changed since last night. There is still someone out to hurt you and we still haven't figured out who it is. Why are you so happy and relaxed?"

"Oh, for a couple of reasons." She sat back in her chair as she thought about her meeting with Robert at Carter's Grove. "Jane, I know you won't like this either, but I think I am falling for Robert. He found me yesterday at Carter's Grove and we had a really good talk. I'm not sure I trust him completely, but I know I'm attracted to him and unless he's a great actor, he's attracted to me."

"You've got to be kidding," she sneered. "It was only a little over a day ago you were so mad at him and at Fran you couldn't speak civilly to *me*. Now, you're falling in love? Give me a break. I suppose you've decided Fran is a model sister, too," Jane said contemptuously.

"We actually did have a good talk. She tried to convince me of her goodness, but I've had too many years of her lies to believe that. Still, we shared information and worked out who was involved in my accident on Cassidy. So, another piece of the puzzle is solved. Soon we will have the whole picture and we can put all of these incidents behind us."

"You've certainly been busy. Who did that horrible thing to you and your horse?"

"I'd rather not say, yet. I have to decide what to do with the information. What I have to say will be very damaging. It needs to be handled very carefully."

"Thanks a lot, Darcy. You don't think I can keep a secret? Wow, how everything has turned upside down here in the lazy Virginia sun. Yesterday I was your trusted friend and advisor and today you're full of secrets. What gives?"

"Jane, you're overreacting. Nothing has changed. You're still my best and trusted friend, that's why I am telling you all of this. I just need to deal with the Cassidy incident in my own way, OK?" Darcy paused and looked toward the house. "I guess I shouldn't say nothing has changed since everything has changed in the last few weeks. I now live in Virginia and I am making my own life." Her voice softened, as she looked her friend in the eye. "I have invited you to join me, but so far you have decided to stay in Minnesota. So, maybe we are finally growing up and apart, but you will always be my best friend. Do you believe that?"

"I'm not sure what I believe any more," Jane snapped. "Things have happened so fast and I feel caught in a tidal wave that's carrying you away from me. I need some time to think about all of this."

"I have to get to work, so I'll leave you alone. Jane, you're the keeper of my soul and the person to whom I turn for everything. I don't want to lose your friendship." She patted her friend's hair and walked into the house.

Jane watched Darcy go. As soon as she was out of sight Jane headed for the dock and stood watching the sun sparkle off the water. She tried to keep her temper in check, but she was angrier than she had ever been. How could Darcy be so blind? Didn't she see that everything was changing? By Darcy moving to Virginia, Jane was losing her comfortable life forever. She might be the keeper of her friend's soul, but it looked like Robert was winning her heart. She didn't begrudge Darcy some happiness in love, but she didn't want to lose her friend. And that bitch Fran. Somehow she was worming her way back into her sister's life. How had things gotten so far out of control? She needed to get a handle on things here before she lost everything.

Robert wiped the sweat from his brow. The old Ford tractor started up on the first try, and he climbed back aboard. From his seat high above the ground, he took a moment to survey his land. The spring planting was completed except for one field on the other side of the land. In this field little green buds were already poking through the soil. It felt good to see the results of his labor.

A helicopter thundered overhead and flew down river toward Newport News. He no longer felt any anguish at the sight. His time in the Marines had been both an exhilarating and horrifying experience, but here on his farm he felt part of something more elemental, that his work here mattered as much as flying. He put the tractor in gear and got back to the road in time to see Beth driving up to the house.

She waited until Robert joined her on the front porch. "Well, Brother, I hear you are escorting Ms. Jeffers to the dinner tonight. Have you completely given up on your family? How can you be so fooled by her?"

"Nice to see you too, Beth," Robert drawled. "To what do I owe this honor and outrage? I've just been out in the fields and need to get the last one planted."

"I came out here on behalf of the rest of your family to find out just where you stand. You have to know we are not giving up on getting rid of Darcy and we still need your help. Why have you given in to her?"

"Look, Beth, we gave it a good try. But things have gotten out of hand. The violence, the threats, the smear campaign, it's just too much. If we can't break Mother's will legally we need to gracefully handle our defeat. After all, what have we really lost? It's not like Darcy can do anything with the house and that we don't have access to it. Why are you all so bent on continuing this? I'm sick and tired of fighting. I have my farm and maybe Mother was right. Maybe Darcy is the right person to deal with the plantation."

"It's our inheritance, Rob. Doesn't that mean anything to you? There's been a descendant of the Moore family living on that land since the seventeenth century! How can you just turn your back on that kind of history?"

"I'm a descendant, and I'm here on the farm and that was part of the original plantation. Why can't that be good enough for you? Is this worth Darcy's life?"

"You are so naïve. Do you really think Ms. Jeffers will continue to allow us access to the plantation once her position is secure? Do you want to be banned from our own home forever?"

"The way to win Darcy's favor isn't by trying to get rid of her. Don't you realize that only makes her more determined to stick it out? She feels a real obligation to Mother and terrorizing her is only making her plant her feet more firmly in the soil of Winterview."

"An interesting thought, Rob. I suppose we could try killing with kindness, so to speak, but I don't think that will be successful, either. So, I take it this means you are now on her side?"

"I am on the side of reason and sanity. Whatever that makes me in your eyes and the eyes of my brother, I can't say. That's up to you to determine." He glanced at a van pulling up to the barn. "I see the vet is here to look at Cassidy and some of the mares, so I need to talk to him, then get back out to the field. See you tonight, Beth."

Grant picked up the telephone on the first ring. "Hastings & Hastings. How can we help you?"

"Grant, is that you? This is Fran Jeffers. Do you have a minute to talk?"

"Sure, Ms. Jeffers. What can I do for you?"

"I'm just wondering if you were going to the Raleigh Tavern Society dinner tonight. And if so, is anyone going with you?"

"I am going to the dinner, and actually, my father was going to go, but he just got a call from a client and said he won't be making the dinner. Are you looking for an invitation? I'd be happy to escort you." He was already figuring out how to use this new situation to his advantage with Darcy. Maybe she'd be jealous of him with her sister. That idea held real appeal.

Fran laughed a deep, sexy laugh. "Why Grant, that would be lovely. I know I'm not being very subtle, but I would like to keep an eye on my sister. There has been too much going on to not keep her in sight. It would be my pleasure to attend the dinner with you. There's also some information I need to discuss with you."

"Then I will pick you up at five thirty. Drinks are at six and dinner at seven, and we don't want to miss any of the fun, do we?" He smiled as he thought about all of the players who would be at this dinner.

"What do you know that I don't, Grant?" Fran was intrigued. "You sound like a cat that just found a bowl of cream. You're positively elated about something, so give."

"Oh, it's just that everyone is going to be there: Jonathan, Beth, Andrew, Robert, Darcy, and us. Seems like a mixture that could spark some fireworks. Are you up for the show?"

"Again, it would be my pleasure," she purred. "I'm always up for some extra entertainment. And, if everyone is going to be there, we certainly couldn't miss the main event, right? See you tonight, Grant."

He slowly put the phone back down. Yes, this made tonight complete. It should be very interesting to see how this story would end.

The telephone rang again and Grant picked it up without a thought. "Hastings, is that you?" a nasal, coarse voice shouted in his ear. "Where's my money? I want it now!"

Darcy sat in her room trying to get her hair to behave despite the heavy humidity. All afternoon the weather had gotten hotter and more humid, and she was having a hard time trying to look her best. A knock on her door brought Anita into the room.

"Miss Jeffers, would you like some help? Jane said you were having some trouble with your hair. In my younger days I was quite good at styling, so if you'd like me to make a try I'd be happy to."

"That would be fabulous. I can use all of the help I can get with this weather," Darcy laughed. "Maybe we could put it up somehow so I don't have to worry about it at all tonight, but I'm not sure it's long enough to do anything. I have a feeling I will have plenty of other things taking up my time." She grimaced at herself in the mirror. "I usually look forward to these dinners, but I am afraid tonight may turn into a confrontation with the Fulton children."

Anita took Darcy's fine, blonde hair in her hands and started to work. She deftly twisted the fluff into a ponytail of sorts, then dropped it and started all over. "I think a French roll would look best. There are pins in the middle drawer. Will you hand me some?" Darcy complied and Anita continued to comb and sculpt her hair.

"Marjorie would be so proud of you. The way you have dealt with all of these problems reaffirms her choice. You are the right person to help her legacy continue. The children are right about her choosing you as the child she wanted. But she did love them all, that's why she left them so well off. As a mother she would never have left her children without means, but Marjorie knew that they were not interested in anything but the money, the inheritance. Keep your chin up, Miss, and you'll get through tonight as well. You're going with Mr. Robert, aren't you? You might just have some fun. You two sure seem to throw sparks off one another." Spraying a coating of hair spray, she announced, "There. All finished. What do you think?"

Darcy looked into the mirror and marveled. Her hair was beautifully pulled back into a roll that was artfully pinned to her head. "It's lovely, Anita! Thank you so much for the styling and for the kind words. Now, I can get dressed."

A few minutes later Robert swung out of his silver Jaguar and put on the coat of his tuxedo. As he did so, the door of the plantation opened and Darcy came out, Jane coming with her. He looked at Darcy's hair pulled back in a sophisticated style, then noted her beaded cream, sleeveless blouse cut low in front with a simple gold choker around her neck. Continuing down he took in her creamy arms adorned only with a gold watch on her right wrist, then down to her long, black skirt where he was teased by the length of leg made visible by a slit up the right side. Looking back at her face, he was mesmerized by the beautiful smile and shining eyes. She was a vision to behold.

"You're staring," Darcy laughed. "Something out of place?" She made a show of looking at her clothing to see if there was a problem.

The stunned man finally found his voice. "You look truly beautiful, Darcy. You take my breath away."

Darcy was shocked and thrilled by his words. "Why, thank you. What a nice compliment. And let me return the favor. You look good in that tux. Maybe good enough to eat." The fitted, smooth black material fit Robert's lean frame perfectly. His amber eyes looked intense, to say the least. Darcy found her throat getting dry. She came down the steps regally and took Robert's waiting arm.

Turning back she waved at her friend. "Goodbye, Jane. We won't be out late. Are you sure I can't talk you into attending? I've been after you all week to go with us. I would very much like you with us tonight. Are you sure you won't reconsider?"

"No thanks, Darcy. I wouldn't want to be a third wheel. Besides, someone has to stay behind with the dogs when the thunder and lightening start. You know what big babies they are. It's not my kind of event anyway." She waved her hand and said, "Go on, have a good time. I'll be just fine."

The ride into Williamsburg was mainly silent until the song "Don't Stop" by Fleetwood Mac came on the radio. After Darcy cranked up the volume, she and Robert sang together "Don't stop thinking about tomorrow, don't stop cause it will soon be here" with the radio at the top of their lungs until they were laughing so hard they could barely breathe. It was a great way to release tension. They were still laughing when they reached the Williamsburg Inn and boarded the bus to the Historic Area.

From the Inn the group was driven to the front of the Governor's Palace. As they disembarked, footmen in eighteenth century costume awaited them and pointed the way toward the receiving line just inside the palace doors. It was hard to say hello to the dignitaries in line while trying to look at the magnificent building. The main hall of the recreated palace contained hundreds of guns mounted on the ceiling in a circular pattern and also on the dark paneled walls. Darcy and Robert passed through the hallway to the main staircase, then into the ballroom where they were greeted by the sound of a harpsichord playing a gavotte. The couple continued out the back door, down the stairs and into the garden where the bar had been set up.

The setting could not have been more charming. The scent of boxwood permeated the air, and flowers Darcy had never seen were placed in exact patterns, which made the garden a joy to behold. "Oh, Robert, I can't believe how lovely the palace looks tonight. I've been here so many times, but never on a night like this."

He squeezed her hand and started to speak when someone spoke from behind them.

"Hello, Troops, nice to see you," Fran drawled. "Surprised? I knew you would be, but I just couldn't miss this event and Grant graciously invited me along." She looked directly at her sister for the first time. "DJ, you look gorgeous!"

Fran, even more fabulous than usual, stood before them in a sapphire blue off the shoulder gown that hugged her lithe body and flowed like water to the ground. The color set off her blonde hair, which she wore in ringlets that bounced down her back. The smile on her blood red lips did nothing to detract from her shining beauty.

"Fran! What a surprise," Darcy said when she regained her equilibrium. "I had no idea you would be here. You look stunning as always, Sister. On the prowl?" she asked, smiling sweetly.

"DJ, I look no more stunning than you do. I had no idea your wardrobe was so up to date. You really do look elegant." In spite of herself, Darcy was touched by her sister's praise.

Grant showed up at Fran's side with drinks in hand. Passing around champagne to all of them, he said, "I propose a toast. To these beautiful sisters and to the beauty of Colonial Williamsburg." They raised their glasses, then drank the cool, bubbly liquid.

The foursome walked down the shaded arbor on one side of the garden, then back up the other talking about everything from Grant's lack of a secretary to the ominous weather. To the west a large, dark bank of clouds was forming, and they all hoped the rain would hold off until after dinner. Darcy and Grant stopped to speak to several acquaintances before the dinner bell sounded.

"Oh, Ms. Jeffers, I'm so glad I caught you," a young woman in a business suit said as she rushed up to Darcy. "I work for the Virginia Historic Preservation Department, and I wanted to give you this in person." She smiled as she handed the other woman an envelope.

Darcy opened it and read the letter inside. She beamed as she looked up and announced to the group, "Well, here it is. This is for the slave quarters. We've received a temporary designation as a Virginia Historical Site! Isn't that wonderful?" She stepped closer to Robert and gave him a big hug. "Your mother would be so happy," she said quietly.

"Good work, Darcy," Robert whispered. "Seems you really are the right person for this job." He wiped away the tear that had slipped from her eye.

"DJ, you're a miracle worker. Way to go," Fran added her congratulations.

"That is quite impressive, Darcy," Grant said. "I had no idea you were this far along in the process. Why wasn't I kept informed? Isn't this part of my job?" He was clearly angry about being kept out of the loop.

"I'm sorry, Grant," she replied contritely. "Remember when we were at the Colonial Williamsburg offices the other day? They helped me fill out the application, so I sent it in that day. I know we were going to talk about this, but I was worried about reports of development in the area and I wanted to be sure to get the slave quarters protected. It's still vulnerable without permanent designation, but this is a huge step."

"I accept your apology," Grant said, not wanting to make a scene. "I am glad it all went so quickly for you. Shall we go in to dinner?"

Darcy thanked the courier and the group made its way from the garden onto the Bowling Green where a huge tent had been set up. Flooring covered the green grass, making walking to the tables easy. Tables were set with crystal wine goblets and lovely china with centerpieces of fresh flowers and candles. It was like entering a fairy tale. The sun was just setting, and strings of white lights all through the enclosure added to the charm.

Robert and Darcy had almost reached their assigned table when they ran into Jonathan and Beth. "And here we all are, one happy family," Beth said sarcastically. "It makes me feel so warm and fuzzy. At least we don't have to sit at the same table."

"Where's Andrew, Beth? Not able to make it from the bar to dinner?" Robert retorted. He did have to admit that his sister looked as sharp as her tongue tonight. She was dressed in a black silk pantsuit with a sheer black and white jacket over the top. The whole outfit flowed nicely on her thin frame.

Darcy saw several people turn toward them as their voices rose. "Stop it, all of you," she commanded. "This dinner is about Colonial Williamsburg, not about the Fulton family. We can fight later." Smiling at them all, she moved past and sat down at her table.

"Are you sure you'll be all right here alone, Miss Jane?" Anita asked. "It looks like a storm is coming in and this can be a scary place if the power goes out. George and I can go to dinner another night if you want us to stay with you."

"Don't be silly, Anita," Jane replied. "I'm not a child and I love storms. I will be just fine. If the power goes out, I'll light all of the candles. Go out and have a good time like everyone else tonight. No need for you to ruin your evening for me."

"All right, then we'll be on our way. I've cooked up some food and left it in the oven for you. Have a nice evening."

Jane watched their older Buick pull away before reaching for a bottle of champagne. At long last she was alone. She needed the time to relax and make her final plans. She was tired of all of this nonsense in Virginia—it was time to go home and Darcy needed to come with her. They had such a good life in Minnesota where she didn't feel so outclassed or poor. Jane needed Darcy to do this for their friendship this time, and she was going to be sure it happened.

Jane took a long soak in the tub in the master suite, sipping on champagne. When she dried off, she slipped into a party dress from Darcy's closet, sat down at the vanity and put on a thick, vivid coat of makeup. Looking in the mirror she wasn't satisfied with her hair, so she twisted it up and around until it looked as Darcy's had when she'd left for the evening. Tonight she would be in control, be the wealthy landowner; she would be Darcy.

The dogs lay at the foot of the bed asleep. She made sure they would not be in her way by adding a few ground sleeping pills to their dinner.

A knock on the back door brought her off the stool, her transformation complete.

"Andrew, how nice to see you," Jane greeted her guest. "I wondered if you could tear yourself away from your wife long enough to drop by. Come on in." She stood aside and let Andrew stagger past her.

He turned around and stared at Jane. "You look a lot like Darcy tonight, do you know that? You also look pretty damn good. Why don't you get all dressed up more often?" Realizing she was glowering at him, he made his way into the family room. "Mind if I have a drink?"

"It's all laid out for you. Help yourself, but do it quickly. We have much to discuss and not a lot of time. Andrew, just how much do you despise Darcy?"

Seventeen

Do you enjoy reading mysteries, Darcy?
They are my favorite genre. I am one of those
readers who never realize who the guilty party is
until the end of the book. That is, for me, what
makes the story so entertaining.

Dinner was a lovely affair. The courses were well presented and accompanied by excellent wine. Darcy enjoyed the salmon mousse and the flavorful steak, but she took devilish delight in the dessert, a dark chocolate torte with fresh raspberries. Many conversations flowed around her, but she was content to be silent. Robert was talking to the woman on the other side of him about the state of the country, but he occasionally glanced her way or gave her knee a squeeze under the table. Others were discussing Colonial Williamsburg, but the main discussion was how to solve the problem plaguing many volunteer organizations—how to get younger people involved. No one had any ready solutions, but many ideas were offered. Darcy could not remember the last time she had felt so relaxed and happy.

Occasionally she glanced around at other tables and waved at friends. Unlike most of the people, Grant and Fran were tense and talking only to each other. Darcy wondered what that was about, but as soon as Fran realized her sister was watching she smiled and conversed with the man beside her. She then glanced at her watch and back at Grant who nodded toward the clouds building in the east.

The dinner concluded with Dr. Caine giving recognition to Raleigh Tavern Society members. New members were recognized for joining the group, and others who had been members for many years were honored for their service to the Colonial

Williamsburg Foundation. People accepted awards for their service of ten and twenty years to the foundation, and Darcy was proud to be a member of such a group. The number of people willing to give their time and their money to preserve not only one piece of American history but also other such causes around the country awed her. The members of the Raleigh Tavern Society made a difference.

Deputy Marcia Benson rushed into the Sheriff's office. The young woman was eager to make her report. "Sheriff, I don't know if this is anything of real value, but I thought I should report it. I was interrogating our friend Nick Martine again when he remembered something about his employer. When he was first hired, the person was angry and wanted to hurt and scare Ms. Jeffers. But, the last few times he talked to this mysterious person, it seemed to Nick that he or she was more out for revenge and wanted to see Ms. Jeffers dead. He didn't think anything of it at the time because he was too afraid of failing, but now that he's had time to ponder it, Nick thinks he might have been talking to two different people, or something might have happened to make his employer really upset."

"Well, that's certainly something new," the sheriff said as he mulled over the information. "Did Nick give you any indication of when the voice changed?"

"Let me think. Yeah, when he talked to the person after the accident in the swimming pool things seemed to be different. Each time after that, the person's distress seemed to rise. Do you think this might help us break the case?" the deputy asked.

"It could. Remember, a couple of those people at Winterview didn't arrive until after Ms. Jeffers had that little accident in the pool. Makes you wonder, doesn't it? Looks like we need to do some more checking. Benson, get a hold of the state police in Minnesota. Let's find out a little more about Winterview's guests."

"Thank you all for coming to this spring's meeting of the Raleigh Tavern Society," Dr. Caine said. "I would normally invite you to linger and enjoy this beautiful locale, but we have been advised by the weather service that the storm they have been predicting all day is almost upon us. So, please make your way to the coaches and we will get you back to your cars and hotels without getting wet. Good night, and thank you for your continued support of the Colonial Williamsburg Foundation," he concluded.

Robert pulled back Darcy's chair and waited for her to stand before moving toward his brother. Jonathan looked worn out, and good old Beth still looked mad. When would they ever be a family again, he wondered. He hoped it was soon, as he was tired of worrying about everyone and tired of the nightmares. He had been awakened by that same dream of Jorge and the helicopter crash every night this week. The rumble of thunder in the distance did nothing to make him feel better. "All right, Jon, if you really need to talk to us, let's get going. Do you want to meet at the farmhouse?"

"If Darcy will allow us, I would prefer we talk at the plantation house," Jonathan responded. "Beth, you will be there, correct?" he asked his sister.

"If you insist. You know how I feel about all of this, and I have an appointment again with Graham Hastings in the morning. But if you need me there, Big Brother, I will attend. Darcy, are we to be allowed into the plantation house?"

"Of course," she replied, trying not to react to the venom in Beth's voice. "I'll call ahead and let Jane know we are coming. Do you want Fran and Grant there too, or would you prefer they come home later?" She looked around for the couple and saw them moving quickly toward the palace exit.

"I would like everyone there, I think," Jonathan responded. "Rob, will you catch up with them? We'll all meet back at the Inn before heading to Winterview."

As they were boarding the coach, Robert caught up with Fran and Grant. "Wait, you two," he called. "Where are you headed?"

Grant backed off the bus. "Fran and I were going to stop at my house before I took her home. Is that all right with you?"

"What's wrong with you two tonight?" Robert countered. "You both look like you are on pins and needles about something." Waiting for a response but getting none he continued. "Jonathan has something he wants to say and he would like you and Fran to hear it as well as the rest of us. Can you head over to Winterview instead? You can always go out afterward."

Grant glanced up at Fran's worried face and smiled. "We can do that for Jonathan," he replied. "I think Fran would want to be there for anything that happens. We'll meet you there shortly." He got on the bus as the first raindrops began to fall.

Robert met up with Darcy at the Williamsburg Inn and together they raced through the warm rain to the car. "I could have brought it up to the door, you know," Robert said as they looked at each other and broke out laughing. "We could have at least avoided you looking like a drowned rat."

"I'm not the only wet rat in this car, Rob. Have you looked in the mirror?" She laughed at his expression before continuing. "It was exhilarating running through the rain. There hasn't been a good storm since I moved to Virginia, so this is wonderful! I feel so happy, Rob. This has been a terrific evening." She looked up to find him staring intently at her.

"And it's not over yet," he promised. "As soon as we get through with Jonathan and the group, you and I are going to do some serious talking, among other things." He leaned over the console and kissed Darcy's wet, shining lips.

"I'll hold you to that, Mr. Fulton. I hope that was only a teaser for the rest of the evening." She laughed breathlessly as he swooped in and kissed her more deeply, molding her body to his as best he could with the car's gearshift between them.

Breaking apart, Robert started the car. "Let's get going." The thunder roared as they sped out of Williamsburg.

Andrew jerked up at Jane's question. He gave her a long, assessing look as he finished filling his glass with vodka and ice. He decided to wait to see what kind of game she was playing.

Jane continued, "Do you despise her enough to want her out of the way? Enough to hire someone to do your dirty work? It's been you all along, hasn't it, Andrew?" She laughed at the wary and frightened expression on his face. "I've known since the first time I met you, you know. You have a peculiar little sound you make when you're trying to be quiet, and I remember hearing that sound when Darcy called me from here. You were on the line listening, weren't you? You were trying to figure out how to make this all work out, and she gave you the perfect opening when she gave me her itinerary for returning to Minnesota."

"What do you know about anything," Andrew snarled. "Darcy Jeffers is just like that bitch of a mother-in-law I had. They both thought they were the boss of everyone around and neither had any time for me. They thought I was a waste of time just because I have a few drinks and I don't always know what to do with myself." He threw back another shot of vodka.

"Well, you have certainly tried to get back at them in your own way, I'll give you that. I thought you would succeed with that pool accident. Darcy's terribly afraid of drowning." Jane paused. "I knew I was helping you with that information about her parent's car crash when that private investigator called. Unfortunately, the people on the Plantation Trust board are too trusting and again you have failed. What I don't know is why you've done all this. I mean, I know you despise her, but this is going a bit far for that, isn't it?"

The telephone rang as Andrew continued to stare at Jane. She was so different from her usual self. Why was she saying all of these things to him? He needed to make a plan fast to get out of this situation before he ended up in jail. Was there a chance he could make her help him, or was this just a trap?

"That was Darcy on the phone," Jane reported. "It seems Jonathan wants to have a talk with all of us, so everyone, including your darling wife, are on their way here." She sat back in her chair and closed her eyes. "Ah, just listen to that thunder. It's a perfect night for mayhem." She opened her eyes again and addressed Andrew. "Are you planning more for tonight or calling it quits? You don't have much time to decide."

Sweat popped out on Andrew's brow as he tried to make sense of all she had said. "You don't know what you're talking about, Jane. What's wrong with you? You're different. Why are you talking about your best friend as if you want to harm her?"

"I don't want to hurt Darcy, Andrew, but I do want her back in Minnesota where she belongs. You may have to trust me so I can help you get rid of her."

Grant and Fran drove out of the parking lot as fast as the rain would allow. "We have to get to Winterview before they do," Fran cried. "If we don't this is going to turn into the worst night of all of our lives. Grant, did you call the Sheriff?"

"No. You're not sure about any of this, Fran, and I didn't want you to look like a fool. Darcy would hate you for sure then. I called my father and let him know what we know. He will make the correct call with the information."

"How can you be so dense? Why do you care what DJ thinks of me? She's not going to be yours, Grant—she's in love with Robert." Seeing him glower at her, she continued, "Don't look at me like that. I know when a man is after a woman, and you've been after DJ since I've been here and probably before that. But it's never going to happen for you. As for me, she already hates me and I don't think I can make that any worse. We've got to call the Sheriff. Grant! What's happening? Oh, my gosh, we're going off the road!" Fran screamed as she felt the car sliding off the pavement. Grant fought to keep on the road, but the water lifted them up and sideways. They hit a signpost on the side of the road, and the jolt brought the car to a rest across both lanes.

Jonathan and Beth were quiet as they headed out of Williamsburg. "What is so important that we all have to hear, Jon? You're scaring me. You look as if you have just survived a war. I've never seen you like this. Are you all right?"

"I'm fine, Beth. It's just been a long couple of days and I have had the time and the occasion to rethink some things in my life. I need to change my priorities and take more time with Lucas. He's in bad shape, and he's what I need to tell everyone about. When Linda left us I knew he was hurting, but I thought he was young enough to get over it. Apparently he took her desertion a lot harder than I realized, and I haven't been there to help him through it. I now realize I need to be there for him first and foremost."

"So, you're giving up on Winterview, too?" she asked her brother. "I thought you would be with me all the way, Jon. Well, I am not going to stop until that plantation is in Fulton hands, no matter who abandons me."

"I am not abandoning you, Sis," he said, a sad smile on his face. "I am just facing up to my familial responsibilities. It is not just you, Rob and me any more and it hasn't been for a long time, but I keep acting like it. I need to give Lucas the time and love that he needs to grow into as fine a man as he can be. Can you understand that? Winterview is no longer the priority."

The melodious sound of Beethoven's Fifth Symphony filled the air and Beth dove into her handbag to find her cell phone. "Andrew, is that you?" she asked into the phone. "I can hardly hear you over the storm. Speak up. Yes, we are on our way to Winterview. You're already there? Is Jane there too? All right, we'll see you shortly." She put the phone back in her handbag.

"That's odd," Beth murmured, "I wonder why he's already at Winterview."

"Who's at Winterview? I thought we were all going there? What's going on Beth?"

"That's what I want to know. Andrew didn't come with us this evening because he had a business meeting, he said. Now he calls to tell me he is at Winterview waiting for us. Don't you think that is quite a coincidence? What can he be up to this time? He's been acting so crazy lately."

"Beth, I'm sorry things are not going well between you two. Is it that bad?"

"I honestly don't know where we are. Andrew drinks so much and is so bitter about Mother's will that it consumes him. He was happy to be of help to you and to be involved with the smear campaign. I fear for his sanity and sometimes my safety." She turned toward her brother. "But he hasn't deserted me like you and Rob have. I don't know how this will all work out, but I think he's involved in something else. He's hiding something."

"What's that in the road? I can't make it out through the rain."

"Slow down, Jon. I think it's a car. Can you stop before we run into them?"

"Hold on, Beth! Here we go!"

"There are no lights on anywhere, Robert," Darcy commented as they reached the farm area. "We must have lost a transformer somewhere. I wonder if Jane has called it in. She probably has, as she's always so on top of every situation." She looked at the man next to her and wondered why he looked so uncomfortable. "What's wrong? Don't you think Jane can handle an emergency?"

"Darcy, we are having such a nice night. Let's not talk about Jane, all right?"

"What aren't you saying to me? Do you have a problem with Jane? She's my best friend, Robert. She's been my rock for these past ten years. I would not have made it through my grief if not for her. What do you know that I don't?"

"Nothing specific. That's why I don't want to talk about it."
Seeing the look of determination on Darcy's face, he sighed. "All
right, I give up. Jane is a very nice person, but she seems to need to
control what's happening in your life. I think she assumed that position all of those years ago, and now that you have finally moved on,
she's having trouble accepting it. I know she sure doesn't like you
around me. I think she is afraid she'll lose you to me."

Darcy thought about what Robert said. It was true that she had
basically handed over the reigns of her life to Jane after her parents
had died, and as the years went by they remained in that relationship. Why, Jane was not only the keeper of her household, she was
the executor of her estate and the person who would make Darcy's
health decisions if she could not do it herself. Jane really did have
control of her life, and it suddenly made Darcy feel uneasy. She
had not noticed that she had given up so much of herself to Jane,
nor had she noticed that her friend had not reciprocated. She did
not know if Jane even had a will, but she knew she was not desig-
nated as any decision maker for Jane. How strange.

Did Jane have anything of her own? Darcy wondered. She
knew Jane had lost everything to her ex-husband. That was over
thirteen years ago. Certainly she must have built her savings back
up by now, hadn't she? Darcy realized how little she knew about
her friend's financial situation. She had never taken the time to
find out how Jane was doing, and it made her sad that she had
been so selfish.

Darcy's distress showed in her face, so Robert tried to change
the subject. "The house sure looks gloomy in all of this rain,
doesn't it?"

Darcy glanced up to see they were in the Winterview drive.
The rain was coming down in sheets so she had not realized how
close they were. Robert stopped the engine, and as he started to
get out, she laid a hand on his arm.

"Wait," she said quietly. "I think you have a point about Jane.
Do you have any more to tell me about her?"

"Only that Fran has been suspicious of Jane for quite some
time." He continued quickly, "I know, Fran was also very jealous

of Jane's role in your life, but she was also worried about how much control she had. Your sister came down here with Jane to make sure your friend didn't upset your plans. You probably don't believe that, but Fran actually had to quit her job in order to make this trip. She really does care about you."

"I'm not sure I can believe all of that good stuff about Fran any more than I can believe all of the bad about Jane. But you have certainly given me lots to think about." A crack of lightning illuminated the sky behind the house leaving it in cold shadow. Darcy shivered. "Let's get in and see if everything's all right."

Eighteen

Never underestimate your effect on the lives of the people surrounding you. Have you seen the play "Six Degrees of Separation"? I believe all of our lives are intertwined, and each decision we make causes a reaction in the people around us.

Jonathan shook his head as the car came to a crunching halt, the driver's side hitting the driver's side of the car already stopped on the road. "Beth, are you all right?"

"Yes, I'm fine," she replied. "Just some bruises and some shaking up. Do you see any movement in the other car?" She tried to peer through the curtain of rain but could see nothing but blackness.

"No, and my door is pinned shut," her brother replied. "We both have to get out through your door. Can you get it open?"

Beth shoved her door open and was greeted by a gust of wind that ripped the handle from her hands. She was immediately soaked but dutifully got out of the car and helped her brother over the seat and out her door. Brother and sister stood side-by-side looking at the car in front of them.

Shouting over the wind and rain Beth said, "Do you think anyone can still be in there?"

Jonathan walked over to the other car without answering. He ran his hand down the length of the car and looked at the license plate. "Oh, my God, Beth, this is Grant's car! Grant and Fran must be in there. We've got to help them."

Running back to his car, he dove back in to find his cell phone. A tug on his legs brought him back upright. "They aren't in there, Jon," Beth called to him. "Wait. I see a shape moving over there." She moved away from the road. "They're right over here by the big tree. I can just make them out from here. It looks as if Fran might be hurt. Come on!"

Racing over to where Grant and Fran were huddled, they became aware they were both sitting upright and talking. "Are you two hurt?" Beth asked, trying to wipe the rain out of her face. "Your car is totaled. Did you hit something?"

Fran looked up, startled to hear familiar voices. "Oh, thank goodness. Beth is that you? Is Jonathan with you? We heard the crash but couldn't tell who was involved."

"Yes, we're both here and relatively unharmed. What's going on?"

"You have to get to Winterview as fast as possible," she cried. "We hit something on the side of the road, and our car is now blocking the way. But you have to find a way to get around it. I think something terrible is going to happen tonight."

"Fran, calm down," Jonathan said. "You're hysterical. Why do you think something is going to happen? And what?"

"Grant, tell them. Tell them what you have found out," Fran pleaded with the man sitting beside her. "They have to know so they can help."

Grant just stared at her. "They won't believe me, you know that. We have to get there ourselves."

"Stop this," Jonathan roared. "Has anyone called the sheriff about this accident? That's the first thing we need to do. Then, you will tell us what is going on. We can try to squeeze into my car to get out of this rain. Let's go."

"Wait. Let me go," Grant said. "I'll make the call and start down the road to find us some help. You stay here and make sure Fran is all right, unless you want to try to find a house nearby."

"We'll stay here. Once you call it shouldn't be long before help arrives," Jonathan replied. "We can't get any wetter than we are now, and I don't think Fran should be moved yet."

Grant nodded in reply and headed toward the Fulton's car.

"When you call the sheriff, have him come out to Winterview right away," Fran begged.

Darcy and Robert ran from the car, up the steps and into the kitchen. She tried the light switch, but nothing happened. "As we thought, no electricity. I wonder where Jane is." She crossed to the doorway and called out for Jane.

"I'm here, Darcy," said a voice beside her. She jumped as she saw Jane appear next to her, candle in hand. There was something different about her, but Darcy could not identify it with just the light from the single candle.

"Oh, thank goodness you're all right," she said to her friend. "Was it spooky to be in this big house all alone without lights? I know you're not fond of being alone, Jane."

"I'm just fine. Robert, would you be so good as to run down to the basement and check the fuse box? I didn't get a chance to do that. Maybe we can get some lights on after all."

"The storm has probably knocked out a transformer," he replied. "But if it will make you feel better I'll check it out. Do you have a flashlight or an extra candle handy?" Jane handed him another candle and lighted it.

"We'll be in the family room waiting for you," she said. "Come on, Darcy. I want to hear all about your evening, then I can tell you about mine." Her smile made her look almost angelic in the candlelight.

"Jonathan, it's been quite a while since Grant called the sheriff. Do you think we should call again?" Fran asked, shivering. "We really need to get out of here."

"OK, Fran, if it will make you feel better I will call again." Jonathan left the cover of the trees, reached the car and dialed the Sheriff's office.

"Sheriff Matthews, there's a call coming in from Jonathan Fulton. Seems there's been an accident on Route 5 and he, Beth Page, and Fran Jeffers are stuck out there. He says Ms. Jeffers is real agitated about something happening at Winterview tonight and they have to get there right away." The deputy paused for breath. "Do you want to talk to them?"

"Put it through to my office and get Deputy Jackson on the radio right away. I think we'll head out to Winterview tonight."

"Yes, sir," the deputy replied. "Here's the call now."

"Sheriff Matthews here," he said into the telephone. "Is that you, Mr. Fulton? I can hardly hear you."

"Yes, sheriff, it is I. My cell phone is losing its battery so I will speak quickly. Did you send someone out after Grant called?"

"We didn't get a call from Grant Hastings tonight. Was he supposed to have called in?"

"Yes. He came to the car to call twenty minutes ago. How strange. He must have gone to get help instead of calling. Let me tell you where we are." He reported the location of the accident to the sheriff, then added Fran's plea to have someone get out to the house as soon as possible.

"Why is she so upset, Mr. Fulton?" the sheriff asked. "What does she know?"

"She is worried about Darcy being there with Jane. She's afraid Jane is responsible for some of what has happened here lately. Can you assist?"

"Deputy Benson and I will head out there immediately. Can the cars be pushed off the road?"

"Yes, with enough help, it shouldn't take long. Please hurry."

"Jackson, this is Sheriff Matthews," he called into the radio. The static from the storm almost drown out every other sound. "Jackson, come in! What is your location? If you are at the plantation, please be alert for trouble. We are on the way." He paused to listen for a response. All he heard was static.

Andrew looked down at Robert's form slumped at his feet. He had smashed him on the head when he entered the room. Well, one problem down, several more to go, he thought. And where was that partner of his? He wasn't going to go down alone. He pulled out his cell phone and dialed.

"Where the hell are you?" he barked into the phone. "That Jane woman is putting some of the pieces together and now she's upstairs with Darcy. I don't know if she's helping me or setting a trap. She seems to have gone off the deep end tonight and things are getting messy around here. I've just gotten Robert out of the picture, but I need help to get out of this one."

"I'm almost there, Andrew," his partner replied. "I have everything else under control. Sit tight and we'll take care of both women when I arrive." The phone line went dead. Andrew felt relieved that he wouldn't have to deal with the women alone, so he looked around for rope to tie up Robert. Not finding any, he settled for moving him into the corner and shutting the door.

Grant wiped the rain out of his eyes and looked around to get his bearings as another flash of lightning split the black sky. He had been running steadily for over twenty minutes, so he had to be getting close to Winterview. Good thing he was so in shape from his marathon training or he would never have been able to make this run. The accident had occurred not far from the turnoff to the plantation, but that was still several miles from the house. He knew help would get to the others soon, but he had to reach Darcy.

What was happening at the house now? He shivered as the rain increased again, hitting his already soaked body like needles. He had taken off his tux jacket in the car, and he had lost his tie somewhere on the run. Grant hoped he would get to the house in time. His whole future depended on it.

Darcy was sitting with Jane in the family room when Andrew appeared. She was shocked to see him in the house, but she was more concerned about Robert. "Have you seen Robert?" she immediately asked. "He went down to check on the lights and he's not back yet."

Andrew glanced at Jane, then replied, "No, I haven't seen him. I was upstairs checking on a noise we heard. Nothing but the wind, though." He tried to laugh it off. "I wonder what could have happened to him. Maybe it's more complicated than we realize with the fuses."

Darcy saw the look that passed between Jane and Andrew, and suddenly she was really afraid for Robert and for herself. Something was happening with these two and although she couldn't believe it of Jane, she sensed her life was in danger. She heard a faint whine and wondered where the dogs were.

"Jane, what's going on here? Why is Andrew here and why are you acting so strangely?" She looked closely at her friend and gasped. "That's my dress you're wearing and my jewelry. Jane, what's wrong?"

Her cry tore Jane from her trance. "Oh, stop it, Darcy. This time there's no one to save you from a terrible situation. I warned you, but you wouldn't listen. You need to make your own way tonight. I'm not the evil one here—that's Andrew. He's hated you since you arrived, and tonight I am going to help him convince you to leave Winterview, leave Virginia, and come home where you belong."

Jane's eyes were glazed over and she moved as if she were acting out some kind of fantasy. It was clear to Darcy that her friend had snapped. She was in big trouble and she needed to escape, fast. Turning to Andrew, she said, "Is this true? Are you responsible for my accidents?" Seeing the grin on his face, she asked, "Why? What have I ever done to you? Oh, never mind. It's all about this place, about Marjorie's will, isn't it? She slighted you, so I am paying the price."

"That's part of it, Doll," Andrew replied, warming to the topic. "You are Marjorie's chosen one, so you get everything that comes with that distinction. But there's so much more that none of you has even begun to realize. Just wait. My partner will be here soon, and he'll explain it all to you before we get rid of you once and for all."

Fran saw the flashing lights and tried to jump up to meet them. She was brought back down to the hard earth by the pain in her knee. Beth rushed to her side and helped her to stand. The rain had let up, but the latest round of thunder and lightning was nearby. Jonathan assisted the women to the Sheriff's vehicle. Blankets were tossed to them as they got into the warm car.

"You two wait here, and we'll get these cars out of the way," Sheriff Matthews instructed. "Mr. Fulton, we'll need your help." After several minutes the officers and Jonathan succeeded in moving both cars far enough off the road to get the other car through.

The front door opened and the soaked sheriff entered the vehicle. "Now, Ms. Jeffers, can you please tell us what is going on at Winterview? You seem to think Jane is a part of the problem, but from what you've told us over the telephone, it's not the real story," Sheriff Matthews said. "Who is really behind all of this trouble?"

"I'll fill you in as we go, Sheriff," Fran replied. "We're not far away and if we don't get there soon, I think I may lose my sister!"

Darcy slowly got out of her chair and moved toward the front door. The wind had picked up yet again, and the rain returned with a vengeance. If she could just get outside she might be able to get lost in the storm. She moved slowly, as if pondering her situation and looking at some of the paintings on the walls. Deciding that she needed help to get out, she turned toward her captors.

"Jane, what has happened to you?" she asked, trying to distract her. "I thought you were my best friend in the whole world and now you're acting like someone who hates me. Why are you doing this to me?"

Jane leaped to her feet. Andrew was right behind her, listening with obvious pleasure to the confrontation. "I don't hate you at all, my dear. I want what's best for you," she whined. "That's why I can't bear to see you stay here with all of these people who don't care about you. Don't you understand? I keep losing everything in my life—my husband, my money, now you. I don't have anything of my own, and you have everything. It's only right you continue to share it with me. All I want is for you to come home with me so I can live the way I've been doing all of these years. Then, everything will be all right. Isn't that true, Andrew?"

As Jane turned to look at the man behind her, Darcy saw her opportunity. She grabbed Jane's hand and brought the candle up into Andrew's face. He howled in pain, and grabbed Jane, leaving Darcy free to run for the front door. She murmured a prayer of thanks that it was unlocked as she pulled the heavy door open. For a split second she was stopped by the thought of the dogs, but she needed to keep going. She'd find the dogs later.

Stepping out into the rain, Darcy was immediately drenched. The night was pitch black except for the lightning, so if she could get far enough away from the house she'd be safe. Hating the thought of being out on such a raw night, Darcy made her way toward the only other shelter she could think of—the slave quarters.

Grant was reaching for the back door knob when he heard cries from inside the house. He dashed around the end of the wing just in time to see Darcy running toward the woods. Torn between which direction to go, he headed after the fleeing woman. He was already drenched and tired, but he could run a little further, he told himself.

Andrew finally untangled himself from Jane. "Damn it, woman, she's getting away. Now look what you've done. I've had enough of this." He picked up Jane's candle, pulled it out of the silver holder and came toward her, the candlestick raised in his hand. "You're in my way, now, Jane. You've lost your meal ticket now that Darcy knows you tried to harm her, so you might as well give up."

Jane, who had been staring at the huge red welt on Andrew's face, sank to the floor, sobbing. She realized he was right. It was as if she'd been in a trance, Jane decided, and she had now awakened. She knew he was right about losing her friend, and she no longer cared about her own life. The woman glanced up again at Andrew's angry face in time to see it change to surprise as Robert caught his arm and spun him around.

The two men fought for control of the candlestick, with Robert finally forcing Andrew to drop it. It rolled outside of the light provided by the remaining candle, so the two men resorted to their fists. Andrew outweighed Robert by a good forty pounds, but the younger man was quicker, and in better shape. His Marine training came back to him. He kept out of the way as his brother-in-law tried to get him into a bear hug and drop him. Finally, Robert landed a sucker punch, and his opponent went down with a thud.

"Jane, what's happened to Darcy?" Robert asked the woman gently. He could see she was in great distress. "Where did she go? Did Andrew harm her?"

"NNNNooo," Jane sobbed. "Sshee fled out the ffrront door." Trying to get herself together she got to her feet. "Andrew said he had a partner, ssso someone else is after her ttooo. Oh, Rob, what have I done?" She rushed out of the room.

Robert didn't wait a second longer. He ran to the front door and down the steps. The rain was directly in his eyes so he could see nothing in front of him. Where would she go? At once he knew—the slave quarters. Taking a deep breath and getting himself under control, he headed for the woods as fast as the rain and lightning would allow.

Nineteen

Your urging has, at last, made me take action. I have spoken to some of the preservation groups in the area, and I have met with experts from Colonial Williamsburg. Everyone is in agreement that saving the slave quarters is a worthwhile project. If I could be as successful in getting my children involved, the project would be perfect.

Darcy

couldn't breathe. Her lungs felt as if someone had them in a vise and was squeezing them as hard as they could. The last burst of lightning let her know she was still on the right path. Any time now she would arrive at the village. Then she could hide in one of the structures and away from the rain. Gathering what little breath she had left, she took off at a jog and soon came to the outskirts of the village, slowed to a walk, then fell over the threshold and into the foreman's house.

How long she lay on the cool, compact dirt Darcy had no idea. She sat up and tried to look around, but it was so dark inside the decaying structure that she couldn't see her hand in front of her face. She could, however, make out the door opening. Carefully she moved away, into the darkness.

Grant was tired but still breathing easily as he trotted into the slave quarters, the place that had caused him so much grief. Now, where was that woman? Didn't she know it was a bad idea to hide in a place like this? He had to find her. He crept around all of the buildings trying to see anything in the wet, black night. A sudden burst of lightning gave him one glance around, but it was enough. He could see her footprints. He followed them to the foreman's house.

"Darcy? Is that you?" he called out quietly. "It's me, Grant. We're all so worried about you! They sent me out to look for you when I got to the house. Everything is all right now. You can come out."

Darcy held her breath while she contemplated her next move. It was Grant, for goodness sakes. Of course he was here to help her. She was being paranoid because Andrew had said he had a partner. He could have been making that up for all she knew. She let the air out of her lungs and called, "I'm over here, Grant."

Jane saw the flashing lights on the Sheriff's car from her bedroom window. She rushed down to greet the car's occupants, hoping Andrew was still unconscious in the family room. She assumed Robert had gone after Darcy and wished this were all over.

Fran limped out of the passenger side of the car and turned toward the agitated woman. "Where is she, Jane? What have you and Grant done with her?"

Jane just stared at Darcy's sister. Why was she talking about Grant? Andrew was the one who had done all of this. "Fran, I am not proud of myself tonight, but I did nothing to your sister. It was Andrew. He hit Robert, and he was going to kill Darcy, then me! Robert knocked him out. Andrew is in the family room."

"Oh, my God! Sheriff, I've really messed this up. It's been Andrew and Grant all along! Jane was acting crazy so I thought she was the one helping." Turning back to the distraught woman she asked, "Has Grant been here tonight?"

"If he's here he didn't show himself in the house," Jane replied. "Of course with no electricity he could have been here and we would never have known. Darcy escaped out the front door a little while ago and Robert followed. I have no idea where either of them is."

Sheriff Matthews stepped forward. "Have you seen Deputy Jackson? He was supposed to patrol around the plantation tonight." Before Jane could reply, a noise to his left made the sheriff turn in time to see the deputy jogging up the driveway.

"Sheriff, someone slashed my tires tonight and cut my radio. The tires didn't go flat until I was out on the road and then I couldn't call for backup because my radio was out. I've been jogging across the fields for some time. Sorry, Sir."

"Well, I hope we're not too late," the sheriff replied. "Darcy Jeffers is still missing, as are Robert Fulton and Grant Hastings." He turned to both deputies. "Spread out and search the property for them," he ordered. "I'll take care of this one," he continued as he turned to the distraught woman. To Jane he said, "Jane Marshall, you are under arrest for attempted kidnapping. Come with me and get in the car where I'll read you your rights." To Deputy Benson the Sheriff finished, "Go see about Andrew Page."

"Oh, thank goodness you're OK Darcy! I was so worried," Grant fussed as he made his way to her side. He gave her a big hug. "Are you hurt?"

"No, I'm fine," she replied. "How did you know where to find me?"

"I saw you run toward the woods just as I was reaching the house, so I followed you." He wiped some mud off her cheek.

"I thought you said everyone was worried about me. Didn't you talk to anyone in the house? Where is everyone else? Where is the Sheriff?"

"What do we need him for, Darcy? It's just you and me, the way it should be."

"Now you're talking nonsense again, Grant. What is it with everyone tonight? I'm so confused."

Pulling her to her feet, Grant said, "Look, the rain is slowing down. Let's walk back to the house and I'll fill you in." Reluctantly, Darcy stepped out into the damp night. The air had finally cooled, and she shivered from the breeze against her sweat soaked skin. Or was something else making her shiver?

Stopping in the middle of the village, she faced the man who had found her. "How about filling me in right now about what's happening? I've been in the dark far too long."

"All right, Darcy, but remember you asked for it." He pulled a gun from his pocket. "I didn't want things to turn out this way. If you could have only done what you were supposed to do, none of this would have happened."

"What are you talking about, Grant? And why the gun?" She looked into his face and realized that he was, indeed, Andrew's partner. She had given herself up to the one person who was still trying to kill her. Darcy could feel the black fingers of oblivion reaching out for her, but she pulled herself back from the edge. She needed to find out why this had happened to her before she died.

"It all began with Marjorie, of course," Grant said with a sigh. "She was supposed to leave the plantation to the kiddies and then it could have been divided up among them with Andrew and Beth getting the land upon which you stand. If that had happened, life would have been good for everyone.

"But no, Marjorie left all of this to the Trust with you in charge. So, we needed to get you out of the way. At first I thought I could work some magic as your attorney, but my father had drawn up the will, and he was watching me like a hawk. My hands were tied, so I couldn't do anything. Andrew and I also decided to scare you away. He hired Nick and the games began. But did you cooperate? No, you held your ground. Do you know I admire you for that?

"After a while I realized I was falling in love with you, Darcy. You were strong, intelligent and compassionate. My next plan was to marry you. If you and I married I would be able to make all of this work out for everyone. However, you wouldn't cooperate with that plan, either. You had to fall in love with Robert, which just complicated things further. So, you left us no alternative but to kill you. And here I am."

"But you still haven't told me why all of this was so important to you, Grant. What is worth killing for? Certainly you don't want this land for its historic value."

He snorted at the thought of that. "Quite the opposite, My Dear. Andrew and I are partners in a new development. It's a grand place right here next to Winterview. Big lots, huge homes, great money rolling in. There was just one fly in the ointment— we need the land on which the slave quarter sits to complete the development! As land goes, it doesn't mean much, but in the big picture this land is necessary to provide access to the James River. The whole pitch for the development is its exclusivity in plantation country, and its private access to the river.

"We've already sold most of the lots, but without this piece of land the whole development is, in effect, useless. Andrew and I put a lot of money into this project and if we don't secure this land, we will not only lose everything, but will be sued for much, much more. People hate it when you don't come across with what you promise. So, you see I have no choice but to kill you. Too bad. I was looking forward to having you as a wife. We could have had lots of fun together."

Darcy stared at Grant. She couldn't believe she knew so little about the man standing in front of her. She would have sworn he was a good man and would never get involved with any of this. "I know Andrew has a drinking problem and Marjorie cut him off so he's low on funds, but why would you get involved in this scheme?"

"My weakness, Pet, is the races. I believe we discussed those lovely horses. I go to the track as often as possible. How do you think I know so much about horses? The Richmond track is my favorite place to be, but it seems I got in a little too deep with some of the lending officers up there. I needed to pay my debts and this seemed like another sure bet."

"But you didn't count on Marjorie throwing me into the mix. Oh, Grant, how sad for you. You're such a great person and you could have had so much if you had just stayed away from gambling. You're to be pitied as much as Andrew. You both have a disease that destroyed your life. I'm sorry."

"I don't want your pity, woman!" Grant yelled. "I am not to be pitied. I'm going to be the biggest real estate developer this area has ever seen. The only thing stopping me is you and I'm going to deal with that right now." He pointed the gun at her.

Realizing she was about to die, a spurt of adrenaline hurled Darcy toward the surprised man, and she sat him down in the mud before kicking him in the stomach. The gun went off wildly. Grant dropped it in the mud as she twisted his fingers. Finally recovering, the furious man grabbed Darcy's wrist and twisted her down into the mud beside him. She roared with pain and frustration as he had grabbed her injured arm, but the two continued to struggle. Grant pushed and twisted until he was on top of Darcy, and she was face down. He grabbed her head in both hands and pushed her face into the sticky mud.

Thankful that the rain had stopped, Robert got his bearings and ran into the village. The sight that greeted him made his stomach turn. Grant Hastings was sitting astride the unmoving, prone figure of Darcy! Gathering all the strength he had left, he threw himself at Grant and they both rolled off the woman. He had just enough time to see Darcy's head come up slowly and hear her take a deep breath before Grant landed a punch to his jaw.

The two men rolled over and over on the wet ground. They fell into a nearby creek, a tributary of the James River. Usually tame, on this night the creek was swollen with rainwater and running rapidly. Robert grabbed onto a tree limb to keep from being washed away. Grant used the other man's change in focus to punch him again and head back to shore. As he tried to get up, Grant stumbled and fell back to the wet ground where he froze. A copperhead snake lay next to him on the creek bank! He again tried to pick himself up. As he did so, the reptile struck at him, biting him until the man managed to roll off its slippery body. Grant cried out in pain and shock, looking to Robert for help.

Robert watched the whole scene in terror. He found himself back in Columbia in the river watching Jorge being swept away in the coils of an Anaconda. He had to help. He had to help the man who had tried to kill the woman he loved. Sweat popped out on his forehead, but he gathered his courage and let go of the tree branch. He tried to find footing in the rushing water. Slowly he made his way to the bank where Grant had now passed out. Robert grabbed onto the other man's pant leg and inch-by-inch pulled him back into the water, away from the snake. Grant was almost completely in the water when the copperhead lunged again, this time at Robert. He froze and his heart raced, but the snake was not close enough to reach him.

Once the unconscious man was in the water, Robert floated down with him until they found a place to land without any waiting reptiles. Dragging Grant onto the bank, he tore his shirt and made a tourniquet, placing it around the man's arm above the snakebite. Then he ran back toward the village.

There he found Darcy, covered with mud, trying to find him. "Are you all right? Where's Grant?" She launched herself into his arms.

"There's no time, Darcy. We need to get back to the house and get help. Grant is in real trouble. A Copperhead has bitten him. Come on." Grabbing her hand, he led the way back to the plantation house.

Twenty

*The garden is in full bloom as it was
a year ago when you were here. I cannot believe
how fast this year has passed. I would never
have believed then that I would be an e-mail
expert in such a short time, and have gained
a trusted friend in the process.*

When Darcy and Robert arrived back at the house, the deputies were immediately dispatched to the slave quarters. The ambulance arrived quickly after that, having been called in case of trouble.

Grant Hastings was still alive, thanks to Robert. The family watched the ambulance depart for town. The Sheriff called Graham Hastings with the news, and while he headed to the hospital to be with his son, the others, weary from the night's events, moved back into the house and tried to make sense of it all.

"If y'all come sit we'll try to tie up the loose ends," Sheriff Matthews announced. "Anita and George, good to see you back here safely. You should also hear about what's happened."

"I'll get the coffee on," Anita replied. "Please don't start without me."

The group was silent as they waited for Anita. Everyone was tired, and Darcy's sense of loss was painful. Thinking about the evening's events, she didn't even notice she was still covered in mud. She knew Jane had always been there for her, but Darcy had taken advantage of her friend. It had been a shock to see Jane so far gone. Robert squeezed her hand and apparently read her mind as he said, "You know, Jane was doing much better after you left. I think she will be all right. She needed you more than you knew, more than was healthy."

"That may be true, but I wasn't a good friend. I never tried to find out what was wrong if Jane wouldn't tell me on her own, and I just brushed aside her needs." Tears filled her eyes as Darcy thought of her friend. "I feel like I've lost her forever. Silly, isn't it?"

"No, DJ, it's not silly," Fran said as she came to sit beside her, the beautiful dress torn and her knee taped up by the EMTs before they had gone to get Grant. "She was your rock, and you were both her hero and her nemesis. You had no way of knowing just how much she depended on your dependence. Sounds convoluted, but it's pretty straight forward. I'm sorry I wasn't around more to help you. Maybe things wouldn't have gotten so out of hand if I had been."

The two sisters gazed at one another, tears in their eyes. "Fran, do you think we can really try to be friends and sisters again? I do need you in my life, but only if you want to be there. And, you quit picking on my boyfriends."

Holding out her hand, Fran said, "It's a deal. Anyway, I have a feeling there won't be any more boyfriends for me to steal." She glanced at Robert who was silently watching the exchange. The two women shook hands as Anita came into the room, followed by the Sheriff.

"All right, then. Let's see if we can tie all of this up. We'll start with Jane Marshall". He spoke directly to Darcy. "I think it's safe to say she felt threatened by your new life without her and did what she could to get you to go back to Minnesota. It seems she made some very bad investments in the last decade, so she could no longer live on her own income. She depended on you to provide her lifestyle." The Sheriff paused to accept the coffee Anita offered.

"Jane will have a psychiatric evaluation in the morning, and we'll proceed from there. The most serious charge against her will be attempted kidnapping and her part in getting Lucas to act on his insecurities." He saw the looks of surprise on the faces in the group. "Yes, I'm afraid Jane encouraged Lucas to act on his feelings and go after Darcy. She had no idea what he would do, but she did encourage him."

"I am so sorry about Jane," Darcy whispered. "She has taken care of me these last years, now it's my turn to take care of her." She looked up to Sheriff Matthews. "I will do all I can to help Jane, so please keep me apprised of her situation."

"Of course, Ms. Jeffers. Now, on to Lucas." Turning to Jonathan he asked, "Mr. Fulton, would you like to tell us about your son?"

Jonathan stood up in front of the fireplace. "On behalf of my son," he began, "I would like to apologize to Darcy for the horrible accident she suffered because of him."

"What are you talking about, Jon?" Beth asked. "What did Lucas do?"

Sighing, he went on. "I have not been around my son enough to know how he was thinking and feeling. I had incorrectly led him to believe that his grandmother would leave him this house when she died, and when that didn't happen Lucas turned all of the anger and frustration he felt at both Marjorie and me toward Darcy.

"Apparently Jane saw that when she arrived, and after she determined that the situation was getting out of her control as well, she encouraged Lucas to act on his angry feelings. As a result, it was Lucas who planted the ball of nails under Darcy's saddle when she was at the slave quarters. He had learned all about horses and what hurts them from working with his Uncle Rob, and he used that knowledge to try to hurt Darcy. He certainly came very close to succeeding, and I can assure you he and I are both more sorry than you can imagine. I hope one day you can at least forgive him for being a teenager and acting rashly." Jonathan paused. He was uncomfortable with what he had to say.

To Darcy he said, "I doubt you will ever be able to forgive me, given my role in not only Lucas' behavior, but in trying to get you out of the Trust and out of your new home. To put your mind at ease, I will now concentrate on being Lucas' father, not on trying to keep Winterview in the Fulton family." Jonathan sat down in his chair, a great weight seemingly lifted from his shoulders.

"That clears up the last 'accident' you had, Ms. Jeffers. So let's now talk about the others," the Sheriff continued. "It seems that Andrew Page and Grant Hastings formed a partnership two years ago in a business venture called Great River Plantation Estates. This was to be a huge development next door to Winterview, very exclusive in nature, very pricey. The only piece of property they lacked to complete the development," he went on, "was the slave quarters and the area to the west that led to the James River. This piece of property was needed because they advertised private access to the river and a marina. Without that property there was no river access, so no development.

"Hastings was trying to figure out how to get the property legally and had sent people to Winterview to try to talk Marjorie Fulton into selling. She was a tough nut to crack, and they were still planning ways to work on her when she suddenly passed away. This was what both men were waiting for, and they thought their problem solved until the reading of the will. Enter Darcy Jeffers, another enormous problem for them.

"Ms. Jeffers became more of a problem because she was determined to start working on the restoration of the slave quarters right away. This couldn't be allowed, so Andrew took charge of getting rid of her and hired Nick Martine." The Sheriff continued, "Seems at first they just wanted to scare you away, Ms. Jeffers, but you wouldn't scare. Then you scared them by going to the Colonial Williamsburg Foundation for help in the restoration of the village and getting the property placed on the Virginia list of historical sites. Once that happened, there would be no way to get the property for the development."

Deputy Jackson interrupted, "And that's when things really started to happen around here. You getting that temporary designation today threw them into high gear. Somehow Andrew learned of it earlier in the day. Then, there was also the problem of Mr. Hastings getting pressure from his buddies at the track."

"Thank you, Deputy. I'll take it from here," the Sheriff insisted, giving the deputy a look of irritation. "Now ya'll probably know more about what was going on with them than we do. You had problems at the Trust, right? Also, when Nick was caught, everyone got desperate. But what made tonight so important was what Mr. Hastings found out from Fran." He looked at her for confirmation.

Before Fran could reply, a muffled thud at the doorway announced the arrival of two sleepy dogs, with George following. They half-heartedly wagged their tails and immediately staggered to Darcy. After receiving a pat, both lay down in front of their master.

"George, where did you find them?" Darcy asked. "And, what's wrong with them? They'll be all right, I hope."

"The dogs were locked in your bedroom," George replied. "Miss Jane told us where they were before she left. They are fine, just a little sleepy from a dose of sleeping pills." He pointed to the dogs. "Look, they're already waking up." Both animals had their heads up and ears alert.

"I'm sorry you got interrupted, Fran," Darcy apologized. "Please go ahead with your information."

"The Sheriff is right about my part in this," she confirmed. "I was shopping in Williamsburg at the outlet mall and I heard two women talking about the grand new development going in by Winterview. I asked them about it, and they said lots were already sold, quietly, as it was very exclusive, and they had the inside track because of someone from the Fulton family being involved. Well, that got me to thinking. I started to snoop around. It didn't take long to figure out the person was Andrew.

"But I couldn't figure out who his partner was. I originally traveled down here with Jane because she was acting out of character and I was worried about what she would do in Virginia. I began to suspect that she was involved. It seemed like confirmation when the complete story about our parents' deaths was used against Darcy. Only Jane would have that much detail, so she had to have been the source.

"The problem came in when I confided this information to Grant this afternoon. I thought he could help keep Darcy safe and get Andrew and Jane out of her life." Fran looked over at Darcy. "I'm so sorry, DJ. Tonight was my fault. Can you ever forgive me? I led Grant right to you." She grabbed for her coffee cup as it started to tip off her lap.

"Fran, it wasn't your fault," Darcy said to her sister. "Grant fooled us all and you only did what you thought would help. We were caught in a bad situation. Also, don't forget how upset he was when that woman gave me the letter about the historical designation for the slave quarters. One way or another he was going to come after me tonight."

Sheriff Matthews once again took the floor. "Are there any other loose ends we need to tie up?" He looked around at each person. Slowly, Beth raised her hand and stood up.

"Darcy, my brothers and I did all that we could to legally keep you from this house. I was all for going further, but Robert wouldn't hear of it. Then, Jonathan also thought better of it, so I am left as the only Fulton who believes you should not be here. I have lost my husband tonight, and I assume all of my money since I will have to pay for Andrew's share in this mess. I don't want to lose my heritage as well. Can you understand that?"

"Of course I can, Beth, but you don't have to lose your heritage," Darcy replied. "I am hoping you will join us on the Plantation Trust board and continue to make decisions for this property. Together we can keep your family's legacy alive and well. And, you will still have your money from your mother's will, you know. That money cannot be touched to pay Andrew's debts."

"That is very generous of you to offer under the circumstances. I hope you will give me time to think it over. You're right about Mother's money, though, so that's good news. However, I still believe it should be a Fulton living in this house."

"Knock it off, Beth," Robert said quietly. "Hasn't all of this taught you what is really important and what isn't? Mother left us all comfortable, left us able to pursue our dreams. We still have access to our family home, but now it will be protected for all time. How can you possibly want anything more?" He looked at Fran, then at Darcy. "As far as I'm concerned, I hope you both decide to stay in Virginia and become part of the life of Winterview."

"Thank you, Robert," Fran replied for them both. "I know Darcy is already a part of this life, and it's a nice offer to stay here, but I'll have to think about it. Maybe it's time I go home and take care of our family heritage. What do you think, DJ?"

"You would move to the farm in Minnesota?" she asked, surprised. "That would be great, Fran. Although I'm not sure it's better than you being here with me. But, whatever you decide to do I'll support you."

"Well, I think that wraps it up," Sheriff Matthews said. "Let's all go home. I have arranged transportation for those of you without cars. Good night everyone."

Darcy and Fran escorted everyone to the door. They watched the cars depart before going back into the house. Seeing Robert standing in the kitchen, Fran discreetly headed for the stairs. "Good night, DJ. Tonight we can all sleep well."

"Good night, Fran. Thanks for being here and helping me out. You really went all out even after I told you I didn't trust you. I'll never forget that." She hugged her sister for the first time in ten years, and watched as Fran tromped up the stairs.

Darcy turned to the man waiting for her. "What are you still doing here, Sir?" She asked holding out her hand. "Care to go back into the family room?"

Hand in muddy hand they walked back through the silent house. They passed a mirror in the hallway and broke out laughing as they saw their filthy state reflected there. In the family room Robert said, "Maybe I can help out my sister with her problem. I had hoped to speak to you under more romantic, and cleaner, circumstances, but since we are tying up loose ends, what's one more?" He kneeled in front of Darcy's chair.

"Darcy, in a fairly short amount of time we have learned so much about one another, learned to trust one another and even to love one another. We've sure been through a lot together, and tonight, thanks to you, I even faced my greatest fear. I cherish the time we spend together and I would like to continue that for as long as I live. Will you marry me?"

Darcy could not have been more surprised. She looked down into Robert's eyes so full of love and joy, and she could not resist a smile. "I'll consider it. We'll see how useful you are to have around before I make my final decision." She threw her arms around his neck and gave him a big, smacking kiss.

"I think I'm going to like living in Virginia more than I ever dreamed. And tomorrow, we start work on the slave quarters. What more could I ask for?" As she kissed Robert again, the two rested dogs ran into the room, knocked Robert over and licked him mercilessly. Darcy laughed, and dove into the fray.